ONLY A LODGER . . . AND HARDLY THAT

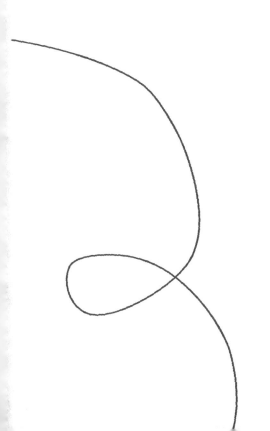

ONLY A LODGER . . . AND HARDLY THAT

A Fictional Autobiography

VESNA MAIN

LONDON NEW YORK CALCUTTA

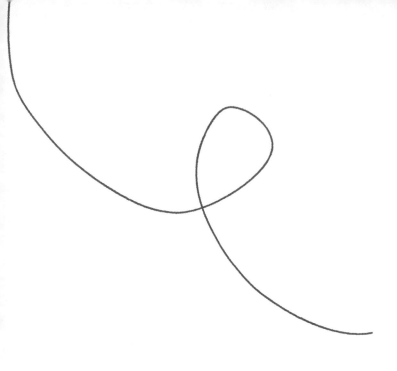

Seagull Books, 2019

Text and photographs © Vesna Main, 2019

ISBN   978 0 8574 2 646 8

British Library Cataloguing-in-Publication Data
A catalogue record for this book is available from the British Library.

Typeset and designed by Seagull Books, Calcutta, India
Printed and bound by Versa Press, East Peoria, Illinois, USA

To the memory of my grandparents

Marija Ondruš
(1898–1968)

and

Franjo Josip Genus-Pistotnik
(1897–1970)

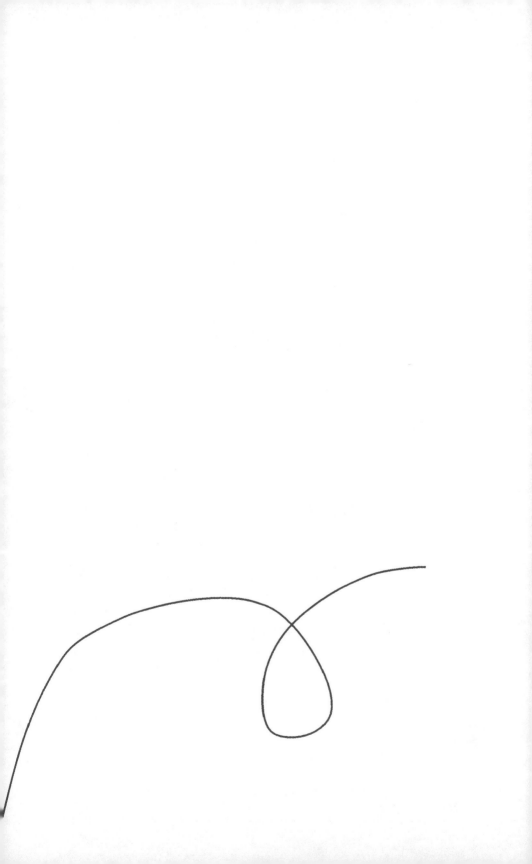

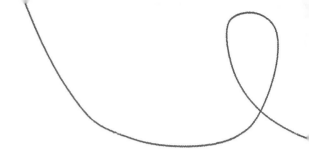

CONTENTS

I am only a lodger—and hardly that.

Ignatius Sancho

*We are the living proof of everything that has befallen us in our
lifetime. Getting a clear view of existence—not just seeing through
it but throwing the brightest possible light on it every day—is
the only possible way to cope with it . . . it is
a daily process of making order.*

Thomas Bernhard

The Eye/I
A Story to Love Her

For a long time, her mother read to her. Since the time she had learnt to speak, every morning for the next three years they spent two hours together, with the mother reading stories and poems to her and after each story her mother asked questions. My Little V— her mother always called her My Little V even when her mother was not happy with her; her mother always called her My Little V—can you tell me why Marcela ate the cake that her aunt had kept for her brother's birthday and why did Franz, who was only five years old, why did Franz have to work in his father's garden even though his fingers hurt and he never had enough time to sleep and was that right for such a young boy? She remembered her mind racing as she had to think quickly through the stories to answer her mother's questions, and to answer them correctly, remembering the details and turns of each story and then commenting on each story in the way that her mother liked. There was no time for her mind to wander off or listen to those voices running around; the voices that she could hear through the open window; the voices she knew she should not listen to. Her mother was not in the habit of uttering explicit words of praise but she could tell that her mother was invariably pleased with her answers and that pleased her too. At the age of not-yet-four she was sufficiently needy—without knowing the word and therefore unable to articulate her feelings verbally—to understand that if she could show why it was wrong for Pinocchio to play truant, or why it was not right for Franz to work so hard in his father's garden, if she could think of the right comments, her mother would show affection to her. She wanted to be loved and she had to get love from her mother for there was no one else around: her father was out working most of her waking hours and at the time she had no siblings who could give her love even if siblings were ever inclined to give love.

In the years to come, she understood that her mother believed living was about improving oneself and the only way her daughter could improve herself was by being serious and working hard to acquire knowledge. The way she learnt to talk about the stories her mother had read to her made her mother think that there was hope that she would one day—but only if she worked hard—that she would one day make something out of herself. Her mother said those words while nodding half-heartedly; and that was important, she understood that kind of nodding at the time, she had a hunch that the half-hearted nodding meant her mother was not sure that what she was saying was true; her mother doubted her own words, the words saying that there was hope for her. That she would make something out of herself. That was important. She could tell from the tone of her mother's voice. She knew then that she should remember those words. They were the words to guide her in life, and she did not have to make a special effort to remember them. But when it came to poetry, her mother's hopes were severely challenged and she knew that her mother must have worried that her daughter would not make something out of herself and that pained her mother very much but despite all her efforts, despite all the willpower she could muster at that age, the words of poems came and went or, as her mother used to say, the words of poems entered her head through one ear and went out at once through the other. Her mother expected her to learn a poem by heart every few days, and when more often than not she failed to do that, her mother despaired. It is your fault, why are you not paying attention, why are you resisting my efforts to teach you? You do not want to learn. That much is obvious. What will become of you? Those were the questions she heard repeatedly; she heard them every day, every morning, every afternoon. Her mother was not a cruel woman by any means, she said. If such a thought crosses anyone's mind, they misunderstand her mother's reasoning and her mother's intentions, and very good intentions they were, and they misunderstand her mother's love for her and had someone at the time said anything about her mother being cruel—not that anyone could have, since no one was around during their mornings, those mornings when her mother worked with her—her mother would have been horrified at the suggestion; her mother would have been hurt; her mother would have considered the idea absurd, so absurd that her mother would have waved it off, perhaps even laughed at it, her mother would have said it was most unfair to say something so untrue, for she loved her daughter, she loved her more than she could ever love anyone else and her sole desire was to educate her daughter and help her improve, help her improve by increasing her motivation, help her improve by encouraging her to push herself to make more effort, to make more effort so that something would become of her. That was what life was all about: improving oneself, making sure that no day passes without learning something new, something that would make her a better person. Ignorance was embarrassing and most people had no excuse to remain ignorant, that is what her mother said, she said. Telling her to kneel in the corner of their kitchen for ten or fifteen minutes at the time when she was not-yet-four years old, and the ten or fifteen minutes facing a blank wall, while she was not allowed to talk, seemed much longer—as they would to a child of that age—but she had to do it because she could not remember a poem her mother had read to her several times, a poem that her mother had expected her to recite by heart, and that punishment—for it looked like punishment when she thought about it years later, but not at the time—she is certain that her mother would not have used the word because she would not have intended the kneeling and facing a blank wall as punishment—that kneeling, that punishment, was intended to, and it did have that effect, to make her daughter feel ashamed, ashamed in front of herself even though she was not-yet-four years old, and that shame spurred her to try harder, to make an effort, to push herself, as her mother kept saying, she said, and in that sense her mother was right and her mother's method was right. It was not the fault of the mother or of the method, for the mother did not know at the time and neither could she, since she was not-yet-four years old, she could not know that she was already a visual person, one of those people who find it easier to memorize words if they see them written down. It was no one's fault because her mother had tried and she had tried; they both had tried, they both had tried very hard but she still could not recite the poems her mother had read to her, she could not recite them by heart without stumbling and without prompting or at least not beyond the first few lines. But in no way was the kneeling in the corner of the kitchen cruel for it was not intended as such and if anyone wants to look at it as punishment, they would have to admit that it was an enlightened punishment, yes, that is what it was, enlightened punishment, because it was designed to further her education and in doing that her mother was inspired—indeed she could see that later, years later, and she knew that her mother was compelled to act in such a way by the desire to improve her education and to help her make something out of herself. That was the most important wish her mother had for her. There was no question of cruelty because cruel parents were the ones who let go of their children—her mother would never let go of her—who let go of their children completely, such as the parents of Hansel and Gretel.

Apart from the shame that she felt while facing the blank wall—the shame that in itself would have proved constructive, a shame that would have been motivating had she not been a visual type, but that is something no one knew and no one could have known at the time—the kneeling was not painful in itself and the mother always made sure that her daughter's white tights did not become stained and so her mother always, always without failure, slipped a clean, white sheet of paper, A4-size, under her knees, and that was kind, that was very kind indeed, she knew that at the time and she knows that now, she said. It was love, it was love that motivated her mother to slip a clean, white sheet of A4-size paper under her white-tighted knees and the shame she might have felt became part of that love that her mother was giving her. Those who might think that her mother might have been cruel should know that the floor in her mother's kitchen was never dirty, in fact it was immaculate, one of those floors that people would say *you could eat off it*, that is how clean it was, and once they knew that they would understand how much the mother cared that her daughter would not have her white tights stained, and although it was unlikely, it was still a possibility, a chance event, a freak occurrence that a speck of dust or soot—where would soot have come from?—floated unseen from somewhere and landed in the corner of that kitchen, but mother cared so much that her daughter would not have stained tights, the mother cared so much that she kept a sheet of white paper, A4-size, ready and always slipped it under her daughter's knees before she knelt. That was love. Her mother cared so much that her daughter would not be dirty, she cared that her daughter would not become ill, for being dirty would lead to becoming ill and that could lead to dying and that was frightening, that was frightening because the mother's first child had died when he was a baby, a tiny baby and that was before the daughter was born and now that the daughter was a child, her mother experienced a terrible fear that the daughter could die too. And so her mother kept everything clean, everything immaculate, everything white, everything pristine, such that there was nothing to make her daughter ill, that is how much her mother cared, that is how much she loved her daughter. Her mother loved her so much, so much that she changed her clothes three times a day, regardless of whether they were visibly dirty or not and so three times a day she had to put on a clean dress, she said, a navy dress, a freshly ironed dress, and a white pinafore, a starched white pinafore and white knee-highs, or white tights, and white knickers and a white vest and everything was white except the dress, the dress that was navy but the dress had a white collar, a crisp white collar. The floor in their kitchen was covered with lino and so it was not too hard, not hard at all, and her knees never hurt when she knelt for that might have been cruel if she had to kneel on a hard surface, or even a rough surface, something that might have grazed her soft skin, her skin that was always pale, as pale as the white sheet on which she was kneeling, her skin that seemed indistinguishable from the white sheet on which she was kneeling. But there was no question of the floor leaving indented marks on her soft skin, definitely not, there were no marks left on her pale skin after kneeling for ten or fifteen minutes facing a blank wall and although she was not allowed to speak— her mother expected her to reflect on her bad behaviour, on her inability to recite a poem by heart, on her inadequacy as a not-yet-four-year-old child of a mother who worked with her—and she had to stay still and that was something her mother never specified but she knew it was expected from her and in any case she was not a fidgety child and so it was not a problem and she did not mind kneeling and facing a blank wall. Had it not been for the shame, the shame that played a crucial part in her mother's method, the shame that was intended as a constructive shame, the shame that was not only a motivational shame but also a shameful shame because she knew she had failed her mother, she had not lived up to her mother's expectations, she felt that shameful shame even though at the time she could not have articulated her feelings in such words and the shame, the shameful shame, which she felt strongly but was unsure as to why she felt it, nevertheless she felt ashamed, she is certain that she felt ashamed and had it not been for the shame she would not have minded kneeling in a corner and facing a blank wall.

She remembered how glad, relieved even, and how grateful she was when her mother, despite threatening to tell her father that she had to kneel in a corner because she could not recite a poem by heart without stumbling and without prompting, how grateful she was that her mother never carried out the threat and so her father never found out how bad she had been, for had her mother told her father, she would have been shamed in front of him as well, she would have been doubly shamed. That sense of gratefulness is something she felt at the time but she had no name for it then, all she felt was a sense of something like a relief, a burden falling off her chest and she was grateful to her mother. It would have been a double shame and perhaps a triple shame as her failure would have counted much more in front of her father. Although not-yet-four years old, she was aware that her father thought of her as *his clever little girl* when she really was not, and she would have been shamed had he been told that she was not really a clever little girl. She remained ever-grateful to her mother that her father had never found out about her inability to recite a poem without stumbling and without prompting, that is, he did not find out until many years later and by that time she had other achievements, other considerable achievements which, at least on the face of it, at least in the eyes of her father, and perhaps in the eyes of her mother, too, but never in her own eyes, those other achievements compensated for her inability to recite a poem without stumbling and without prompting. Sometimes in the eyes of her mother and in her own eyes those other achievements overshadowed, but in her own eyes they were never completely obliterated, her inability to recite a poem and therefore her inadequacies of that time no longer mattered as far as her mother was concerned. But the shame she had felt at the age of not-yet-four years old, that shame stayed with her. Had it not been for the shame, she would have thought of that time facing the wall as part of a game, a game that—thanks to her own resourcefulness, thanks to her own imagination, thanks to her ability to enjoy her solitude even at the age of not-yet-four years old, thanks to all of that, the game of facing the wall, for she had made it into a game—that game was enjoyable, that game was something she could have looked forward to if only that game had been the result of something else and not of her failure to recite a poem. But how could she look forward to that game, the game that she enjoyed, how could she look forward to it when she knew that the game was only possible because she had disappointed her mother? Sometimes, for at least half of those ten or fifteen minutes she had to spend kneeling in a corner of her mother's kitchen, and sometimes for three quarters of that time, she forgot about the shame or the shame was not the predominant preoccupation of her mind and she imagined that there were shapes on the wall in front of her. Although the wall was white, she could see patterns and forms in front of her when in her mind she connected tiny specks that had been ingrained in the wall or in the texture of the wall paint as it dried and linking those specks, drawing lines between them—and with the number of specks she had noted, probably up to twenty, although she could not remember exactly, but certainly no more than twenty-five, she thought, and this calculation is based on memory and is certainly not reliable for she had not really counted all the specks as she could only count to ten at the most at the age of not-yet-four—and with the number of specks, the possibilities for creating different shapes were numerous. Those shapes, the shapes that moved in front of her, like an ever-changing flock of birds in flight—she used to watch birds when she had free time and her mother allowed her to look out of the window and she used to find the sight of the ever-changing pattern of birds in flight pleasurable, even magical—that could take on as many forms as she wished, all depending on the way she linked the specks and that allowed her to create objects and people, images of objects and people because sometimes those shapes reminded her of the people she knew or of the people she imagined, and those shapes gave her a great deal of pleasure, the pleasure that by far surpassed both the feeling of shame and the slight discomfort she occasionally experienced on her knees, on her thin knees, on her bony, unpadded knees, the discomfort that was not significant as the lino was thick and not hard—not hard at all. There is no doubt in her mind, she said, that those ten or fifteen minutes kneeling in the corner of her mother's kitchen and facing a blank wall, for despite the specks that she perceived, it was a blank wall, a completely blank wall, and that is what any observer would have noted, any fair and detached observer would have said it was a blank wall, and therefore those ten or fifteen minutes, a few mornings a week, with a clean, white A4-size sheet of paper under her white-tighted knees, those minutes were if not all about pleasure, at least half of those minutes, and sometimes three quarters of those minutes were about pleasure, for no cruelty was intended and no cruelty was experienced, she said.

The shapes were not her only amusement. She had other sources of joy, numerous other sources of joy. When she was not connecting the specks on the wall into shapes, she thought of the stories her mother had read to her during those mornings and here she had yet another game. Among the stories her mother had read to her—either fables and fairy tales or simplified classics—was Mark Twain's *The Prince and the Pauper* and while it was not the story she liked best, it was a story that proved more rewarding than any other she knew at the time. She imagined that, like the Prince, she had changed places with someone else but in her case it had happened when she was a baby, perhaps even immediately after birth, in hospital, and so she could see someone else kneeling in the corner of her mother's kitchen, someone who was bad enough not to be able to recite a poem without stumbling and without prompting. With that game the possibilities were truly infinite for she could use anyone she had ever met, or anyone from another story, or anyone she imagined, to be the person taking her place, while she, despite not being able to recite a poem without stumbling and without prompting was somewhere else, perhaps sitting on the ground, in the dirt, without her collapsible stool that she had to carry in case she needed to sit down during those rare occasions when she was allowed to go out and even then only to walk in the little communal garden in front of their house. That collapsible stool proved to be a rich source of mockery for those neighbourhood children, but while kneeling and facing the blank wall in her mother's kitchen and playing the Prince and the Pauper game she could see herself sitting on the ground, in the dirt, and her white pinafore was stained with thick brown splodges, splodges of dust and caked mud, and she would make stories about the splodges, about the dirt, about the stains that marked her immaculate clothes and sometimes she could see herself playing with those children, those children who were always on the road, *like horse manure*, her mother's exact words, *those children who were street urchins*, again her mother's words. The thought that she, her mother's daughter, could be sitting on the ground among *those street urchins*, those children who were always on the street *like horse manure*, while one of those dirty street urchins was kneeling in the corner of her mother's kitchen, that thought amused her, that thought was so pleasurable that she almost giggled but something held her back. The game made her happy, so happy that on more than one occasion after her mother had read her *The Prince and the Pauper* again, she had almost told her mother what she was thinking while kneeling in the corner of their kitchen, she had almost told her how she could see an urchin kneeling down on a white sheet of A4-size paper (but would her mother had put a clean A4-size sheet underneath the urchin's knees?) with their dirty and sometimes even torn trousers and crying—yes, crying, something she never did—and protesting—again, something she never did because she knew she would be in the wrong to protest—but she stopped herself from telling this to her mother. Some part of her told her that she should not tell her mother but she did not know why she should not tell and years later she still could not find the answer but perhaps there was no single reason why she did not tell her mother about the Prince and the Pauper game. Imagining she had been swapped at birth was her secret, a pleasurable secret that made her all warm inside and had she told her mother, the game would not have been pleasurable any more, or not to such extent. Or perhaps she feared, and yes that was a fear, that her mother would have told her off for using the time in such a profligate fashion—*profligate* was the word she had heard from her mother and the word she was made to understand when her mother complained about people being profligate with their time and going to football matches when they could be reading poetry—and had played a game when it was a time meant for reflection, the time for reflection on her bad behaviour, the time to make promises to herself to be good and try harder, the time to make a decision, a resolute decision to put more effort. She could see that clearly at the time; and she can see that now. But perhaps there was something else as well that prevented her from telling her mother about her game: she sensed that the joy at the thought that she had been swapped at birth would have hurt her mother, would have made her mother think that she wished she had not been her daughter, or that she would have preferred to have been one of those street urchins, one of those horse-manure children. That was not the case. How could that possibly be? How could she possibly wish to have been born a street urchin? She was lucky to have had mother like her. She knew that then at the age of not-yet-four years and she knows it now, she said, and she knows for certain, there is absolutely no doubt in her mind that the main, the most significant, long-term and far-reaching benefit of those mornings when she was asked to kneel in the corner was that she learnt early on—and early on is important because *you have to catch them when they are young*, that is what her mother said, as young as she was, not-yet-four years old—she learnt to enjoy solitude and she has to thank her mother for that, she said. As the pleasures of what she could do increased proportionally to her growing awareness of herself and the world around her, and as the pleasures increased proportionally to her developing skill with words—and to the as yet only emerging skill of observing and perceiving beyond the perceivable—that pleasure of solitude increased too and so that in her teens she craved to be alone more than to be with anyone else. Ever since then she could not understand how anyone could say that they were bored in a particular situation, especially so when they were alone and left to create whatever they wanted, create in their mind, just as she did when kneeling and facing a blank wall in her mother's kitchen. She believed that a person who could be bored in one situation, could be bored in any situation since it was not the problem of the situation but of the person themselves. She understood the pleasure and the benefits—in this case, the two words were synonymous—of solitude and she knew that there was a great deal that she had to be thankful for, and thankful to her mother, she said. That would not have been the case had her mother been cruel. Anyone should be able to see that, she said, but people often do not know the facts, they do not know what is going on, and so they should stop insinuating, they should stop being malicious; it is such insinuations that are cruel. But she understands, she said, that if anyone has seen a child, not-yet-four years old made to kneel in a corner of a kitchen for ten or fifteen minutes, which is a long time for a child not-yet-four, and had that person assumed that the child was kneeling on a hard floor, for it might have looked like a hard floor, the yellow lino in their kitchen might have looked as though it were a hard surface, those observers would not have seen what was going on in the child's mind, those observers would not have been aware of the pleasure of the child at being able to make up stories using the shapes created by linking the tiny specks in the white paint of the wall, those observers would have no idea of the long-term benefits to the child, for such observers would only be thinking of the situation, of the situation as seen from the external point of view and so those observers might have thought the adult was forcing the child to kneel and face a blank wall and that the adult was cruel. But that was not the case with her mother. Her mother had never forced her to do anything. Her mother said she should kneel on the floor and—it was advice, not an order—so she did, she followed willingly, she said.

Her mother worked with her, and that is what it was, she said, and *working with her* were the words her mother used for reading of stories and poems and all the efforts her mother was putting into their mornings, all the encouragement, such as the kneeling in the corner of their kitchen, that were part of helping her improve, she said. Other people did not work with their children, certainly none of the neighbourhood children had parents who worked with them, her mother had said, and the parents of Hansel and Gretel did not work with their children either, and her mother wanted her to understand that what she was doing was for her own good and she should always remember that and she should know her mother was different from those who did not work with their children but let them be on the street all the time *like horse manure*, her mother's exact words, and she was different from those parents who let their children run around *like street urchins*—her mother's exact words again. Sometimes she thought that those parents, the parents of the street urchins were like the parents of Hansel and Gretel, cruel—that's what cruel meant, the parents who not only did not work with their children but also sent them away to fend for themselves, just like the parents of those street urchins she could see running around and playing together let their children fend for themselves. That was cruelty, but having poems and stories read to her and then being asked to kneel in a corner of her mother's kitchen on a floor that was immaculately clean and not hard, not hard at all, on a yellow lino, soft lino, with a clean sheet of A4-size white paper between her white-tighted knees and the lino—that was not cruelty. As her mother said, those parents of the street urchins were bad parents. She was pleased to be different; she was pleased to have a mother who was different, and even at the age of not-yet-four years old, she knew it was a good thing, she said. Mornings were for working with her, for reading poems and memorizing them, for reading stories and talking about them, mornings were for improving her. Afternoons started with a nap. Her mother had it all planned, every hour of her waking day was to be used meaningfully and working with her was crucial for her development, for her improvement and in that area nothing could be left to chance. She does not know, and it was something she began to wonder about later in life, whether by the afternoon her mother had become bored with her or whether her mother was tired, or whether her mother had something else to do, such as attend to domestic tasks, but every day after lunch a girl came to sit with her and watch over her while she had to have a nap. Her mother believed that having a nap was important for her growth, for her healthy development, for she was always pale, as pale as a white sheet of paper, her mother used to say, and although she did not feel she wanted to sleep, she had to go to bed and the girl sat next to her holding her hand. Since she was not sleepy, since she could not fall asleep, she had to pretend that she had fallen asleep, for there was no question of not sleeping, because her mother believed she needed to sleep to grow and develop and not be so pale; she was always so pale, *as pale as paper*, her mother used to say and at first she was not good at pretending to be asleep and she would scrunch up her eyelids, it was hard to keep them closed, scrunch them up so hard that her mother would laugh at her and laugh loudly, making fun of her, telling her not to be silly and that was right, she was silly but gradually she learnt to close her eyes and make the eyelids appear sufficiently relaxed to fool her mother and the girl. Fooling the girl was much easier; she always succeeded in making the girl believe that she was asleep. Her mother had instructed the girl to let go of her hand as soon as she was asleep but at the moment the girl did that, she pretended that she had been woken up. She had seen her father wake up with a sigh and a stretch, and she enacted the same and she knew then and knows now that she could not have been good at pretending to wake up, not at the age of not-yet-four, but the girl was easily fooled, and that too amused her, for as soon as she sighed, stretched and opened her eyes, opened her eyes slowly—that was the key—the girl believed she had woken up and the girl would immediately take her hand again and wait for her to fall asleep. She never fell asleep and so the game of pretending to fall asleep and pretending to be woken up by the girl, after the girl had let go of her hand, the game continued and that in itself kept her awake, for it was amusing, so amusing that even had she felt sleepy she would have made an effort to stay awake and not to miss the chance of the game. Her mother, who put a great store in her belief that children have to have regular periods of rest in order to grow physically and develop mentally, was annoyed and so she told the girl off, she said *you should not do that, you should not let go of my daughter's hand, I am not paying you for letting go of my daughter's hand too early, too suddenly, too roughly.* The girl had to make sure that her charge was asleep, the girl had to be sure of that before the girl was allowed to let go of her charge's hand and the letting go had to be gentle so that she did not wake up. The girl had to be careful because she was looking after a sensitive child, and a child who was pale, *as pale as a white sheet of paper,* her mother's words, and her mother told the girl to make sure not to do anything that could be detrimental to the child's development since that could not be tolerated under any circumstances. Her mother could never allow that her child lagged in her development because of anything, let alone because of the girl's lack of attention. The poor girl genuinely believed that she was wrong in judging when her charge was asleep and that the girl's letting go of her charge's hand had woken her up and the girl apologized each time and promised to be more careful. *I know I am looking after a sensitive child,* the girl said, repeating the words of the mother. That she was a sensitive child might have been the case but it was also beyond the girl's innocent and good self— could she say, as she later came to think, even simple-minded self—

to imagine, let alone consider that the child was being playful, and that the child could be cunning too, so cunning at the age of not-yet-four years old. But there was no question of her disliking the girl and trying to make things difficult for her, she said, and she is certain of that for she remembered feeling uncomfortable each time when her mother told the girl off and the girl apologized so sweetly, so innocently—so stupidly, she thought later—and with-out a trace of anger or annoyance. The game with the girl amused her and truly it did not make life difficult for the girl; she said, she could see that the girl was not upset at being told off and besides her mother always paid the girl even when she was annoyed with the girl, but the question of whether she was making life difficult for the girl was not something that would have crossed her mind at the time. Despite being not-yet-four years old, she was aware that the girl was being paid by her mother and she knew that the girl really wanted the money, she had to have it, that is what the girl's parents had said, she had heard them say that they had to have the money, the girl's parents had said when they had first brought the girl to see her mother and it was them who had arranged for the girl to look after her, she said and she knew that her mother, a doctor's wife from the capital, living temporarily—her mother always stressed it was only temporarily—in a small provincial town, her mother had power over the girl, although power is not the word she would have understood at the time of being not-yet-four years old. And she too, being her mother's daughter, she too had power over the girl and that amazed her since the girl was so much older than her, and that awareness was pleasurable for she was surprised how easy it was to fool the girl and how easy it was to control the situation, how easy it was to make the girl do what she wanted, the girl who was a child like her but an older child, very old in the eyes of her who was not-yet-four years old. But she was not cruel, she was not bent on exercising her power, for she did not know what it was, and she was not bent on exploiting her social superiority for she did not know what it was until much later when they were no longer living in that provincial town, nor did she want to be unkind, nor did she want to be hurtful, for she liked the girl, truly, she liked the girl, the girl who was a bit like street urchins because the girl might have come from a family like those of the street urchins but—unlike them—she was clean and calm and meek and the girl was in her mother's house and the girl was doing something, rather than running around aimlessly and she was not on the road like horse manure and she was not completely a street urchin. She liked the girl and indeed she looked forward to the girl coming to the house every week day after lunch, and what she liked was not just a game—an amusing game. As her mother had said, and the girl acknowledged, she was a sensitive child, an emotional, deeply feeling child, not a street urchin, rough and hard, and so the warmth of the girl's presence by her afternoon bed, the touch of her hand, a soft hand, a moist hand, a small hand but bigger than hers, and the sound of her voice, gentler than her mother's, all of that was pleasurable to her. With her eyes closed, she was free to think, free to think her stories, to revisit *The Prince and the Pauper* and sometimes, although not so often, *Hansel and Gretel* too, and with that latter story she imagined two of the street urchins, two of the horse-manure children, being sent away by their parents, the parents who were bad because they did not work with their children, her mother said, and the children, the street urchins, were lost and they walked to the witch's house and then one of them was being fattened up to be eaten, and here she dwelt on the oven scene, on the moment when one of the street urchins is about to be pushed in and the other one is terrified, and she made that bit of the story longer, imagining how the fattened-up street urchin would have been trying to free himself and he, or sometimes she, would have been screaming in fear. She could see the face of the street urchin and sometimes it would be the face of a boy and some-times of a girl and sometimes she would choose a street urchin whose name she had heard being called when she and her mother passed by the horse-manure children. Sometimes it happened that she dwelt for so long on the scene when the witch is about to push the child into the hot oven, and she imagined the situation with such intensity that she too would be scared for the street urchin and the more she was scared, the more pleasurable it was to remind herself that she was safely lying in bed and that her hand was held by a girl looking after her and that it was someone else who was being pushed into a hot oven and who was going to be roasted and eaten by the witch. At such times, she felt good, she felt safe and she would squeeze the girl's hand as if to reassure herself. But the real beauty of the situation, something that she was not able to articulate at the time when she was not-yet-four years old, the beauty that she felt instinctively, was that the situation allowed her access to two worlds at the same time: her own private, secret world, the world of stories that went on and on and the world that offered comfort that came from the presence of another person, even if that person was only a hand—but a warm and smooth hand.

Thinking about it years later when she started writing, when writing became her life, and sometimes, though not often, but from time to time, sometimes she felt lonely for writing always had to be done in solitude, her writing always had to be done in soli-tude, and it struck her that making up stories while having the comfort of another, of another who was warm and kind, was a unique situation, never to be repeated. The girl was holding her hand, while she had her eyes closed and the girl and the mother thought she was asleep and therefore did not make any demands on her and in that situation of being left alone she was able to think her stories, she was able to make up narratives, she was able to cre-ate like a writer while having love from the other. Even writers who work with other writers, writers who collaborate, even they have to work alone because collaboration does not mean that they write together at the same time at the same place holding each other's hand. And then there are those writers who co-author a text, but they too have to work alone, without the constant presence, the presence that is warm and soothing without being intrusive. But she had it all there, and from a writer's point of view it was a perfect situation: the peace and quiet to make up stories while having the presence of the other, the presence that was caring and entirely submissive to her needs, the presence that never threatened her story-making, the presence that never interfered with the world in her mind. But it was only in the years to come, many years later, when she started writing in earnest, when writing became her life and she understood what that situation, when not-yet-four years old she was forced to have an afternoon nap, she understood what that situation was about. But hang on, she said. These days she does not want the presence of the other, she does not want anyone around ever, at any time. These days, she detests most people, all those vulgar herds, *vulgar herds* that is what she calls most people, and when she thinks about that, she thinks that her mother would have liked that, would have liked her calling people vulgar herds, and it is those vulgar herds shouting on their mobiles and eating smelly food on trains, all those vulgar herds reading tabloids, all those vulgar herds . . . No. Stop. She needs to put a stop to such thinking, to such ugly thinking, otherwise she will be tormented by the smallness of her thoughts.

That warm, soft hand, that girl's hand from her childhood holding her hand was lovely but these days she can do without love, and she wants to say that she is unlikely to fall prey even to friendship, certainly not to a friendship from a woman, oh, she knows about those, those treacherous Eves, but best not to go there now, she said. Best not to go there now but still the question is why it is always women, why it is always women who abandon her, why it is always women who offer her friendship and then disappear without even having an argument, without having a disagreement, without falling out and then these treacherous Eves disappear without an explanation, with not a word of goodbye. Without a word they disappear and that puzzles her, and that used to hurt her, she said, but not any more. Men do not do that to her, men stay friends (or most do) but women, women turn their rough backs on her, she said. It has always been like that, from very early on in her life and it remained so through her teenage years and adolescence and continued through her mature years. But not any more. Not any more for if she has mastered anything, if she is good at anything, she knows how to be alone, to be alone and not to need anyone. And so she can say, she can proudly say that she would not fall prey to their friendship, the false friendship of those treacherous Eves, the friendship that would lure her in only to throw her out again.

While she lay in bed for her afternoon nap, the street urchins ran around and, when the windows were open, she could hear their running, their shouting, their squabbling, their singing, their laughing and she amused herself by trying to guess what was going on and she amused herself by matching the voices she heard to the faces she remembered. She had never dared have a close look at them when she and her mother passed them by as she did not want her mother to think that she was interested in those children, her mother would not have liked that because they were bad children, the street-urchin children, the horse-manure children. Sometimes she passed those street urchins on the way out to town with her mother and sometimes with both of her parents, but that was less often, and she always wanted to look at them but did not dare, and that became much easier when she was given a pair of sunglasses with dark lenses and she knew that if she looked at the children quickly, without turning her head, no one could know that she was looking at the children. She was interested in the street urchins but not because she wanted to be like them. She only wanted to use them in her stories, she would tell herself. She only wanted to see them kneeling in the corner of her mother's kitchen, facing a blank wall, and crying, protesting, none of which she had ever done. She only wanted to see them so that she could imagine their faces as the witch from *Hansel and Gretel* was preparing to push them into the hot oven. But she could not show in front of her mother that she was interested in the street urchins and so she made sure that she was not looking at them, and if she did glance at them, she made sure that no one could see her doing that, and she made sure that she was not saying anything when she and her mother, and sometimes the father as well, were passing by the street urchins and she hoped that her parents would not ask her a question and expect her to speak while they were within the earshot of the horse-manure children. It was best to pass by the street urchins as quickly as possible since there was no way of avoiding them, they were always outside whatever the weather, *like horse manure*, the phrase that she liked to repeat loudly as it was so evocatively visual, the phrase that also pleased her mother when she heard it from her, the phrase that could only have been said in a place like that provincial town in those days when people from neighbouring villages drove in their horse-driven carts on the way to the market and where horse droppings, fresh or hard, in various stages of decomposition—the images that came to mind each time she saw those children—were a daily sight.

When the afternoon nap had run its course and it was time to get up, usually after one hour, and her mother came to wake her up with a cup of hot cocoa, so hot and steaming that her mother had to stir it for a while and blow at its bubbling surface before she could take a sip. She pretended (what a good little actress she had to be for sleeping, for waking, for drinking, but all that pretending and acting was pleasurable) that she was looking forward to drinking the cocoa. Her mother often commented how good sleep was for her and how fresh her cheeks looked, not as pale as before and almost a touch flushed, and not as pale as a white sheet of paper, and her mother said *that makes me happy, very happy to see my little girl, my little V, looking so well rested* and her mother often added that her cheeks were the proof that sleep was good for her and she felt pleased and did not contradict her mother but she knew it was all those games she played, all those games she played in secret, all those stories she made up using people she imagined or borrowed from among those she knew, all the excitement from playing games with the girl sitting by her bedside and holding her hand that made her cheeks flushed. But she did not say that, she did not say that because she liked her secrets and above all she liked her mother being pleased with her and that was enough, enough pleasure. She drank her cup of cocoa with a thick foaming top, a cup that she had to be encouraged to drink with her mother pretending that the foam left on her upper lip as she took sips of cocoa, that foam was a moustache, a real moustache and her mother pretended that she was surprised that her little girl had a moustache and that was funny her mother said, very funny, and so her mother laughed, but her mother pretending was not real pretending, not like her pretending that she was asleep and that she was waking up. She knew that even then at the age of not-yet-four years old. Her mother's voice was not her real voice, it was a voice that she made up for that occasion only and it was an exaggerated voice and even her mother's face had a smile that was not her mother's real smile and her mother kept asking her to show her the moustache and to make more and more moustache and show it to her, urging her to take more sips until the cup was empty. Her mother laughed each time she was shown the moustache but she did not laugh in the same way she laughed when her father said something funny, this was a pretend laugh in this game they shared, a game that was a silly game, it was a game for her mother and a game not as good as those games she played on her own while kneeling in the corner or having an afternoon nap. It was not a real pretend game but a pretend-pretend game. And because it was a silly game—she did not say that because it was her mother's game—she did not want it to last a long time and so she drank the cocoa that she did not like, that she had never liked. After the cocoa, it was time for a walk, for fresh air, she had to have fresh air every day as it was essential for her development, for her who was pale, *as pale as a white sheet of paper*, her mother said, she said.

She has a photo, one of those black-and-white pictures with serrated edges, in the style of those days, with her mother wearing a summer dress—she remembered it was a yellow summer dress with the pattern of black sprinkles and smudges, the yellow summer dress that always reminded her of the scrambled eggs that her father sometimes ate for dinner, the scrambled eggs, that were soft and almost runny and on which he ground lots and lots of black pepper—high heels and short white gloves, the same type of white gloves that she too, at the age of not-yet-four wore when the two went out for a walk. And she still has the white gloves, she said, and sometimes she wonders how the gloves have survived all those decades of her life and how they have survived with her since she herself does not remember making any effort to keep them. Years ago, when one of her daughters, aged five or six at the time, acquired a magician's kit, she gave the gloves to her, she said, and she did that because the gloves made her daughter look special, the gloves made her daughter look unusual, the gloves helped her daughter play a role—just as her mother must have played a role and just as she herself had played a role when she wore them as a child—and as soon as her daughter donned the gloves, she looked different, she became someone else, as if she belonged to another world. Her daughter wanted to belong to another world, a world less ordinary than her everyday one and the gloves made her feel special, helped her think of herself as a magician. And she remembered how glad she was to be able to give the gloves to her daughter, the gloves that her mother had given to her, the gloves that thirty-five years after they had been used for the first time were still white, immaculately white, and she thought that was unusual and she thought that there was magic in them, and that idea amused her. She remembered being glad to give the gloves to her daughter, she remembered being very glad to hand over the gloves, as if there was something else that she wanted to hand over with those gloves, and she tried to think what that was but could not decide and sometimes she wondered whether the pleasure of handing the gloves to her daughter meant that she hoped her daughter would be like her, like she had been at the age of five or six or whether there was some other reason. But since then the daughter has grown up and abandoned magic, abandoned magic a year after she had taken it up, and the magician's kit was lost somewhere on the way but the gloves, the gloves that the daughter had given back to her were hers again and something about the gloves coming back to her made her uncomfortable. Why could she not shake them off, those gloves that made her stand out, those gloves that made her different? When she thinks about it, she finds the idea of those white gloves staying with her, living with her, without her wanting to keep them, without her making an effort to keep them and even after she had given them to her daughter—the daughter that would usually have forgotten to return even something she had lent her and the gloves were not a loan but a present—she finds it irritating that the gloves are hers for good. How come the gloves, the still-immaculate white gloves, have not been lost; how come they have not been misplaced; how come they have not been left behind in the course of one of her journeys from one country to another? And how come that the gloves are still unstained, and so immaculately white?

In the picture where she and her mother are wearing white gloves, her mother's dress is much too fashionable, much too elegant for an ordinary walk in a small provincial town and that is obvious when one looks at other figures passing by, other women wearing ordinary, everyday clothes, loose skirts and blouses tucked in, blouses that were not well cut and that did not look elegant and men are in navy-blue calico trousers—trousers that did not have the ironed line—and shirt-jackets, shirts that were meant for work, manual work but were worn on other occasions as well. Her mother's high heels are too impractical for the rocky ground of the small provincial town where only the main street and a few neighbouring ones in the very centre were paved. Her mother's clothes and shoes are ignoring the landscape just like her mother is ignoring everyone around, not looking at anyone, not talking to anyone as if her mother wanted to pretend, pretend to herself, that the family were back in the capital among fashionable friends. She, the girl, is wearing a navy-blue dress—one of a series of navy-blue dresses that she wore for years as if they were her uniform, one of those dresses that the street urchins used to make fun of—a navy-blue dress with a white, gauzy pinafore on top, and her hair is tied in a ponytail with a white silk ribbon. But the *coup de grâce* of their outfits are the white gloves, the gloves that they wear, or so the mother says, to prevent the dirt of the town marking their hands, and while the gloves protect them from dirt, the gloves also mark them out from other people. At the time she sensed that she and her mother were marked out but she could not have been aware of what it was that marked them out. Or if the thought occasionally crossed her mind, she would have attributed it to the fact that she and her parents were strangers in that part of the country as they had come from elsewhere. Later in life, whenever she looked at that black-and-white photo with serrated edges, the question that was to occupy her, she said, the question was what other people in the town thought of the two of them when they saw them so beautifully dressed, in clothes that were more beautiful than any Sunday best that they had ever had, not that those people, not that most of those people had a Sunday best and instead had to do with one outfit for winter and one outfit for summer, wearing the same clothes every day. And that black-and-white photo with serrated edges reminds her of those fashion photographs where a model, or a Hollywood star, is filmed somewhere in Africa or in a very poor area of Asia, or South America, and the attraction of the picture comes from the contrast between the environment and the local people on the one hand, between their poverty, the poverty that is made to appear exotic and therefore not real, not the poverty of deprivation, not the poverty of suffering, the living poetry, and the model wearing designer clothes on the other hand and where the local people are no more than the backdrop, the stage setting, where the local people are reduced to the function of making the Hollywood film star, like an Angelina Jolie in rural Cambodia advertising Louis Vuitton, in her perfect make-up even more glamorous than she could be if she were not standing next to the natives with their simple, primitive lives. In a similar way, she and her mother with their white gloves during the summer in a place where most people could not afford gloves in the middle of winter, despite the fact that winters were particularly bitter, she and her mother appeared even better dressed, even more elegant, even more special than they would have been elsewhere, as if they had been unjustly transported into the place with which, as her mother made sure, the two of them had nothing to do, the place which they treated as if its only function was to provide a background to their lives, albeit not an exotic background in the eyes of her mother, but the background that allowed them to stand out, the background that allowed them to separate themselves from everyone else and to make themselves different, and different meant better, she knew that even at the age of not-yet-four years, she said. And who could tell what that being different, and even more so that knowledge that she was different from others, that awareness even at that early age of not-yet-four, who could tell what that did for her becoming as she is, never belonging, always sitting in a corner, never being picked up when teammates had a choice, always feeling like an impostor, for ever being an outsider?

One day, when she was close to reaching her fifth birthday, she said, the girl who looked after her during the afternoon nap did not turn up and she had to have a nap without anyone watching over her, lying in her room with the shutters pulled down and while she missed the girl's presence, the softness of her small fingers, smaller than her mother's, stroking her even smaller hand, and while she missed the girl's words urging her to sleep, the girl's soft voice, softer than her mother's, for a couple of days she stopped playing the Prince and the Pauper game because all she could think was the girl's absence. She asked the mother where the girl was but the mother ignored the question. She knew that the mother had heard the question and she wanted to ask whether the girl would come back the next day but she knew better not to repeat the question and so she had to get used to being left alone for an hour every afternoon because her mother would not sit with her but would only come and check on her during the hour of the nap, tiptoeing softly, so softly that she could barely hear her and so she had to carry on pretending that she was asleep.

When the window was open, which was most of the time except in the middle of winter, she listened to the voices from the street and when the street urchins happened to be near the house, she heard words she had never heard before. Once she repeated those words in front of her mother and her mother frowned and she knew she should not repeat them again, for they were street-urchin words, the horse-manure words, bad words. They were not the words from the poems and stories her mother read to her, they were not the words for someone who had a mother who *worked with her*, that is what her mother said, she said. Around that time, soon after the afternoon-nap girl had stopped coming and just before her fifth birthday, she started attending a kindergarten several afternoons a week and there were no more naps. Some of the children she had met there were street urchins, and she wondered whether her mother would have been aware of that, and she thought that it was not possible that her mother did not know something like that and so she wondered why the mother had arranged for her to attend the kindergarten and it was that question that preoccupied her mind at the time, or at least that is how she remembered it. She was puzzled as to why after all her mother had allowed her to be with the street manure and while she expected her mother to say something, perhaps give her a warning to stay away from them, nothing like that happened. She could not tell whether she was happy or not to attend the kindergarten or indeed if she had any other feelings about seeing those street urchins there. At the time, she was an only child and perhaps she was shy in front of other children. After all, she had not had much experience of playing with them. Or perhaps it was because even at that early age she had a sense of being different. Sometimes she accompanied her father on his home visits to the villages surrounding the town and the family of the patient would always offer her a cake or sweets but her mother had forbidden her to accept anything. She had to stand by the door and wait. Her mother believed that most people in that area had poor hygiene and that her child could become ill from consuming their food. The daughter gradually developed a feeling that her family were not only different but also better than most other people around them. She was certainly better than other children since their parents did not work with them and that realization gave her confidence. She did not remember whether she had played with those street urchins in the kindergarten, in fact everything about her time there, a few months altogether, all of that is a blur, gone from her mind, it is all forgotten except for one memory.

That was the episode—she always thought of it as an episode, the word carrying connotations of something dramatic and unpleasant, also something that was a one off in her early life—that was the episode when a child, she thinks it was a girl, for in her memory it does not look it could have been a boy, boys always seemed more amenable, appreciative of the way she talked and of what she said, boys were always curious about her but not aggressive towards her, she said, and so that child, that girl, that girl who will no doubt grow to become one of those treacherous Eves, she pushed her into the swimming pool. It was a winter day and she was wearing her brown duffle coat, a coat that is in some of the pictures surviving from that period in her life. She did not think she had had an argument with the other children and she could not remember what it was like to be in a pool of cold water, a pool that would not have been deep but then she was small and the water would have reached up to her waist at least, but she remembered that two older girls from a nearby school were asked to take her home, and on their way they made her walk in the middle and they held her hand, one each, as they must have been instructed to do. They held her hands very tight as if they feared that she might escape. She did not remember being cold or shivering while they walked and she would have been cold because it was winter, and winters were bitter in that part of the country, and she thought later that it was significant that she did not remember being cold, and she did not remember it because she must have been so shocked,

shocked by the novelty of the situation. When she looks back, she wonders why no one, not even a teacher, had not taken off her coat and given her something else, something dry to wear, or at least wrapped her in a dry blanket. The house where they lived was not far from the kindergarten and it would have taken her and the two girls only a few minutes but it seemed strange to her now to think that they would have allowed a child, a child not-yet-five years old, to walk home wearing wet clothes and in the middle of winter, in the middle of what had to be a bitter winter. When the girls pressed the bell and her mother opened the door, there was a moment of silence as the two girls looked down, nudged each other as if neither dared to speak or was afraid of how her mother would react. Her mother stared at them, her mother stared at her as if the sight of her daughter in a wet winter coat was a proof of what she had expected to happen and her mother waited for the girls to say something. But whatever it was that one of the girls said was not important since her mother seemed to understand what had happened and since whatever words the girl had uttered made no difference to the scene. Her mother remained calm—and when she thought about it later, it surprised her that her mother was not surprised at the sight of her young daughter standing in front of her in a wet winter coat—and her mother carried on staring at her, at her dripping brown duffle coat and at the puddle that had formed on the marble floor and her mother's face remained calm. There definitely was a puddle, she is certain of that, for her first thought was that her mother might think that she had had an accident by their front door and the thought horrified her, and she felt ashamed that her mother might think—even if that thought existed for a split second only—that she had had an accident. She remembered standing right outside the front door of their flat, flanked by those two girls and the mother staring at her, staring at the puddle underneath her and fearing what her mother might think and that thought, that fear, made her shiver. She had never had an accident, she was potty-trained very early on, as her mother had said many times, and she had never had an accident, not even at night. Other children had accidents, and later on her baby brother, not yet born at the time, he had accidents, but she never did. Her mother stared at the puddle on the floor, stared for what to her seemed a long time and her mother's face was blank and that blank face, that very calm face of her mother's, that face with no questions, that face with no surprise stayed with her for the years to come. That was her mother's face not because her mother was not concerned for her daughter not-yet-five years old but because in the eyes of the mother nothing unusual had happened and, as she was to understand later, her mother had expected something like the pool incident to happen. Her mother had expected that the street urchins, those awful children with whom no one worked, those awful children who were on the street all the time like horse manure, she had expected those awful children to do something to her and she might have even been waiting for that to happen. Could that have been the reason why she had sent her daughter to the kindergarten? And when it did happen, when the street urchins threw her daughter in a pool of water in the middle of winter, and a bitter winter, her mother had no questions to ask, her mother had no surprise to show. It was all clear to her mother. Years later she wondered whether her mother had sent her to the kindergarten so that she could see what those bad children, the street urchins, the horse manure were capable of. Her mother could tell that her daughter was looking at them, she was looking at them surreptitiously and her mother knew about it because her mother knew her daughter, her mother loved her daughter and that is why she could see that her daughter was interested in those children and that sometimes she wanted to play with them, her mother could tell that, so, let her play with the horse manure, let her get dirty, let her play with the street urchins and see what they were really like.

For many years after that day she has wondered what the mother was thinking when she saw her daughter not-yet-five years old wearing a dripping, brown duffle coat, standing on the threshold of their home in the middle of winter. What was the mother's first thought when one of the girls said that someone had pushed her daughter into a paddling pool, and what was going through the mother's head when the mother nodded, when the mother thanked the girls, what was the mother thinking when she took her in? Whatever she was thinking, the mother had not asked either the girls or her daughter why someone had pushed her daughter into a paddling pool, she never asked whether it was an accident or whether someone had done it deliberately. Her mother did not have to ask, she said, because her mother knew the answer. Seeing her daughter not-yet-five years old, standing in front of her in her dripping duffle coat was the proof to the mother that after all she was right: her family was better than those people living around them and that was why they were not liked, that was why those people hated her daughter and wanted to hurt her. What else could you expect from the parents who did not work with their children? What else could you expect from the children no one worked with, from the street urchins, from the children who were left on the street all the time, like horse manure? No stories, no poems, nothing structured in their days, nothing planned in their upbringing, no wonder they were bad children, vulgar children, the horse manure, her mother said and that was the lesson that stayed with her, that was the lesson that stayed with her for life.

This recollection, this recollection which is fragmentary and incomplete, incomplete of necessity but no less valid, this recollection has another one attached to it, that of her parents kneeling by the side of the paddling pool in the evening of the day of the incident and poking the bottom of the pool with a metal measuring tape. They did not speak to her, they did not look at her but they whispered among themselves. She could not discern what they were saying to each other but that did not matter to her then and it was only years later that she understood that they were kneeling by the pool to ascertain whether she could have drowned and although she had not drowned, the possibility that it could have happened would have been on their minds and so they needed to measure the depth of the pool and determine the likelihood of that possibility but why, why did they need to know that, why did they have to be so theoretical, why were they interested in a mere hypothesis, she wondered years later when she understood what that night outing was about, or what it was about for her parents. And she, their child, their only child at the time, their child not-yet-five years old, the child who was the victim of a violent incident, the child who could have been scared, who could have stayed traumatized for life, that certainly could have been a possibility then, the child who could have developed a phobia of water, that child stood there on the other side of the pool, in the dark and watched them, thinking that they have forgotten about her and longing to be hugged. But hang on, did she really long to be hugged or is that her older self looking at herself not-yet-five years old standing in the dark, on the edge of the pool, her older self imagining that her younger not-yet-five-year-old self longed to be hugged and could it be that she is seeing her not-yet-five-year-old self longing to be hugged because her older self had been told by someone, a friend, or a so-called friend, her older self had been told that her parents should not have been theoretical, that her parents should have hugged her? If anyone had ever asked her later in life about the first occasion when she remembered being lonely, feeling alone and abandoned, feeling forgotten by the world of which she was not a part, had anyone asked her such a question, she would have described that night, that evening after supper when she walked with her parents to the kindergarten and that evening when she was left alone by the side of the pool while her parents poked the floor of the pool with a metal measuring tape. But that does not mean that she had such feelings at the time. It is easy to say that the trip after supper should have been about her, as someone did say to her years later, a friend or a so-called friend, and so she began to think that, she said, and whenever the memory returned and she saw in her mind that image of her parents kneeling by the side of the pool, and poking its floor with the metal measuring tape and then taking it out and looking at the measurements, doing their theoretical business, their hypothetical business, the business that had nothing to do with her, as that friend or so-called friend said when she told them about the incident. Sometimes she felt guilty when she thought about her parents in such a way but she always knew that there was no point being sentimental, there was no point wishing to have been hugged and comforted because that was kitsch, that was allowing your emotions to become kitsch—the word her mother had introduced to her very early on—that was in bad taste and it was even worse to have thought that her parents were deficient or that she had expected something from them that they did not provide, she thought at the time and she still thinks so, and besides, what was the point of wishing that some things were different when they had passed and there was nothing one could do to change them, she said.

When she thinks of guilt, she thinks of guilt that she did not feel at the time, she thinks of guilt that came later. When she thinks of guilt, she remembered the afternoon when she was not-yet-five years old and her father drove home from a village where he had been visiting a patient, a village where the land was green and soft and not as hard and as rocky as where they had lived, and they had cherry orchards and someone, the patient, or someone from the patient's family, had given her father three wooden crates, the kind that greengrocers sometimes use to store their wares, such three wooden crates full of cherries. Her mother washed a plateful of fruit for her but she did not want to eat them, which was not unusual, and she played with the cherries, using the double-stalked ones as pairs of earrings. Her mother watched her play with the fruit, still nudging her to eat just one: *My little V, have one for me, just one, my little V*—and when that failed, her mother fetched an old pot from the pantry. She can still see that pot, a big red pot with low sides and the grey-blue enamel inside, she remembered that clearly because the enamel was worn in the groove where the side of the pot met the base of the pot and to her it looked as if a huge black worm, or a slug, was stuck inside and the worm interested her but she would never eat from a pot like that. She did not have to eat from that pot, a pot with a worm, or a slug, living inside and she did not have to because her mother did not cook in that pot and only used it to store onions in the pantry and when her mother came back, she held that old pot in front of her and the pot was filled with cherries and her mother said she should offer it to the children outside. Not to the street urchins! What would the horse manure do with cherries? They eat thick slices of bread spread with lard—why would they want cherries? They have never eaten them, her mother said. They may never have seen them. It would be good for them to try something new, her mother said. Perhaps that is what they need, her mother said. Why would the horse manure need something new? Here, offer them the cherries. She went without saying another word and she does not remember whether it was because she was too surprised to consider what was happening, what was happening with her mother showing interest in the horse manure or whether she went out looking forward to seeing the children, looking forward to at last having a chance to be with those children, those dirty children who were running around, free to do what they wanted. As soon as she stepped out, holding the bowl in front of her, close to her body, embracing it with both hands, the street urchins, eight or ten of them, she cannot remember the exact number, the street urchins looked up from their game of hopscotch, or something similar, something that they played jumping around in the dust. They stopped playing and were looking at her, one or two moved closer. It would have been easy to offer them cherries and they might have been nice to her, but she was a child not-yet-five years old and she did not think like that, she did not think at all, when she stood there with her pot of cherries and the street urchins smiled at her, and she thought they are smiling because they wanted her cherries and looking at them from such proximity she could see how their ruddy cheeks, as ruddy as her cherries—the cherries which were clean, her mother had washed the cherries clean, and the cherries were shiny and the cherries were glossy and smooth—but the ruddy cheeks of the street urchins were dirty, dirtier than she could ever imagine, some with snotty upper lips, snotty green stuff under their lips with sticky bits, sticky snotty green, and that was the only thing on her mind, their dirt and snot and the thought that she had not noticed it before and it was that realization that they were dirty, that their ruddy cheeks were dirty, that they were real horse-manure children, that realization, that realization made her not want to give the cherries to the street urchins—or at least that is what she said to herself then and that is what she carried on believing—she did not wish to give them the beautiful cherries, washed and glossy; how could she have given the cherries to those dirty mouths, those horse-manure mouths? They were smiling mouths but they were dirty mouths, they were snotty mouths, they were sticky mouths under those ruddy cheeks. As she was looking at the dirt on the street urchins, as she was looking at the dirt around the street urchins, it occurred to her that they would become ill from all this dirt and that they would die, all of them would die, just like her little brother did, not that he was dirty, not at all, he was clean, a very clean baby, a baby in white, a baby lying in its clean white coffin, a clean baby with a white teddy bear, a clean baby surrounded by white flowers. She could see the street urchins lying in coffins but they were brown coffins and the street urchins were wearing their dirty, their scruffy clothes, and there were no soft pillows under their heads, there were no toys in their brown coffins, nothing that her little brother had. And when all of the street urchins died, she would be alone, she would be the only child and she would be able to go out on her own and no one would laugh at her white pinafore, no one would point at her collapsing stool, the stool her mother made her carry so that she did not sit on the ground in the dirt, so that she would not die, unlike those street urchins who were going to die. All of them would die.

Did the cherries come before or after the swimming-pool push? But what does it matter? What does it matter whether she played a trick on the horse-manure children or whether they hated her even before she had done anything to them? She is telling her story and her story is not about justifying herself. Her story, and this is *her* story, her story is not about looking for excuses and assuaging guilt. Why is it that even when she says so, and she believes it and she wants to believe it, why is it that she feels guilty for not being nice to the children who were born to the parents who did not work with them, the parents who did not know better than let their children be street urchins, the horse manure? But no, she does not feel the guilt, she is bored with thinking that she should feel guilty, for she has grown to be her mother's daughter and making an effort, improving herself, reciting poems by heart without stumbling and without prompting, that is what she cared about, that is what she valued, that is what she still values.

She cannot remember which of the street urchins facing her and her bowl of cherries asked first to have a cherry, she cannot remember whether it was a boy or a girl, but she remembers saying no, you cannot have it. How could they place a glossy, shiny, beautiful cherry next to those snotty, dirty lips? She remembered the street urchins stepping forward, standing close to each other and she watched this moving wall, surrounding her, slowly closing in on her. If they wanted to, they could have grabbed her cherries, they could have grabbed the bowl from her hands and run away. But they did not. Why not? Because they did not dare. The street urchins, the rough, dirty street manure did not dare take the cherries from her. She wanted to laugh at them. They were afraid of her. All ten or twelve of them—she did not count them—and some were bigger than her, stronger than her, but they were dirty and she was clean, her hair was combed and tied with silk ribbons. And she was a doctor's daughter, everyone knew her father, everyone knew her. Of course the street manure did not dare snatch cherries from her. They did not even try. But they asked to try the cherries. Can I taste one, only one, just let me taste one, someone said and the others echoed him. No, she couldn't give clean cherries to their dirty mouths. A pause. They were looking at her. A silence. Their eyes on her, pleading, unthreatening. She covered the cherries with her hand. She stepped back. The street urchins were still smiling at her, smiling their dirty grins, their snotty grins. You can have some of my chocolate, next time when I have it, someone said. She did not want chocolate, she did not like chocolate and she would not have taken anything from his dirty hands. Anyway, being so dirty he was bound to die. What was the point of having a promise of chocolate from him? She shook her head and she knew she blushed. She is all red. Look, look, someone said and then they laughed at her, pointing at her, taunting her, these dirty, snotty, street urchins, stinking street manure. Why did she ever think that she would have liked to play with them? She turned to go, they followed. She ran, they ran after her, the bowl bobbed in her hands, a cherry fell out, and someone screamed. She has dropped it, she has dropped it. She ran and someone picked up the cherry. But that was all right, they would have to pick it up from the dust. A dirty cherry. No glossy cherries for the dirty street urchins. Dusty cherries for the horse manure. Death, certain death. She ran, she ran in circles, she ran to the left and to the right, up and down, with no pattern, zigzagging left and right to evade them, she ran in the directions she chose and they followed, they had to follow if they wanted her cherries, the cherries which were falling out of her pot, falling into the dust and now that the cherries were as dirty as the street urchins, the dirty street urchins could have the dirty cherries. They could have them all, they could stuff themselves with dust. If this was not revenge for the paddling-pool episode, what was it? Was it really the snot, the dirt that made her think they could not have clean, glossy cherries or was that part of the story that she kept telling herself years later when she wondered what it was that guided her that day, what kind of perverse desire for control? Was she such a nasty child or was there something else she had learnt from her mother even at the age of not-yet-five years old, something about having to earn one's treats, something about having to work hard for what one wants, and therefore she was making the children run in exchange for the pleasure, the pleasure of eating the cherries? But there was pleasure, there must have been pleasure for her, too, in this running, this evading, this teasing, this control, this being in charge of a herd of street urchins. Soon the bowl was empty and all the cherries were picked from the dust and eaten, and they were eaten whole, eaten with stones. That was stupid, that was very stupid, did they not know that? She was not going to tell them, she would wait and look out, look out for a tree, many trees growing out of those dirty bottoms. She had never swallowed a stone, not once. Her mother had warned her: If you swallowed the stone, it would grow in your tummy into a tree and as the tree grew, its trunk and its branches would stick out from your bottom and you would have to walk around with the tree growing out of you. Now that would be embarrassing, everyone pointing at you and laughing. And your bottom painful, sore. But how come that she had never seen anyone with a tree coming out of their bottom? Everyone must have been very careful. But not this time. There will be street urchins, if they were still alive, if they did not die from all that dirt, all that dust on them, there will be street urchins walking around with a cherry tree each poking through their trousers and skirts. She waited and waited but it did not happen. She asked her mother how long it took for a tree to grow and when her mother said that it took a few years, she knew she would have to wait a long time. She waited a bit more but she could not wait long enough because her family moved back to the capital. Sometimes in her mind she saw the street urchins running around with trees growing out of their bottoms and one day she drew a picture of the street urchins with trees, cherry trees with fruit hanging of its branches and the trees sticking out of the children's bottoms. She loved the picture. When she showed it to her mother, her mother laughed and said she was silly to believe such things. How could a tree grow out of someone's bottom? Trees could only grow from soil, did she not know that? What a silly girl she was, and ignorant too, her mother said, she said.

Working with her, the words her mother used for their mornings of structured activity, usually reading stories and reciting poetry, was not only about improving oneself. Working with her was about love, she knew that even at the age of not-yet-four years old: her mother worked with her because she loved her, her mother was giving her love. Her mother made her kneel in a corner of the kitchen when she could not recite a poem by heart without stumbling and without prompting because she loved her. Those street urchins, those awful children—*and you know, my little V*, her mother said, *we should not forget that it was not their fault to have been born to such parents*—the children who were always on the road like horse manure, they were not loved by their parents. Learning her poems by heart and being able to recite them without stumbling, without a prompt, was also about love and she came to understand that one day when she was called back from the kneeling in the corner and when her mother had read her a poem not just once, not just two times, but three times and then had given her a chance to recite it without stumbling and without prompting and she still could not do it, her mother said that if she carried on like that, and like that meant being ignorant, being incapable, not very clever, inadequate, useless, she said all those things, if she carried on being like that no one would ever love her and she would be alone for ever, alone and unloved. She was not-yet-four years old and there was a long life in front of her and that life was going to be without love. That was not good. That was scary. That was serious. She could clearly recall the moment when her mother said those words, she could see that scene in the kitchen many times later in her life: her mother was sitting by the kitchen table, a poetry book open in front of her, and she, not-yet-four years old, she was standing by the door, with the hall behind it, and there was a saucepan with a soup simmering on the stove. The window was closed, the sun was shining outside and there were three flower pots on the ledge, begonias, two with red flowers and one with white in the middle. When her mother said the words, *no one will ever love you, V*—this time it was not *My Little V*, the endearment name—she believed her mother and she did not say anything, and her mother kept looking at her and the expression on her mother's face was serious, it was the expression of concern, concern for her. She remembered that suddenly the kitchen disappeared from her view, and all she could see was a geometrical pattern on the oil tablecloth and that pattern started moving and that gave her comfort, made it possible for her to breathe again, the pattern was moving and the pattern went still, but she liked it even when it had gone still and because of that pattern and the pleasure it gave her, the weight of her mother's words did not touch her as much as it might have had she not seen the pattern, or had the pattern not given her pleasure. But later, later that evening when she was lying in bed in the dark, the words came back and they were loud, much louder than when her mother had said them and she tried to think of the flowers on the window ledge and she tried to think of the pattern on the oil cloth but she could not remember the pattern and even the flowers on the window ledge appeared in her mind in black and white and she could not recall which colour they were. And then her mother's eyes came back into her vision and her mother was staring at her and her mother's eyes became bigger than any eyes she had ever seen and she was scared. *No one will ever love you, V. Not My Little V.* That was what her life would be like. Without love. Always alone. She pulled up her legs, bending them at the knees, and she hugged her legs and she made herself small and she told herself that if no one loved her, she would love herself, she would hug herself, she would kiss herself. That made her feel better and she fell asleep, and when she woke up, again she thought of the flowers on the window ledge and she thought of the dancing pattern on the tablecloth but when the next evening came and she had to go to bed, she could not sleep. She kept hearing those words and she was scared that she would always be alone and unloved as she was that evening lying alone in bed in a dark room. And so again she pulled up her legs, bent at the knees, and she hugged them, making herself small. And that is how she made herself fall asleep that night and many nights after that. But the words never went away and even when she stopped believing in them, she did not stop believing in them fully, she always believed in those words in part at least and that was enough to make her take the threat seriously, for it was a threat, a prophecy almost, a curse even—her first curse because there were others to come, other curses from bad fairies—and for the rest of her life she would think of her mother's words casting a spell on her and she believed in that spell, she believed enough to push herself, to fight the spell and to get rid of her ignorance because she wanted to be loved. She wanted to be loved more than anything else. And in those years of striving to make sure that the spell did not come true, she came to think that her mother was right to say those words, those painful words, because those painful words were the words that made her want to improve herself, those painful words made her want to better herself. She did not want to be without love and she was going to work on herself to get love. Her mother's words were a spur to her improvement, they were the words that encouraged her to work harder and learn more so that she would be loved. That was kind, that was kind of her mother, that was about the love her mother had for her.

Those painful words were kind words and let no one, some friend, so-called friend or other, tell her otherwise. If that friend, or so-called friend, needs proof that improving oneself is about getting love, they should read Kafka's letter to his father. He too was someone who wanted to be loved, and loved by his parent more than by anyone else and, like her, he feared that he was too ignorant to get love, and he lived his life fearing that his ignorance would be discovered and he worried that one of his teachers, or someone else, would expose him. The consequence of being exposed, for ignorance, was not being loved. That is what he understood and that is exactly what she had felt, she said, for many years she felt that. Throughout her education, throughout many years at different universities, and during the years that followed, she feared that someone would come and say that they had made a mistake and that they would have to withdraw her grades, they would have to ask her to leave and tell her never to come back because she was a cheat, an ignorant cheat, an impostor, and it was a miracle and also a shame, a great shame and really a terrible oversight that no one had ever discovered the extent of her ignorance. That is what they would say and the worst was that she knew that they would be right. She feared the door opening on a classroom and expected that whoever came in was about to say those words. She feared letters from schools and universities, she feared telephone calls. And when she stopped attending schools and universities, she was still afraid as afraid as she was on her first day at school, on that very first day when she could not stop her tummy hurting and rumbling as if she were hungry, that is how afraid she was of being seen as ignorant. Being ignorant meant having to do without getting love. Her tummy hurt on that first day at school and on her last day at school and her tummy hurt on every day between the first and the last day of her attending schools and universities. Her fear had nothing to do with being ignorant in any abstract sense, her fear had to do with being a failure, and being a failure, being ignorant, meant that no one would love her, as her mother had warned her that time when three begonias, one white in the middle and two red on the side—her mother was particular about such arrangements—were flowering on the window ledge.

She grew older. She was more aware of being a failure and she did not know what to do about being a failure, she did not know how to cope with being a failure and that really meant she did not know how to cope with not being loved. That is something her mother never taught her. When she was a postgraduate and one of her colleagues, an Iraqi woman, a married woman, a mother of three children, a woman who was a friend of hers, failed her exams, and she talked to another friend, a friend who knew the Iraqi woman and she said that it was amazing that the Iraqi woman's husband still loved her, still loved the Iraqi woman even though the Iraqi woman had failed her exams. And this friend, who was also a friend of the Iraqi woman, this friend laughed and said that the Iraqi woman's marriage did not depend on her passing exams. Did it not, she wondered. How was that possible? And he laughed even more and said she was silly and that she could not have been serious. She was serious. How could anyone love you if you failed your exams? She had never failed an exam, of course not, she made sure she did not fail her exams because had she failed she would not have stood a chance of being loved and she wanted to be loved. She thought about what the friend who was also a friend of the Iraqi woman said, and she thought a bit more about it and then she could see that this friend, this friend could be right, or partially right, for no one was ever completely right, and that even those who fail exams can get love sometimes, or if they did not get love that had nothing to do with their passing or failing exams. The words of that friend, that the Iraqi woman's *marriage did not depend on her passing exams*, those words made her think new thoughts, and those words stayed with her, but they never made sense, or at least not as much sense as her mother's words. She knows she was not unusual in that, she said. She was not the only one who believed that you had to improve yourself and that you had to be clever to be loved. She had come across others who thought that being clever and showing that you were clever, meant that you would get love.

One day, shortly after her fortieth birthday, she talked to a friend, a man past his sixtieth birthday, a retired academic, a philosopher, and he told her that he had written more than thirty books but he told her that they were all failures and they were all failures because he had written them so that he would be loved and yet he was not loved, he was not loved despite writing books that showed his cleverness. He said that he had hoped that a reader might like at least one of his books, if not all of them, and if they liked his book they would like him, perhaps if they really, really liked the book, they could even love its author. But that, alas, he said, she said, had not happened and so his life, his life of writing, staying up every night until two or three o'clock in the morning and writing books of philosophy has been a life without love. He was a failure, he knew he was a failure because the books did not bring him love. But the critics, the critics loved your books, she told him. What did those critics know, after all they were only doing their job and everyone knows that being a jobbing critic is not the real thing, it is not about saying the real thing, it is about saying a bit of this and a bit of that, a bit of good and a little bit of less good and that was it, that is how one was expected to write criticism. But that was not for real. That was not the truth. That was not about love. After the philosopher had talked to her, she wondered whether his mother used to ask him to recite poetry by heart and whether he was not good at it and whether his mother would have asked him to kneel down in a corner and face a blank wall for ten or fifteen minutes at a time. She did not ask him any of that because it did not really matter, things happened, whatever they were, and what happened was in the past and could not be changed and now her friend the philosopher was a successful failure. Or was he a failed success? She could not tell. But it was not all to do with mothers asking you to recite poetry by heart for she had never asked her children to recite poetry by heart and yet her children tended to follow their reports on good grades with questions about whether she loved them, she said. And when they asked like that, so openly and directly and making it clear, unambiguously clear, the link that obviously existed in their mind—and who for god's sake would have put it there, who but her?—she had to laugh and say what a preposterous, what a superfluous question that was but when she was alone she asked herself whether she would have loved her children less had they been academic failures. Of course she would have loved them, she said, of course she would, she always told herself, but she was not sure whether she believed herself and the truth is that she could not answer that question because it was one of those if-questions, one of those suppose-this-or-that question, one of those silly questions, one of those meaningless questions, and she thought it would be better to think of those gloves that she had once passed on to her daughter and the daughter had returned the gloves after she had had them for a year but who can tell what other objects, and more than objects, she had passed on to her daughters, what other objects, and more-than-objects, the daughters have kept and could never return? Who can tell how many objects and more-than-objects daughters retain from mothers and pass on to their daughters?

The words her mother said that morning in the kitchen while the sun was shining outside and three pots of begonias, two red and one white (her mother was particular with arrangements of colour, as she was with any other arrangements and patterns) were flowering on the window ledge, those stayed with her for the rest of her life, she said, and each time the words brought about that longing for love, that longing that was never satisfied but on that day the words did not cause her pain for long. She had found a way out of the fear she felt when she heard the words, she had found a way out of that future without love, a way out that was possible if she worked hard and if she was lucky. She had found a way that could prove to her mother that she was not right to think that her daughter would not get love. She could not tell whether she had found the way out by chance or by design and the latter is possible too because she did think, she did think for days, what she could do to make people love her. At first she thought she should listen harder and try harder and make sure that she could recite poems by heart without stumbling and without prompting but no matter how hard she tried, no matter how hard she listened, she still could not do it. But then she could see that a solution was there, it was with her already: stories, telling stories, stories that would bring love, the stories that she would not have thought of making up had she not been bad at reciting poems by heart and had she not been asked to kneel and face the blank wall in her mother's kitchen. Making up stories about shapes and characters she conjured from the patterns out of the specks in the texture of the dry white paint gave her lots of pleasure, the pleasure that was only made possible because she could not recite the poems by heart. That's where her stories came from, from her inability to recite poems by heart. And if her stories gave her pleasure, they could give pleasure to others, and those others could love her and if not all of those others at least some, one or two, if one or two of those others loved her that might be sufficient. That was worth a try. When she was six, she told a story, a story that she had made up using the shapes that came from joining the specks on the wall in her mother's kitchen, a story about two children who were lying in the grass and watching the sky and watching the birds very closely, watching them fly: two children who wanted to fly and watched birds in flight and watched them very closely and one day the children tried to fly but it did not work, they jumped up and fell down and jumped up again and fell down again and so they went back to lie in the grass to watch the birds and they tried flying again, remembering and copying what they had learnt from birds and this time it worked and so they held hands and they flew, they flew above the place where they lived and they flew round and round and then they flew away from their town and they could not turn back, they did not know how to turn back because that was not something they could have learnt from birds, that was not something they had looked for when they watched birds and now the children could not stop flying, they did not know how to stop flying. People could see them flying above their towns and villages, and after a few days they would appear again, up there in the air above towns and villages, and people began to wonder why those two children were always up in the air, holding hands and flying without stopping. Some people envied them and wished they could do the same and some people even tried to fly, and some people made wings and other implements but could not rise above the earth, none of these people knew that those two children had to fly because they could not stop flying, because they could not turn back. She told that story to a boy from her school, a boy sitting with her on the swings under a sheet, under a sheet which the school's cleaners had thrown over the frame as if to leave it out to dry and it was a red sheet, a red sheet draped over the frame of the swings in the school playground. She remembered the boy's face, a very pleasant face, a face with rosy-coloured cheeks, the colour which might have been reflected from the sheet, and she remembered him smiling when she was telling him the story and when she finished, the boy, the boy with a nice face, the boy who was called Pavel, the boy who had the same name as her dead grandfather, the grandfather she had never known, the grandfather who had died in the war and the grandfather who had no grave, that boy, that Pavel kissed her, he kissed her on the lips. The kiss pleased her, her first kiss from a boy and it was because of her story, it was the best thing that happened, and she felt loved, loved for her story. But when they went inside and Pavel took off his boots, she noticed that he had a hole in his sock and that was not nice, in fact they were two holes, next to each other, one of which was big—big enough for a toe to protrude through—and the sight of those two holes in the socks of the first boy who had ever kissed her was upsetting, that was too much to bear. How could a boy who kissed her, a boy who gave her love, how could he have holes in his socks and she thought that perhaps he was a street urchin, a little bit of a street urchin, a street urchin with a pleasant face and she did not want love from a street urchin, not even a street urchin who loved stories and who was only a little bit of a street urchin. She did not want that love and she decided to forget about Pavel and his kiss—her first kiss from a boy, the spoilt kiss—but she learnt that she could tell her story to someone else and get love from them.

When her parents had visitors around for dinner, she was allowed to stay up and meet them for half an hour and there were occasions when her parents' friends were invited for afternoon coffee and cake and on those occasions her mother would ask her to recite a poem for them but eventually her mother had to accept that her daughter was not always very good at it and that she could not rely on a faultless performance even with the poems that her daughter had previously delivered without stumbling and prompting and that was embarrassing, that was very embarrassing for her mother as her mother told her when they were alone together, that was very embarrassing, that was shameful and therefore she stopped asking her daughter to recite poems by heart and allowed her daughter to entertain their visitors with a story she had made up. She did not know what her mother thought of those stories but her parents' visitors unfailingly praised them and when those visitors came back, they always brought her a bar of chocolate or a packet of bonbons. She was not fond of chocolate and rarely ate it and she was not allowed bonbons as her parents thought eating bonbons rotted one's teeth and she did not mind her parents not letting her eat bonbons because she did not want to eat her presents anyway, she did not want them to disappear, she wanted to see them there, see them as proof that her stories were good, the stories that brought her presents and love, she only wanted her presents because presents meant that the visitors who had heard her stories appreciated her stories, and that meant that the visitors liked her, she was sure of that, for how could you like someone's story and not like them? So that was all right, that was all right for getting love. Reciting poems by heart without stumbling and without prompting was not the only way to be loved. The world would not love her, as her mother had said because she was useless at reciting poems by heart but perhaps the world could love her for her stories, she thought. When the thought came to her, she said, she wanted to tell her mother, she wanted to reassure her that perhaps there was a chance that someone would love her, that even if she could not recite poems without stumbling and without prompting, she could work on her stories, she could make up lots of stories, she could be making up stories every day, making up stories all the time and that would be lots of love but even with just a few stories, good stories, someone would love her and that thought was wonderful to her and she wanted to tell that to her mother but she did not. She thinks, she said, she thinks she might have tried to tell her mother but something always interrupted them, something always came between them, things would regularly come between them when she wanted to say something and she stopped saying what she wanted to say, she said, and sometimes she even worried that her mother had been worrying about her daughter not being loved and she really wanted to speak only to reassure her so she did not have to worry.

But once when she was telling a story to her parents' visitors, a story that she had been thinking about for a long time but never had a chance to tell anyone and in that story there were children who were playing in the street and they played with horse manure, making shapes out of horse manure, making houses out of horse manure, making little sculptures of children from horse manure, making a little world out of horse manure and they played so much, and they loved playing with horse manure and they were shouting and they were singing and then one day no one, not even the children, no one could tell the children apart from horse manure, they all looked the same, the children and the lumps of horse manure, and when she came to that part of the story, her mother stopped her and said that it was not a good story, it was a silly story, a dirty story. One of her father's friends, a man who was usually very quiet and never made a comment about her stories, that man said that he wanted to hear the rest of the story. And she wanted to move nearer him, she wanted to stand by the armchair in which he was sitting so that she could tell him the story and no one else would hear it because it was best to tell stories only to those who wanted to hear them—but how could they know if they wanted to hear her stories until they heard them?—and so it was right, she thought, to tell him a story and not to others but her mother said that it was too late for her stories, for her silly stories, and that it was time for bed. She wanted to tell her that the story was almost finished and she looked at the man and she waited for him to say that he wanted to hear the rest of the story but he did not say anything, for he was a quiet man and then her mother stood behind her and her mother's hand was on her shoulder and her mother asked her to say good night to everyone. Her mother left the room with her and her mother did not say anything when they were alone but she knew her mother did not like the story, the story her mother said was a silly story. She lay in bed thinking about the end to that story but she could not remember the end and so that story always remained in her mind with no end. Perhaps that was a story with no end because it was a dirty story, or so her mother said, and it was good that her mother had stopped her for how could she have told a story with no ending, what kind of story would that have been? A silly story, a dirty story, that is what she thought then but that is not what she thinks now. That is not what she thinks now, now that she knows that stories have no end, now that she knows that all ends to stories are false ends and this story, the story to love her, this story that she is telling now, this story has no end.

There were other ways of getting love apart from telling stories. She remembered being on holiday with her parents and in the middle of that holiday they travelled to a place where her parents had friends and they spent two days and two nights with them and most of the time her parents talked to their friends and cooked together and went for walks and these friends did not have any children and so she was alone and there was nothing for her to do and so she read, she read for hours and when she had finished the reading she had brought with her, she started on a novel that she had found in their bedroom. It was a grown-up novel, thick with hundreds of pages but that did not put her off and although she did not fully understand the story, who loved whom and who did not love whom—something that could not have interested her then, and something that could not have interested her later, and such things never came to interest her in stories anyway—she still carried on reading because she liked the process of reading and the idea of reading and when the man of the house, her parents' friend, praised her and said he was amazed that such a young child could read for so long at a time and such a big book and added that she must be clever and he sounded kind and he smiled at her and it was definitely praise for and approval of her and so it was a bit like love. When he said that, she thought that reading a big book, even if she did not understand its meaning, could make people love her because seeing her read made them think she was clever and being clever brought love and so she carried on reading and although she could not remember much beyond the page she was on, she read and read until she finished it. Those hours were worth it for they were about love, they were about getting love, she thought, she said, and it felt good, because her parents' friend had said those nice things about her and it made her feel nice, it made her feel loved and in the end that was all that mattered, for people to say nice things about her and to love her, to love her because she was clever, she was clever even though she could not always recite a poem by heart without stumbling and without prompting.

Reading was clever and so reading was about love, and making stories was about love but sometimes, and she learnt that later, reading was not all about love and telling stories was not about love and sometimes it was about hate but the worst was that you could not tell whether your story was about love or about hate. Some of her stories must have been about hate, about getting hate, she thought, for why else would those children, and some of them might have been street urchins, and that made her understand it better, why else would they have pushed her to that paddling pool? She was not-yet-five and she could not think that it was anything she had done to them that made them hate her but later, years later, she remembered that on the day when they pushed her into a paddling pool, as on other days in the kindergarten, she was trying to tell them a story, the same story that one of her parents' friends liked, a story about a woman who took a wrong child home from the maternity hospital and it was not a mistake, it was not accidental, it was a deliberate act of cheating because the woman in her story had wanted someone else's baby, the woman had preferred someone else's baby to her own and it was a good story, a story that made her parents' friends love her, a story about love, about getting love but for the street urchins that story was about hate and so years later she realized that whether the story was about love, whether it was to make others love you, or whether it was about hate, whether it was to make others hate you, did not depend on the story but it depended on those who listened to it and so any story could be about love and could be about hate. But how could she know? She was telling the street urchins in the kindergarten that story about the woman and her stolen baby, the story that had given her love before but those children, those street urchins, they would not listen and she followed them around, and telling the story anyway and if only they could have heard the whole story they would have liked it, she was sure of that, but they did not hear the whole story, they were too impatient, too silly, running around and then climbing a tree and so it was not her fault that they did not hear the whole story for she really tried but then she had to stop when someone—and she is sure it was a girl, a street-urchin girl—pushed her into the paddling pool. She stopped telling the story and she wanted to cry because she knew they did not like her—and it was not her fault, they would have liked her had they heard the whole story, but they would not hear it and if only she could have made them hear it, everything would have been fine. But when they pushed her in the paddling pool, she did not cry because they all laughed when they saw her scrambling out and dripping wet and she thought that it was sad that they would never know the end of the story. But she would have told them the end even after they had pushed her, had they asked her nicely, she would have told them the story even while she was dripping wet, if only they had asked nicely or had they said something about being friends, but they did not, they laughed and they all ran away and perhaps they were sad that they had missed her story for it was a good story and it was a story to love her, she thought, she said.

Then there came a time when her writing was less about love or about hate—or at least she did not think of her stories as being about love or about hate—and that was a time when she believed—how naive and irrelevant that seems now—that writing was about making people think or do something. She remembered when she was nine or ten years old, her teacher at school had asked the class to write a story, a story that would be read at a meeting of the local council and the school parents would be in attendance too and those people were the people who were to vote on whether a new school, a brand-new school should be built to replace the old building that had a leaking roof and crammed classrooms. She remembered her story being chosen from among the pupils of all three classes in her year and she remembered thinking that there was something special about her story since it was chosen among a hundred of other stories to be read in front of a large audience and she remembered going home and telling her mother that she had been chosen to read her story to all those people who were about to make a decision on whether a new school, a brand-new school, should be built and she remembered speaking very fast and expecting her mother to be pleased with the news. She remembered thinking that perhaps her mother was pleased because her mother was looking at her and her mother seemed very calm, for a few moments her mother did not say anything, she remembered thinking that her mother was thinking that after all her daughter would not be without love because she could write stories that were loved but when her mother spoke, she knew she was wrong about her mother's thoughts. Her mother said something about her not being able to read in front of such a large audience and she remembered that such a thought had not occurred to her for why should she not be able to read in front of such a large audience, she could always read her story, audience or no audience, that did not matter to her even then, it was the story that was important. She said that to her mother and her mother said that it was not the story that was important, it was the audience that was important, and that the audience could confuse her. Her mother said that the story was only a means to make the audience vote in favour of the new school, in favour of spending money on a building, her story was to be used to influence people. And she thought about her mother's words and she had to agree that her mother was right, the story was not a proper story, it was not a story that was to make people love her, it was a story that was to make them give money, not love, and so it was a silly story. She remembered returning to school later that afternoon and standing on the stage in the school hall, on the stage, in the wings, behind the curtains and waiting for her turn to read the story and while she was waiting she thought more about her mother's words and she did not want to read her story, she did not want to read the silly story to those people who were about to make a decision whether to spend money on building a new, a brand-new school. She knew then that her mother was right and that stories should not be used to make people think in a particular way, in a particular way that was about making decisions connected with money. Her teacher, the teacher who was one of the three teachers who had chosen her story to be read out, was standing next to her in the wings, the teacher turned towards her and said that it would only be a few minutes before her turn and she looked at the teacher and she was about to say that she did not wish to read after all but the teacher was smiling and the teacher seemed happy and the teacher said that she was proud that her pupil had written such a good story and that it was not anyone else from the other two classes, from the classes taught by other teachers, it was her pupil who had won, it was her pupil who had been chosen and how right it was that she had been chosen because hers was the best story and that the story would make many people happy. And so she did not tell the teacher that she no longer wanted to read but she asked how the story would make people happy and the teacher said that the story would make people decide to build a new school and that would make lots of people happy and lots of children happy and that was important. And she wanted to say that her mother said that artists create beautiful things and that only stories that are beautiful should be written, not stories that make people do things. An artist creates beautiful things, she said, but the teacher did not hear, the teacher's hand was already on her shoulder and the teacher was pushing her towards the stage and then she heard the announcer say her name and she had to go on. She stood in the middle of the stage and waited for the announcer to adjust the microphone to her height and she was looking at the audience, at the audience that stretched far back to the end of the hall, to the end of the hall behind the seats, to the space behind the seats where the audience stood in a dark crowd and then she noticed her mother in the third row, right in the middle and once again she did not want to read her silly story and she was about to walk away but the audience started clapping and her teacher, her teacher still standing in the wings said, *give them the story*, and then the teacher said her name and she knew that the teacher was being nice to her and helping her and she knew that there was no way back and so she read the story for the teacher but she kept her eyes on the paper in her hands and she hardly ever looked up because she did not wish to see her mother right in the middle of the third row, she did not wish to see her mother disapproving of her reading this story, this story that was not beautiful, this story that was about money. And the story was not beautiful but the story worked, the story did what it was expected to do and she remembered thinking about it days later when her teacher congratulated her for helping the audience decide and decide in the way that would make many people and many children happy. She remembered being pleased that her story helped make someone happy—because being happy could be a bit about love, about giving love and maybe even about getting love— but it still did not make it a beautiful story and she remembered deciding that she would never again want to write a story like that, a story that was not beautiful, a story that was not about love. In the years to come she remembered that day when she read her stilly story to a large audience but the decision she had made on that day, the decision which she had considered a good decision, that decision, as time passed, stopped making sense because she did not know what beauty was and she thought that she should have asked her mother but by the time she was ready to ask that question, her mother was no longer around.

Her mother had taught her many things, she said, and she was grateful for all those days of working with her but there was one thing that her mother never talked about, and that was to do with failure, with being a failure and all that comes with it. Her mother had never taught her how to cope with failure. She has to cope with being a failure because she, like everyone else, has always been a failure, most certainly so, and it has been a while since she has known that. She wants to stress, she said, that knowing and accepting that one is a failure is not a bad thing and she is not concerned about that and it has not been a problem for her, or it has not been a problem all the time, and she is certain that in her case realizing that she was a failure was constructive as the realization kept her on her toes, spurred her on to try harder, to make more effort, to push herself. That realization increased her desire to improve herself, and with time that meant being more creative, that meant developing her creativity so that other people would love her and that was what life was about, that was what life was about for her, about being loved, she said, she has thought that throughout her life. The realization sent her on a journey, a journey that sometimes, often in fact, made her, if not forget, at least stop thinking for a while that she was a failure—which was not necessarily a good thing; it was better to remember being a failure—but whatever she did and whether she thought about being a failure or when she forgot about it for a moment or two, she was still a failure, even when she appeared successful, or successful at first, or appeared so to some people—certainly not to her, most certainly never to her—and even when what she did was praised by others, she was still a failure and being a failure was difficult, and the worst were those days when the realization of failure was so painful that it paralysed her and on those days the realization of being a failure did not lead anywhere, or not obviously so because in order to be spurred on, that is, for the realization of being a failure to be constructive, the feeling had to be less painful, the feeling of failure had to be less painful but when the realization of being a failure brought about a truly difficult feeling, a truly painful feeling that did not lead anywhere, that was the worst part. There is nothing she could do about that feeling, about that difficult feeling.

But perhaps there may have been a time when she could have done something about that difficult feeling, the time before that person, that woman, but she was only one of many, one of many who behaved like that, that woman who was a friend, that woman who was a close friend, and who wanted to be a very close friend, that woman who wanted to be a lover, or so she indicated, but she said that teasingly, playfully, and that woman made her think that there was a possibility of love and then the woman turned her down. That was difficult, more difficult than anything before, and she remembered going to the toilet in the woman's flat, going to the toilet after the woman had turned her back on her, and turned her back on her so suddenly and so unexpectedly, and after that the woman had laughed at her. She could hear her laughter, the laughter that still echoed while she was in the toilet and she knew that the laughter was in her head because the toilet was too far from the room where the woman was and she remembered that she wanted to cry and she thought that once she started she would not be able to stop crying but then she noticed that the toilet was dirty, she noticed brown marks on the inside of the white bowl and she did not want to cry any more and she left the flat, she left the flat as quickly as she could, she left the woman's flat without saying anything. She did remember the woman for a long time, in fact she never forgot the woman, and sometimes she wondered whether the woman, the woman with a dirty toilet was a grown-up street urchin. When she saw the woman next time, the woman tried to be friends with her and she seemed kind but she did not matter any more, her kindness did not matter any more, her love, on offer or not, her love did not matter, for all she could remember was that dirty toilet in the woman's flat. And her question that day, her asking why the woman had turned her back on her did not matter either. It was too late for questions.

With time, she learnt that women, like husbands and lovers, come and go. And only sometimes do they talk about the master of Sienna.

The woman with the dirty toilet did not really matter in the course of her life. In fact, she remembers her only because she was the first, the first of a series of similar women, friends and potential lovers, all of whom turned their back on her for a reason she could never fathom. Therefore, the woman with the dirty toilet was only the beginning of a series of potential loves lost, the first of a series of lost possibilities of love. But there always seemed to be enough time for hope, for a hope to get love and there always seemed to be enough time for making something out of herself since everyone kept telling her that she was young and that she could still achieve this or that but then overnight she was old and the possibilities, the dreaming of possibilities of making something out of herself, that dreaming had to stop. Failure, the failure to get love and the failure to make something out of herself, became her destiny and she tried to teach herself to accept it and she tried to teach herself to turn failure into the motivating project of her existence. These days she keeps going, going and failing, over and over again, telling her story only to elude the anguish awaiting her when she ends.

Knowing that she was a failure sometimes stopped her from getting love or giving love. She recalls the times of hands reaching out and smiles and messages, but she could not take them for she had nothing to give except talk of her failure, talk of her shame. And who would want to listen to stories of failure and shame, the shame of being a failure, she asked herself? She kept telling herself to stop thinking about wanting to be loved but she was a failure at that, too, and her longing to be loved never went away but on some days, on the days when she could write her story, she did not think about the longing to be loved and when she wrote and wrote and did not need to stop, she knew that she no longer cared to be loved because writing was enough. Writing filled her heart, the heart that did not have love and she made herself stop longing to be loved and she did not care to be loved and that was not so difficult because there were not many people, there were hardly any people at all that she wanted to be loved by and from that moment her life was once again all about improving herself and the only way she wanted to improve herself was by writing and whatever she tried, no matter how much better she became, she was never as good as she wanted to be, she was always a failure. She never improved enough and she knew that she would never improve enough for that was in the nature of things, the nature of things that the writing in her head was always better, infinitely better, unimaginatively better than the writing on the paper, and this was also in the nature of things because there was no absolute level that one could achieve, there was no Everest to climb, no Everest to reach and wave from the summit triumphantly, sticking a nation's flag (which nation in her case?) and taking a picture for the papers, there was no perfect standard (no perfect flag) that she could achieve; not that she could do so even if that were possible in the nature of things. She could not succeed, she said, in striving to go beyond the craftsmanship of writing and there was a time when she thought that maybe one day, maybe one day she might convey something, something exceptional and for that she would have to take risks, she needed a high-risk approach, she needed to go beyond the admissible, beyond the desirable, she needed to go beyond the wanted, beyond the house style, she needed to go beyond the run-of-the-mill, she needed to go beyond what they were looking for, she needed to go beyond that with no certainty that she would ever convey anything memorable. Yes, there was a time when she thought that it was possible, that it was just possible, that she would write something memorable but that time, that hope has gone and even that desire to convey something memorable has gone, has mostly gone, mostly gone, mostly but not completely, and that *not completely* is something. (But why? Why is she holding on to that?) That is a little crack of light, a light crack of desire shining, spurring her on. She has always wanted, she has always hoped to write beyond the craftsmanship, beyond the good, beyond the possible, because anything memorable had to be beyond the craftsmanship, beyond the good, beyond the possible, but she could not, or most of the time she could not do that, she could not do that because what was in her head could never be moved to the paper, she could not do that even with a high-risk approach but perhaps it was not high enough, perhaps it was not really a high-risk approach and therefore she had to be a failure, she said, and she would always be a failure, she said, and it was best, not only best but the only way was to accept that she was a failure, she said. That is what she thought but she could not be sure and she regretted not being instructed to learn acceptance, acceptance of being a failure when she was young. Where was the long-term and far-reaching benefit of those mornings when she was asked to kneel in a corner of her mother's kitchen?—She would sometimes ask herself. Her mother who had taught her many things, many things that she needed in life and she was grateful for that, and her mother who had taught her many things that she did not need in life—but they were still things that she was happy to know—her mother had never taught her how to cope with being a failure, in fact, she said, thinking about it, she does not remember that she had ever heard her mother say that word. For even when she was a failure, a sort of failure, even when she could not recite a poem by heart without stumbling and without prompting, her mother never used the word failure, for it was not part of her thinking, for using the word failure would have meant accepting that her daughter could not do something, such as recite a poem by heart without stumbling and without prompting when it was really a case of her daughter not applying herself properly, when it was really a case of her daughter not wanting to do as she was asked to do and there was no question of her daughter not being able to recite a poem by heart without stumbling and without prompting, there was no question of ever thinking that her daughter could be a failure, she said.

But she was a failure, just like every writer, every artist is a failure, although some fail better, and what can she do now, now that she is a failure, now that it is not a case of her not wanting to do something or not applying herself properly, now that the failure is in the nature of things, what can she do now when she does not know how to deal with failure? It is no good punishing herself, kneeling in a corner and facing a blank wall for ten or fifteen minutes or for any time. What can she do but carry on, carry on writing so as to have it done with? So as to have it done with, that is all that her life has become now and that is why she writes, to have it done with, not to improve herself, for why or for whom would one want to improve oneself when no one matters and there is no love to be got and who is to say what improvement is and she does not write to say something, significant or insignificant, for what is there to say and to whom would one say it, and who is she to say anything anyway, and she does not write to produce a good story, for that is for children, that is for children who always want to know what happened next and who want to know what happened after the witch was prevented from pushing the boy into the oven. That is for readers who have not grown up. Had they grown up they would know that it does not matter what happens next, and such readers do not think of other things that matter and that was fine when she was a child, and when she was telling stories but now she is not a child and she cannot tell what happens next and even if she could what difference would it make?

Writing is what she started doing when she wanted to get love and when she needed to get love (but sometimes she got hate) but that need is no more, that need has gone and it has gone for ever and these days she would not even fall prey to friendship, certainly not prey to friendship from women. In any case, she no longer knows what makes a good story and even if she knew, what would it matter since all stories have already been told and all she can tell is her own story—but who would want to hear her story? That is all she can tell and, for the record, she does not write because she is inspired, for that too is for children—to be inspired—and, also for the record, and this is just a metaphor for there is no record, no record of any kind, she does not write because she has to respond to some kind of a muse, real or imagined, no, she has never believed in that sort of romantic tosh, she said. And she does not write because she wants to create beauty, and this could be for the record, too, for if she could do that, if she could write to create beauty— which she knows she could not but even if she could create beauty—what would it matter since no one would see it, no one would be able to recognize that beauty and she does not write because she has something to say about the world, and she does not write because she wants to ask questions, for what good would that do and, no, she does not write to change the world, no, she has grown out of that illusion, and all of these non-reasons are for the record, too. All that is left is to write to get it over with while being a failure at the same time and because she does not know how to carry on, her life is difficult, and daily living is difficult, daily living in that dark room where even when she switches on the light, all she sees is darkness and that is difficult, and sometimes she wishes, she really wishes that her mother had shown her how to cope with being a failure, for that would have been useful to her as it should be useful to anyone—or perhaps not to everyone for some people are not failures because they do not think of themselves as such, or do not allow the world to think of themselves as such even though they really are failures, but that does not matter for they do not think they are failures and so they carry on oblivious to their real status. She would not like to be one of them because, she said, they are superficial people, they are people who need stories, stories where things happen and they want to know what happens next, stories with an ending, such as a wedding or a death, or both, always an ending, and they are people who are still children, interested in who did what to whom and where and what happened next. If that is what they want, they can read children's stories but she wants to do her writing with no plot plotted, she wants to do her writing without a storyline that would tell her in advance what happens next, such as when she used to sit down with a clean sheet of A4-size paper in her typewriter, a completely clean, blank sheet, just like the ones her mother used to slip under her knees when she asked her to kneel in a corner of her kitchen when she could not recite a poem by heart without stumbling and without prompting, and now that sheet is no more, now it is the screen of her computer, a white screen, a clean white screen that she loves and she thinks that those who need a story, those who need a plot, something to guide them, they are afraid of their clean A4-size sheet of paper, of their white-screen page, and that means they are afraid of life, afraid of living a life. But she wants to write without security, without knowing where she is going, for what is the point of producing something that is like everything else others have produced, what is the point of writing what you already know, of plotting the plot that has already been plotted, what is the point of living a life that you have already lived? And it is this uncertainty, this uncertainty of whether she would be able to produce anything at all, let alone anything worthwhile—but what is worthwhile and who is to say what is worthwhile?—it is that uncertainty that guides her every day, it is that uncertainty that makes her get up in the morning and get on with it, so that she could get it over with. She is not afraid of a clean A4-size white sheet of paper, after all, she grew up with clean A4-size white sheets of paper, she is not afraid of the white screen, that is what she looks forward to—if one could say she were in the frame of mind of looking forward to anything—and she is grateful to her mother for that. Because it was that white sheet of A4-size paper that her mother used to slip under her knees so that she would not dirty her white-tighted knees when she had to kneel on the floor in a corner of her mother's kitchen because she could not recite a poem by heart without stumbling and without prompting and it was then that she told herself stories and, yes, those stories did have a plot, but she was only a child and if she knew how to write, she could have written those stories on that sheet of paper. But that would have made the paper dirty, that would have made her white-tighted knees dirty, as dirty as those street urchins, as dirty as the horse-manure children—have they too grown up to be failures and was that not an issue with them?—and her mother would not have liked that and she would not have liked it either. Her mother liked cleanliness, tidiness, orderliness and she, too, liked all those things that her mother liked, that her mother had taught her to like and let no one tell her that liking dirt, playing in the dirt, like those street urchins, would not have made her a failure.

She remembered an occasion when she was five or six and they were visiting friends of her parents in another town and those friends served lunch and she remembered they started with tomato soup and she remembered that she finished her soup, and she remembered that the plate was stained with the tomato soup, she can still see that plate, a deep soup plate stained all around with red, smeared with the red of tomatoes and she remembered that her parents' friends served the second course in those same plates, on top of the traces of the soup and she thought that was dirty and that those people were really street urchins, street urchins in disguise, and she wondered how her parents could not see that. She did not say anything and she did not touch the second course, even though everyone kept nudging her that she should at least try, that she should at least have one bite, one taste, and even her mother kept nudging her and she wondered how her mother had not noticed that the plate was dirty and she wanted to tell her mother, she wanted to warn her, she wanted to tell her that those people had to be street urchins but she did not know how to say it because everyone was looking at her and she knew that she could not say it if others were to hear it and so she kept quiet, shaking her head each time someone nudged her again and she kept quiet, not touching her food. After the meal, when she was alone with her mother and she wanted to tell her why she could not eat but even before she could say it, her mother said that she knew why she did not want to eat. Her mother knew that the plate was dirty and her mother knew the reason why she could not eat. Her mother knew and yet she urged her to eat. She could not understand that. Her mother knew and yet she ate herself and she let her father eat; how could she do that? Could she not see that those people, those people must be pretending that they were all right when they were really street urchins, dirty street urchins? Her mother agreed, yes, she said it was wrong to eat the second course from a dirty soup plate, the soup plate that was dirty, but some people were like that and since they were grown up, there was no point telling them, it was too late to teach them, that is what her mother said, there was no point telling them. They would not change. But their children would do the same, their children needed to be shown how to do things properly, how to be clean and who was going to show it to them if their parents did not know how to do things properly? She did think that at the time and she told her mother she was going to tell their children, the children of her parents' friends but her mother said she should not do so and so she did not. And as for the clean white sheet, clean A4-size sheet of paper under her kneeling, white-tighted knees, that sheet did not become dirty with her stories because the stories remained in her head until she could tell them to her parents' friends—other friends, not those street-urchin friends who served their second course in dirty plates—and they loved her stories and they loved her, she knew that because they brought her chocolates and bonbons, and she told a story to the boy Pavel and he kissed her and that was giving love but she could not love him back because he had a hole, two holes in fact, in his sock. And she is grateful to her mother to have made her different, to have made her clean, she is grateful to her mother to have taught her so many things, she is grateful to her mother to have shown her how to notice holes in people's socks, and holes in other garments, and she is grateful to her mother to have made her mind about those holes, mind about those people who had holes in their socks, she is grateful to her mother to have taught her not to eat the second course from the same plate as the first course and she is grateful to her mother to have introduced her to clean white sheets of A4-size paper at such an early age, at the age when the clean white sheets of A4-size of paper could not cause her anxiety or fear, the kind of fear that many writers feel but she does not, she never does feel that fear but if only, if only her mother had not failed at teaching her about being a failure. Her mother was a failure at that but she does not blame her mother for being such a failure, she said, for her mother did everything for her and her mother knew what was good for her and her mother was not a cruel woman, her mother loved her and everything she did for her was about love, about her getting love. But now that her mother is dead and she does not need to be loved, she writes to have it done with and most days she writes and she does not care, she manages not to care if the room threatens darkness because all that matters is to have it done with.

But sometimes, and there are days when it happens often, she said, sometimes, she decides not to think about being a failure, she decides to escape from such thoughts, and while that is not entirely possible, while she cannot stop thinking about being a failure completely, she can make an effort to reduce the intensity of her thoughts about being a failure and she can make an effort to have a little respite from thinking that she is a failure and when she wants to do that, she needs to focus on a task. Sometimes, and there are days when it happens often, she said, sometimes, she needs to stop thinking about being a failure, sometimes, she wishes to escape from such thoughts, and while that is not entirely possible, while she cannot stop thinking about being a failure completely, she can make an effort to reduce the intensity of her thoughts about being a failure and she can make an effort to have a little respite from thinking that she is a failure and when she wants to do that, she needs to focus on a task, on a task that is very different from her main preoccupation, that of thinking and that of writing, she needs to focus on a task that makes her work with her hands and allows her thoughts to wander freely in a field of wild flowers, which is not really a field of wild flowers but that is what it feels like for her thoughts as they freely move, like butterflies fluttering from one swaying poppy to another and when she thinks of her thoughts freely moving, she sees a field of white flowers in the sunshine, and for a second, for a split second, everything is possible. There are no tasks that allow her to work with her hands and to have her thoughts wander freely, there are very few occupations she can engage in that satisfy both conditions, in fact there is hardly anything that helps her not to think that she is a failure, and even then, not thinking about being a failure is only temporary, a little respite only, and that one thing, that one occupation that helps is baking cakes. So she makes and she bakes a cake, or two cakes, sometimes three, and she bakes scones and puddings, and she rolls out tarts and then there are days when there are quite a few cakes, quite a few puddings, quite a few tarts, quite a few scones sitting on her kitchen worktops, she said, more than she could possibly eat, even if she were to eat only cakes, or only scones, or only puddings, or only tarts, too many baked things for one person. And on such days she thinks, she said, that baking a cake is pure pleasure but having a cake baked is not so pleasurable because it has to be eaten, it cannot be just looked at, and she always has too many cakes, too many puddings, too many tarts, too many scones for one person.

With all this baking, it is no wonder that she has become good at baking and the other day, someone, someone who sometimes tastes her cakes, that someone said that she should be baking to live and not living to bake, and when she did not understand his words because she was living to bake and baking to live and she wondered what the difference was and he said he meant that she should be making her living with baking. She knew that was not possible because baking was too important to her and when something is as important as baking is to her, you cannot turn it into a commercial activity but some people only think of cashing in and for her that was not possible, it certainly was not possible with baking because if she had to bake to sell she could not bake, she would become bored and even before she became bored all the cakes would fall apart or turn into crumbs as there would be nothing to hold them together if she were baking to sell. And that someone who said she should be baking to live—or was it the other way round?—she cannot remember, that someone who actually said that she should be baking to sell, as if baking to sell and baking to live were the same things, that someone also said that she should not be baking to have it done with, only he did not use such words, for they are her words and people do not use such words, even people she knows, even people who would say they are her friends, except perhaps one or two of them use such words. And he was not the first person to say that she could bake for living, that is how good she was, yes, others have said that over the years but they don't understand that that is not what baking is about for her. She needs to bake in the same way that some people need to go for a walk, for a spot of fresh air, like some people need to have a drink, or a puff, or a spliff but she has never said that to anyone because even she did not understand why she was baking. The other day she heard someone say that baking a cake was about love, that baking a cake was about giving love and she almost laughed for how could it be about love if you had no one to whom you could offer a slice, let alone a whole cake, she said. When her children were younger, when they were still children, she was a Jewish mother, she played the role, she was a cliché of a Jewish mother, her children said. She was a Jewish mother without being Jewish, because she was always baking, always offering cakes and then, in those days when her children were children, baking was about love, about giving love. But those days when her children were children are bygone and she is not a Jewish mother any more, she is not a clichéd Jewish mother feeding her children and so there is no one to eat her cakes, no one who would say to her more than those ducks she sometimes feeds her cakes to, no one she could watch eat her cakes, eat them with pleasure, with gusto, smacking their lips as they bite into her cake and that would give her pleasure, as it used to once, but that feeding, that feeding with love, that is no more and so baking cakes is no more about love. Those days are gone and for her baking cakes is about not having love, not getting love, not giving love. But don't misunderstand me, she said, she does not wish for those days to come back but if there were someone she could bake a cake for, if there were such a someone, she would bake it with love and when they ate it, perhaps they could feel the love she had put into it and perhaps she would get their love, too. But why would she do that, why would she put love into a cake for someone, for someone she does not love? No, she does not mean this last bit, that last bit about putting love in a cake, she said, she most certainly does not mean that, she said, for the fact is that sometimes she turns all sentimental and thinks of the days when she was a Jewish mother and she liked being a Jewish mother because that is what her children used to call her, because her children said in those days when they were still children, they said that she had taught them the importance of education, the importance of improving themselves and she had fed them, she had always offered them food, cakes and biscuits, breads and rolls, stews and bakes, she cooked and taught them and that was love, cooking and teaching her children.

But baking for just anyone or baking for no one, as is her case now, that is not about love, that is not special or not very special, although it could be just a bit special, as with that woman, the woman she did not know very well but met a few times, the woman who tasted her cakes because she knocked on her door to ask something about parking regulations, or something like that, because she did not know what they were but perhaps that was just an excuse to knock on her door because no one would come in and ask for an explanation of parking regulations because everyone can read the signs on the pavement. But that woman said that she did not know the parking regulations because the woman said, I do not live in the street and I stay here only from time to time with a friend, a male friend, a gentleman friend, the woman said, and my friend lives down the road but he is not in now and so I cannot ask him but I need to wait for him and I do not know when he will be back and so I need to park and I need to park in this street, the adjoining streets will not do as I have lots of bags to deposit in his house because we are preparing to go on a trip round the world and we need to take lots of clothes with us and we need to take comforting items, the kind of comforting items one needs on a long trip, a trip around the world, such as my favourite bedside lamp—the light of hotel lamps is always too poor for night-time reading or for making crochet—and I am taking my patchwork quilt too, the woman said. I could not be without my patchwork quilt for a long time, the woman said.

That woman had knocked on the door just as she was about to prick an apricot-and-almond-brandy cake—to prick it to check that it was ready, that it was properly baked in the middle, in the middle that had to be moist but fully baked—and there was a chocolate sponge, freshly iced, and a lemon cake, already drizzled, cooling on a rack on the table and an apple pie, still in the tin next to the cooling, rack and the woman made a comment, the woman said something but she could not remember what it was, perhaps something about the lovely smell and then the woman said have you just baked a cake, and she did not say anything in response to the question—because what could one say to a question like that?—and the woman smiled and the woman was looking at the cakes cooling on the rack and so she had to offer a taste, just a tiny taste of something, and she did not mind offering the woman a small piece of lemon cake, although the woman did not interest her and her lack of interest had nothing to do with the woman, her lack of interest had more to do with the way she is, with the way she has become because these days, she said, not many people interest her, in fact very few people interest her and, to be precise, hardly anyone interests her. The woman said something about the lemon cake being good, very good indeed, the woman said, and the woman made one of those horrible noises of appreciation and immediately, while the woman was still masticating the last mouthful of the slice the woman had been offered, the woman glared at the chocolate sponge cake cooling on the rack on the table and the woman glared at the apple pie still in its tin and the woman made a comment, something about them looking good or yummy, yes, the woman used that infantile word, the word that rhymes with tummy, and the word she cannot stand and so it surprised her that she offered the woman a slice of the chocolate sponge and the apple pie as well. Perhaps that was excessive but she felt, she said, that she had to offer the other two cakes to the woman to taste and that is not quite right because she is past the days, past the time, when she felt that she had to do anything that other people expected her to do, she said, because that is the privilege of old age, the privilege that means you can scupper conventions and you can be as eccentric as you wish to be, not that she thinks that offering a small slice of cake to a woman who wanted to know about parking regulations in her street was eccentric. Sometimes she wonders whether this rule—or is it a convention, or an expectation?—sometimes she wonders whether this expectation may be of her own making only, and so she wonders whether this privilege of old age to scupper conventions is true for everyone and whether other old people follow it but she has never asked anyone and so she cannot tell whether it is only she who has thought of this rule and appropriated it for herself but if the former were the case and the world allowed older people a certain amount of leeway to depart from social norms, then, she often wonders, would that be because society does not take old people seriously, or are there some other reasons such as that old people have earned the right to do as they please, she said, earned the right to do as they please by kneeling down in corners of kitchens when they were children, misbehaved children, and facing blank walls, kneeling down and facing a lifetime of blank walls. That is something she will have to ponder, she said but to return to the woman in her kitchen that day, it so happened that the woman tried all three cakes on that occasion but not because she felt that she had to offer her to try the cakes after the woman had been glaring at them and smiling at them, and smiling at her, and commenting on the cakes, but something inexplicable happened and she who does not like other people or has not liked other people for some time now, felt that that woman was not too bad and that was the reason, that was the sole reason why she offered her the cakes. Nothing else was on her mind, nothing else at all, there was no thought of giving cakes and getting love from the woman, none at all, absolutely none, she is certain of that because she is past the days when she offered love and she is past the days when she wished for love from others.

And then there was a next time, oh yes, she said, there was a next time as the woman knocked again on her door and the woman said my friend, my gentleman friend, is not in and I wonder if you would do me a favour and let me use your phone so that I can check when he will be back, so that I can collect my bags from him because our trip around the world has been postponed—only for a month but still postponed, the woman added—and I need to pick up my patchwork quilt and my favourite bedside lamp and my clothes and my shoes. So the woman came in again there were cakes in the kitchen, as there often are, freshly baked cakes—a Battenberg newly iced, or was it a poppy-seed slice on that day?—and there were scones too, a dozen or so herb scones and half a dozen of sweet ones, and again the woman made a comment on each cake and each bake and she offered the woman a taste of each cake and each bake and the woman did taste them all, taking a rather long time with bites of Battenberg in her mouth—or was it a poppy-seed slice that she chewed on for so long?—and the woman did not even make that phone call, and it was not clear to her whether the woman had forgotten about the phone call since there were so many cakes and bakes to try or whether the woman had only come in to taste her cakes and bakes or perhaps, and that is not completely impossible, perhaps the woman came in to talk to her and the woman did talk to her and while the woman talked to her, the woman said that her cakes, yes, the woman said that, she definitely heard the woman say that and the woman referred to her by name, the woman said, V, your cakes me happy. Your cakes make me happy, the woman said, she said. (But how did the woman know her name?) And she did not know what to say not because the words surprised her, and that is not surprising, that is not surprising to her because nothing surprised her then and nothing surprises her these days but the real point of those words was that there was something definitive about them, something that did not allow anything else to be said. That is why the words stayed with her and she thought they were good words, undoubtedly they were good words, the words that were about her, the words that were prompted by her cakes and so she thought that perhaps after all, cakes, or at least her cakes, could be about love. A few days after the woman had said V, your cakes make me happy, she was baking cakes, trying out new recipes, the cakes the woman had not tried before and she thought the woman might come in and try those new cakes, those new cakes the woman had not tried before, and some old cakes, old recipes, tried and tested, like the apple strudel, her famous—her used-to-be-famous apple strudel—and the plum-and-almond cake (the recipe she only just developed). She even thought that those new cakes would make the woman happy and that there could be something, something a little bit like love in that and she had many more cakes, and many more varieties than ever before when the woman had come round but the woman did not come. And the woman did not come a week later and there were so many cakes, too many to take to the ducks at the pond in Putney and so she threw them out. She threw the cakes out, lots of cakes, many different cakes and bakes, puddings and a cherry clafoutis, a cherry clafoutis that stuck to the mould and would not come out. That was some time ago and she had not seen the woman for a while, for a year or two even, yes, two years it must be and she wondered what had happened to the woman, whether the woman's gentleman friend had moved away or whether the relationship had not survived and so the woman had no reason to come to the street, she said, for really the woman came for the man, the man who was the woman's gentleman friend and not for the cakes and now when she thinks about it, it occurs to her that that whole episode, that whole episode had a possibility of something, a friendship even, a possibility of cakes giving love. Did she mean giving love or getting love? She is not sure but there was something about love and those cakes. Now that she looks back to that episode she thinks of it as a failure —cake baking as a failure?—but even that is fine for she no longer needs to get love and she could never get love from women, the treacherous Eves, always pushing her in the paddling pool, like those girls when she was not-yet-five years old, women always luring her in, always that same pattern of turning up, calling attention to themselves, chasing her with love and then when she wants to give it back to them, when she wants to give love and have love, have their love, they take off, they disappear, they do not return her calls, they cut her out, they cut her out without a word. But not any more, she will not fall prey to their friendship, their false friendship, their temptations of friendship, and now her baking is about her, she tells herself, her baking is about her without love and without the need for love, her baking is about leaving that dark room, that room that always stays dark even when she remembers to put the light on and when she can be bothered to open the shutters. And the woman is not coming back, she is sure of that, the woman could have been run over, she could have had a heart attack, she could have been kidnapped, she could have emigrated, or perhaps she was one of those women who goes around sniffing in front of people's front doors and knocking on those doors when she could smell a cake and that woman must have been in the habit of doing that and perhaps there was no gentleman friend, and perhaps there was no planned trip and no favourite lamp and no crochet and all of that is possible—but not important to her—just as it is possible but not important to her that the woman simply became bored with the cakes and bakes. She does not care what the reason might be for the woman not coming back—she is only thinking about it out of curiosity, silly curiosity, that is pellucid—nor does she care that she will never again see the woman for she knows that she does not like most people, in fact she does not like almost all the people she can think of, except for a very few, very few who know better than to meddle with others, with their baking and their cakes, she does not like people except for a very, very few who keep themselves to themselves, she does not like people with their habits and with their lack of habits. She bakes and bakes more and more without seeking love, without expecting to give love—if it came along adventitiously, she might take it—but she is not seeking it and she bakes and bakes and she makes all those scones, sweet and savoury, herby and fruity, all those cakes and all those tarts that are too much for one person, all those puddings and she makes and bakes for no one, she makes and bakes to have it done with.

But there was a time when love was important and it was not only being loved that was important, not only getting love, getting love with her stories, but also giving love and giving love not only with her stories, giving love in any way. When she was eighteen she dreamt of having a baby, a baby that she would love, a baby that she would be able to give all the love that was growing inside her, the love that she had no one to give to. And the dream of the baby became a literal dream, a recurrent dream, a fantasy and in the dream she would find a baby in a telephone box, lying wrapped up in a blanket on the floor of a telephone box, of a telephone box where she would have gone to make a call and as she opened the door of the box, she would stop and there would be a bundle on the floor, a quiet bundle, quiet but alive, quiet and needy, quiet and helpless, waiting for her to pick it up and love it and she would pick it up and there would be no one else around and she would take the baby to her home and she would look after the baby without ever telling anyone and it would be her baby, her baby to give love to. That dream occurred night after night and it gave her a great deal of pleasure, a great deal of daydreaming that made her feel good and when she felt good it was easier to go on. When she thinks about it now she sees the baby lying on the floor of a red telephone box, the English telephone box, and that surprises her because she had had that dream while she was still living in the country of her birth, in the country of her birth where telephone boxes were blue and not red. At the time, at the time when she was eighteen and the dream was recurrent, the baby had to be lying on a floor of a blue telephone box—or so she thinks but could not be sure—because although she would have seen images of English telephone boxes, red telephone boxes, the idea of those images would not have been strong enough to replace the images of blue telephone boxes that were common in the place where she had lived at the time of her dream of finding a baby, an abandoned baby, no one's baby, lying on the floor of a telephone box. But in her memory of the dream, the blue telephone box, the blue telephone box of her childhood and adolescence was replaced by the red telephone box, the English telephone box, the telephone box of the country where she spent more than half her life, the telephone box that is no longer in use, the telephone box that is not a telephone box any more, the telephone box that has become no more than an image on nostalgic picture postcards that tourists send from London, and the telephone box that is an image in her dream, in her dream of finding someone to give love to. When she thinks about that dream these days, the dream of finding a baby who she could love, she remembers the pain that she felt, the physical pain of the longing to have someone to love and when she thinks about the images in her dream, that someone she longed to love was always a baby, a quiet, helpless baby, a baby that was neither a baby girl nor a baby boy, just a baby for her to love. She is not sure that her dream was really about giving love because it was a dream that was centred on her, not on the baby, it was a dream centred on her need to love and not on the baby's need to be loved. It was a dream to satisfy her nurturing side, she can see that now, the nurturing side which is also her cake-baking side and when she thinks about her nurturing side and her needs, she feels she can say, and say it with satisfaction and with pleasure, and say it with relief, that nurturing side, that cake-baking side is not as needy as it used to be, or at least that is what she would say now.

And she remembered how the nurturing side, the cake-baking side, the side of her that brought about a dream of a baby found in a telephone box, that side sometimes manifested itself in other ways. There were times when her cake-baking side with its needs turned her into a matchmaker and there were occasions, repeated occasions, when she worked to bring people together, people who were friends and who were single—and she always seemed to have friends who were single, most of her friends were single—inviting them around and cooking dinners for them and hoping that they would give love to each other but it never worked, not once did it work and sometimes one of the two people, one of the two of her friends, single friends whom she had invited for dinner would react too strongly against the other person, or against the other person's efforts to get love and then she would be blamed, she would be blamed for thinking that such and such a friend, a single friend, would have been a good match for another such and such close friend. She remembered once while she was on holiday, and in the middle of visiting a Roman amphitheatre in the south of France, she received messages about that C, that woman who talked all the time, that dreadful woman you had introduced me to, that dreadful woman who persuaded me to take her on a picnic and who then proceeded to spoil the whole afternoon with her talking, with her clinging, so much so that I could never again go to Kew Gardens, I could never again have a picnic anywhere and it is all because of you, he wrote, as if this person, this man, this single friend of hers was a minor or had somehow been drugged to take that C woman on a picnic into Kew Gardens and she, their friend, was expected to do something about the failed date between her friend and the C woman and do it from distance, from her sightseeing visit to a Roman amphitheatre in the south of France. And that woman C, she too started sending messages accusing that man H, that single friend, C started accusing him of being unkind to her on that picnic in Kew Gardens. And all she wanted was to bring people together, provide them with opportunities to give love to each other, to get love from each other, and now she was being accused of ruining their future visits to Kew Gardens, their future picnics and who knows what else. And yet she did not give up, that nurturing need, that cake-baking need always prevailed over her experience that was telling her not to try again and so there were other occasions, other matchmaking occasions, other occasions that did not end up with her being blamed, other occasions that were funny as it happened, and it happened more than once that her friends, her single friends whom she introduced to each other, it turned out that they had already known each other and once it even happened that the two friends had gone out together, many years before she introduced them to each other. And on that occasion, she remembered how all three of them laughed, when her friends, her two single friends, told her that they had been a couple many years earlier and not only had the relationship not worked out between them, they had had a rather bitter separation but when they met at her dinner table, with food, good food cooked specially for them, her two friends laughed, and she laughed, and there seemed to be no bit-terness between her two friends and there seemed to be no bitter-ness towards her and they all had a good evening with her food and with her cakes, her gifts for nurturing, and so her effort was not completely wasted although there was no love, no love to give, no love to get, only a talk of past desire for love, of remembered longing for love. Since none of her dating efforts led anywhere, she used to say to herself that she would never try again, but that resolve never lasted for long and her nurturing needs, her cake-baking side prevailed and she tried again and again but eventually the matching of people that was meant to give them love and get them love became the matching of people intended to help them improve themselves, help them find someone that they could improve themselves with, and so she started cooking dinners and inviting friends who she thought might end up working on similar projects, such as the last two who she thought might go on to work on a play, since he was writing plays anyway, and since she was directing plays and that would be good, she thinks if those two, who are both friends of hers could go on and work on a play together. But for her the real question is why she is doing that and she cannot think that there is any other reason except a purely self-ish one which is that she needs to satisfy her own need, her own need to nurture, her cake-baking side, her needy side.

As time passes and she gets older, she likes people less and less and she has fewer and fewer friends and perhaps one day there will be no one to bake cakes for or to invite to dinner and offer nurturing gifts, regardless of the pretext, regardless of whether it would be about love, getting love and giving love or about improving them-selves with someone else. As she turns older, she sees more and more street urchins and it pains her to go anywhere and observe how people's behaviour has changed from the days when learning mattered, from the days when books mattered, from the days when people did not stand up clapping and shouting at the end of a show in a proper theatre, from the days when people did not clap in the middle of a performance, as if it were some silly musical and all because an actor has jumped through some kind of hoop, a real or metaphorical hoop, or performed some other circus-like skill. Street urchins are everywhere, street urchins taking over the world, street urchins who have grown up but remained street urchins, that is what she thinks, she said.

A spot of kneeling on the ground in a corner of a kitchen, a spot of facing a blank wall might have cured these grown-up street urchins of eating smelly food in public, or of putting their shoed feet on train seats, a spot of kneeling in a corner of a kitchen could have cured them of shouting inanities on their mobiles, she often thinks, she said. She was lucky that she had a teaching-poems-by-heart mother, she was lucky to have a mother who took so much trouble with her while the street urchins, the horse-manure children had no one to work with and so they were left with nothing to do and so they never developed and yet now she is not lucky because these people, these grown-up street urchins are everywhere, there are too many of them and she is alone, alone against them all and often she feels that they silently team up against her and there is no end to their smelly food in public places, no end to their shoed feet on train seats, no end to their tabloids and their reality TV shows, no end to their vulgarities. There are so many of them and there is no country that has been spared their presence. If that were not the case, she said, she could move to another country, as she had done several times before, always running away from those grown-up street urchins, from that smelly horse manure, but what good did that do with these people being everywhere and with most countries being the same, so much that there is no point in dreaming of distant lands just as there is no point in travelling any more. There may be benefits to being an exile, but avoiding these people is not one of them for avoiding them has become impossible, she said. She would not say that being an exile has been her salvation as she has heard some exiles say, and she would not deny that they might have been saved if they could tell her what they have been saved from and in any case talking of being saved is going too far as if anyone could be saved (the thief was saved, she heard someone say). But what does being saved mean—saved like the thief?—that is what she would like to ask them. For if they want to be truly saved, truly saved for good and saved from everything, there is only one way, she said, but people are not very careful with language and say things for the sake of saying them without thinking of what they mean, people say things they have heard others say. As an exile, she would never say that moving away from the country of her birth has been her salvation, for how could she possibly know whether it was the case except that living in the country of her birth was suffocating, suffocating her for twenty years, twenty years and a few more and for a long time she could not visit that country, that country of her birth, that country of her accidental birthplace—for it could have been any other and she would have felt the same—and what does it matter in which country one is born except to those who invent a mystical connection with the soil, oh how she shudders at the thought. For a long time she could not visit that country of her birth, her accidental birthplace and she has heard other people say that about their own inability, their own fear of going back, but to imagine that salvation comes with exile or with anything else for that matter, definitely not, that is going too far, that is being careless with language and an exile cannot be careless with language for an exile moves between languages, an exile moves between languages and cannot throw anchor in any, not having a language to call her own, not having a language that she can speak without an accent, always existing in that space between languages, in that space that is forever changing. An exile is always a foreign-language person, an exile is a foreign-language person in the language of the country where she lives and an exile is a foreign-language person in the language of the country where she was born. None of the words an exile utters are the words that a native uses because when an exile says a word, that word in her mind comes with the echoes of its approximate counterparts in the language that the exile first learnt and the exile herself sees herself differently in the new language from the way she sees herself in the language of the country of her birth. The whole world is different in the language of the country of her exile so how could an exile be allowed to be careless with language? No matter how well she knows the language of the country of her exile, an exile is never allowed to forget the language, for her that language, as well as the language of the country of her birth is a thing, a thing that is like a pair of shades, a pair of shades that always interposes itself between her and the world, a pair of shades that is sometimes more transparent than at other times but is always there, palpably there, like a thing, like a thing that cannot be removed, a fixed pair of shades through which she sees the world and people in it. In her case, she thinks, she said, those shades had always been there, fixed on her nose, helping her hide her eyes when she was curious about the street urchins of her early years. Those shades did not appear for the first time when she moved to a country that was not the country of her birth, those shades were there much before that. Those shades have always been on her, ever since she could see, so perhaps there was something about her since birth, something about her that would not let her see the world without those shades. She did not know it at the time but those shades, she thinks, were fixed on her in the days when she was not-yet-four years old, in the days when she could not recite poems by heart without stumbling and without prompting and had to kneel in a corner of her mother's kitchen and it is possible, she said, that the shades materialized, it is possible, she said that the shades intercepted themselves between her and the world because of those poems, because of that kneeling in a corner of her mother's kitchen. But who is to tell whether she was born with those shades or whether she, who was the daughter of a woman who believed that living was about self-improvement, life-long self-improvement, acquired those shades as she was growing up? It took her a long time to stop wanting to be part of the same world as most people, it took her a long time to stop wanting to see the same pictures and hear the same sounds as most people, it took her a long time before she realized that the world looked different to her from how others described it and the voices she heard sounded different from what the others told her they had heard. She had to accept that her shades were part of her and there was no way of living without them. Before that realization, before that acceptance that she could not take her shades off, for many years she had dreamt of a place, near or far away, but it was most likely to be far away, if it existed at all, she dreamt of a place where she would see the same pictures as everyone else and where she would hear the same voices as everyone else and that dream grew over those years, she said and sometimes she likes to think that the dream, which was a vague, undefined longing, that dream crystallized itself one day when she was seven and she took a walk, a short walk around the house of her grandparents, and during that walk a man smiled at her and she talked to him. She does not remember what they talked about and it most certainly was not anything important, not even to a seven-year old, but the man was black and that was unusual, that was very unusual at that time and in that place and she thought that something about him, something about the way he talked to her made him different from the people she knew, and it was not his colour, it was something about his demeanour, some-thing that made her comfortable with him, and years later when she became aware of her shades, of her lenses, she wondered whether he too was wearing those shades, those lenses. And then there were other people, occasionally there were other people who seemed to her to be wearing shades, to be wearing lenses, and she could not be sure whether their shades were the same colour as hers but she knew they were seeing the world through shades and many of them had come from Africa and it occurred to her that perhaps Africa could be her home. It occurred to her that there could be a place somewhere in that continent where she would feel less different from everyone around her than she did in the country in which she was born. It was a dream, a dream she came to believe in because she needed to believe in it and she needed to believe that a place like that existed so that she could hope, so that she could hope that one day she would not be different from other people and that she would belong. But years later she realized that it was a silly dream and it was even sillier of her not to know that it was a dream and that dreams should stay dreams. It was silly of her to try to make her dream real and to look for a job in Africa, and it was even sillier of her to expect her heart to miss a beat when the plane landed in Nigeria, where she was to start her first job, very silly indeed and it was silly of her when she was back in Europe to tell her friends and, her black friends, too, that she was black and she could tell they did not like it, her black friends did not like her saying that but they did not complain, they only turned away from her until one day one of them, a kind friend, who was a poet and a very good poet, one of them said: *Look in the mirror. You are not black.* He laughed but he did not laugh because he thought the situation was funny, he laughed because he wanted to laugh at her, at her silliness, he laughed to show her that she could not be taken seriously and he sounded annoyed and at the time she was annoyed with him and she thought he was being unkind and she thought that it was not a nice thing to reject her like that and it took years before she understood that he was right and that those words had to be said, they had to be said so that she would understand about belonging and not belonging and so those words were kind words. And years later she understood that she did not belong to the black people, and she understood that she did not belong to the Jewish people—as she had wished to for a long time, as she had wished when in her youth she used to hang around synagogues envying the people coming out in groups, envying their togetherness, their togetherness in difference—and she understood that she did not belong to any other group of people and why should she belong to anyone, anyway? What was this belonging to a country or to an eth-nic group?—she might just as well join a stamp collectors' club or the West London Train Spotters' Association, or the Ramblers, or anything like that if she had issues with not belonging. It took her many years to stop being silly, or silly on that account at least, and to learn that she would never belong and that not belonging was fine and that not belonging could be good, could be better than belonging and often she was ashamed of her previous silliness, she was ashamed of her naivety at thinking that it was possible to aban-don those shades, those lenses, that separated her from the rest of the world. She was young and she was naive and that was that, she told herself. And then she was middle-aged and she was naive and that was that, she told herself, she said. But some questions did not go away and sometimes she could not help wondering whether those shades would have been in front of her eyes had she been allowed to play with those street urchins, play with them in the dirt, had she been able to hear them speak, had she been able to see what they thought, had she not have had to kneel in the corner of her mother's kitchen, with a white A4-size sheet slipped under her white-tighted knees facing a blank wall and making up stories using the shapes that she perceived in that blank wall as she con-nected specks dried in the paint or while she was playing games with the *Prince and the Pauper* story. Would there have been the shades, would there have been the lenses, had she not been pushed into the paddling pool, or had she not had to go out for afternoon walks wearing white gloves in the middle of summer in a place where most people could not afford gloves in winter and those winters were very harsh? But these are useless questions for why think about what would have been, why think about what could have been? What matters is that there came a time when she learnt to look at the world through the shades, through her lenses, and these days she likes the colour of her shades, she likes the sound of her shades, she likes their opaqueness, their occasional shrillness; she likes the way they shape the world for her and she accepts she is different, and let the world know that she is different and that she does not belong and that she does not want to belong. She does not want to belong because she could not write if she belonged—for what would she write if she belonged, for what could she write if she saw the world in the same way as everyone else? Oh, the entire questionable business of writing! (But remember, 'questionable' includes a quest, too.) Don't say that if she belonged she would, or she could, write stories about relationships and betrayals and stories about growing up and stories about mysteries and stories where everything would be solved and resolved and everyone got married and the world was a hunky-dory place, no, not for her such stories—and when she thinks about writing and belonging, she cannot see how anyone can belong and write, write in a way that is new, new in some ways at least, otherwise what would be the point of writing if the writing were similar to what is already around, to the writing that is no different from the stories in celebrity magazines, to the stories about how this or that person overcame this or that difficulty or how this or that person betrayed or fell in love with that and this person when they should not have done it—here is the lesson for you, the reader!—what would be the point of writing that turns the reader into a voyeur, a peeping Tom, what is the point of writing that gives satisfaction to the curtain-twitcher? (Readers of such disposition might just as well join their neighbourhood watch.) That is not real writing, that is not the writing that brings love, that is not the writing that gives love, that is not the writing that matters to her, that is not the writing that she wants to write, that is not the writing that she wants to read. When she thinks about what she wants to write, she said, she understands why she could not persuade herself to give in to that supposedly universal longing to belong.

Sometimes, and in the past that used to be quite often but is not so often these days, and that is a good thing, that is one of the very few good things that she can think about, that question, that question is not asked as often as it used to be, since people are more used to exiles, voluntary exiles like her, but it still happens although not as often as it used to happen, but sometimes it still happens that they ask whether she misses her country and she wants to scream back at them, she said. To start with, it is not her country that they are referring to because it is only a place where she was born and that does not make it her country and they ought to think what it means to say that a place is someone's country. They should stop repeating clichés that they have heard from others, that they have heard from their parents, that they have heard from their grandparents, that they have heard from their great-grandparents and they should stop expecting her to answer using the clichés she has heard from her parents and the clichés she has heard from her grandparents and the clichés she has heard from her great-grandparents. They should think about what they are saying and they should see that one's country, mother country, father country, sister country, uncle country, brother-in-law country is a matter of an accident of birth, of being born here or there, or nowhere or everywhere, that it is a matter of being an extravagant stranger of here and nowhere, that it is a matter of a chance event, that it is not a matter of interest, and so why bother, why ask? But people don't think and so they go on repeating words, people are not careful with language because they are not exiles—or people do not think of themselves as exiles and you have to think of yourself as an exile to be an exile, you have to make yourself an exile in your mind—and so it does not cross their mind that what really matters, or used to matter when countries were different from one another, what used to matter, or should have mattered, would have been the choice one made of which country to move to. That is something one could have a discussion about, that is something one could ask about and explain why one has chosen a particular place over all the others, what it is that one has been attracted to, what kind of myth one had harboured before one leapt, for it is always bound to have been a myth and what it is that one has been repelled by—these are valid questions, questions worth asking, she said. And when she thinks of such myths, of the myths that represented England for her, there are many, many myths that attracted her to move to England but none as powerful as one of these, as powerful in her memory which, she has to stress, does not mean that it was the most powerful at the time when she leapt, when she chose England as the country to move to, when she chose England as the country of her exile.

The myth number one—and she wishes to make it clear that it was not necessarily the most powerful myth at the time but it may have been and it certainly appears as such now that she is making a story of her life—that myth number one was that England was a country of Shakespeare. How laughable it seems now to think that she could have believed it and how even more laughable that myth appears when she thinks of another one—except that that other myth did not play a role in making her choose England as the country of her exile—another myth that she believed in: the myth that

On the Buses TV series was representative of the life in England. The juxtaposition of these two myths in her mind may strike someone as absurd, as utterly absurd, such as that friend who asked her the other day: How could you think something like that? Did you imagine Stan Butler reading Shakespeare in between his shifts, did you imagine him going to see a Shakespeare play accompanied by his mother, sister and brother-in-law, that same friend said. She cannot remember whether she ever thought of the two myths in such terms, but the fact that the two myths coexisted in her mind was not that absurd and not only was it not that absurd, it was not absurd at all, and these days she can see that the England of Shakespeare and the England of *On the Buses* juxtaposition is telling, that it is appropriately suggestive of a class separation, of a typically English kind of class separation, a kind that she does not find that much pronounced in other countries, and in that sense perhaps the juxtaposition of her two myths, of her two visions of England, two visions that she formed from afar, was perceptive, in fact, as perceptive as any other view that she has since formed living in the country. But in the days when the two myths coexisted, or supposedly coexisted in her mind, that is, if she can trust her memory, in those days she was not aware of that division, of that social division and so on a day trip to Birmingham, where she was to attend an interview, an interview to be admitted to a post-graduate study of Shakespeare, an interview that was to mark the beginning of the period of her official exile (as opposed to the exile she felt while still living in the country of her birth)—on that day she stepped off the train and asked the first person she saw to show her the way to the Shakespeare Institute. That person was gobsmacked, that person had no idea how to respond to her request and so once that person recovered from her request, he shook his head and went on. Something was wrong with that person, she thought, something had to be wrong with him for he was in Birmingham where the world-famous department, or so she thought, the world-famous department for the study of the greatest English writer was based, so how could it be possible that he would not know. The next person she stopped and asked, more talkative than the first one, the next person said she had never heard of that institute and when the same happened with the third person and the fourth person and the fifth person, she did not know what to think. Was it possible, was it possible that everyone she stopped in Birmingham had something wrong with them, what were the chances that everyone she had stopped had something wrong with them, something that made it impossible for them to be aware that the greatest English writer, was born not far from the city, the greatest English writer was being studied in their vicinity and by scholars of international repute? How could they not be aware of that? It did not occur to her that the people she had stopped in New Street in Birmingham would have come from the life represented by *On the Buses*, except that by the time she realized that, on the cusp of the ninth decade of the twentieth century, some things had changed and the world of Stan Butler, the world that was only a cliché representation of the working-class life even when the programme was first aired, no longer existed. In the post-Thatcher Britain, after years of living in the country of her exile, she watched Stan Butler and his conductor friend replace their allegiance to the working-class solidarity and to trade unionism with consumerism, and so their family life in that TV series, with its petty cruelties, with its roughness and with its sexism, all of which were meant to be the source of humour, but also the family life based around a community, appeared even more dated and unreal. Of course, that is her looking back, she said, for she had no such thoughts on her two myths of England at the time of her alighting at New Street in Birmingham, or in the four years she spent in Birmingham studying Shakespeare. But how could she have lived for four years in Birmingham, how could she have studied Shakespeare without having such thoughts, someone asked her once and she could see that the person was asking a good question, a question that she could ask now. It became clear to her after hearing that question that Stan Butler and his likes were the same as the street urchins of her childhood and that the only difference—the difference that blinded her perception—the only difference between the Stan Butlers and the street urchins from her childhood—the street urchins that she wished to leave behind when she chose England as the country of her exile —was that the former spoke English, the same language as Shakespeare. Blinded as she was, she could not tell that this fact played no part in the life of the Butlers, neither then nor today when she sees these English street urchins communicate via flashy mobile phones, travel in four-wheel drives and own widescreen TVs but she knows that they still could not direct her to the Shakespeare Institute. But what else would you expect, that same friend who asked how she could have lived in Birmingham and studied Shakespeare for four years without realizing the existence of two very different, two very separate Englands, that same friend asked and she wondered whether her myth of the England of Shakespeare and the myth of England of *On the Buses* is not that much of a myth, and the juxtaposition of the two visions of England is certainly not as absurd as it appeared to some natives when she had told them about it, she said.

As for that question, that question of whether she misses her country, that question—now that the world is fuller of exiles than ever before—the question does not come up often, which is a good thing, a very good thing as far as she is concerned, and she knows that question is more to do with people simply parroting what they have heard before and so enabling the world to go on in the same fashion—to the advantage of some people—but those who are disadvantaged by the world not changing are neither aware of it nor can they do anything about it. Such realizations used to upset her and most of her adult life, she said, she wondered why the Stan Butlers of England, as it seemed to her, so willingly accepted what she saw as their inferior position, their exclusion from the myth of England as the country of Shakespeare. For many years she wished she could do something about their exclusion and in some ways she did try to do something—or so she thought—that went beyond joining demos and protests in the name of this cause or in the name of that cause and she thought, like some believer in enlightenment, some naive believer in the improvement of the masses through education, like some naive believer that she had been for most of her life—but what else could a little girl, a girl who was not-yet-four, and who had to kneel in a corner of her mother's kitchen and face a blank wall because she could not recite a poem by heart without stumbling and without prompting, what else could she grow up into than a believer in learning?—that education might help those street urchins even though there did not seem to be real education for them, only exams and qualifications, and then she found out that that was precisely what they wanted, these English street urchins, the Stan Butlers. They wanted exams to pass and the qualifications to gain and that gave them enough skill to read about celebrities in tabloids, and these grown-up British street urchins are now no different from other grown-up street urchins anywhere else in the world—there is nowhere to go to avoid them—and these days it strikes her, she said, that she is immune to whether the world goes on in the same fashion or not, and she does not bother with protests, the world can go to hell as far as she is concerned. What interests her is the realization, and the acceptance, that she is different, as she has always been different, an exile, born an exile, an exile as an outsider—and being an exile as an outsider is much harder, much harder than being a geographical exile—she is an exile among grown-up street urchins, as she was an exile kneeling on the floor in a corner of her mother's kitchen and facing a blank wall, an exile secretly glancing at the horse manure behind her dark shades, those coloured lenses, an exile thrown into the paddling pool, all her life she has been an exile, an exile and an outsider at the same time, an exile among exiles, she said. As for her country, her country in the sense of those who parrot such cliché sentiments, sometimes she wants to tell them that she needs no country, no country as soil, no country of blood connections, for those are real myths and those are dangerous myths, much more dangerous that the myth of England as the country of Shakespeare and the myth of England as the country of *On the Buses* and so sometimes she wishes to tell them that the only country she needs is her library, the only country she could miss is her real library and her imaginary library, an ever-expanding world of words, that is her country, she said and perhaps that is why she had never been able to give a book away once she had read it, even when she knew that she would not read it again. When she travels that is what she misses, her library, not countries, mother or father or brother or sister countries. But she does not say that to those who ask, to those who ask whether she misses her country, for anyone who asks such a question does not have a library, does not understand the importance of library as a home. For how could you have a library, a proper library that you have read, that you have read in a way that was meaningful to you and then ask such a question, such a silly question, how could you go on parroting about missing one's country? It is her library that has kept her going, it is her library that has helped her on the way of having it done with. And when she says that, she recalls that a poet—a poet and a novelist whose name she does not remember—that poet said that library is an act of faith and she understands that so well, for it is her library that is there for her when there is no one to give love to, when there is no one to get love from and it is her library that she keeps because of and despite her growing misanthropic side, it is her library that is the world, the only world she wants: every city she has visited has been a city of books and reading and she thinks of some books as cities she has visited, and she thinks of other books as cities she has not visited.

That other question, that question whether the shades, the shades through which she looks at the world, the shades that made her an exile even while she still lived in the country where she was born, the question whether those shades, those lenses, would not have been there had she not been kneeling down in a corner of her mother's kitchen, that too is a silly question, just like all the if questions, just like all the suppose-this-or-that questions, it is a silly question because who could tell which story, which place or which kitchen corner or which poem brought about those shades?

But the shades were there and the world she saw was different from the world the people around her saw and when at thirteen she fell in love, she fell in love in a way that was different from the way other people of her age fell in love and later she thought perhaps only a person wearing those shades, those lenses, could fall in love in such a way. She loved a poet, a very good poet, the best poet ever in the language of the country where she was born and a poet who was dead and at that time her classmates were in love with pop stars who were alive, very much alive while her poet was dead, dead for fifty years before she was born but that was not a problem for her, that did not matter because what made her fall in love with him was his poetry, his achievement, his cleverness with words, that is what mattered to her, that is what she learnt when not-yet-four years old, she learnt that being clever was about being loved and so she loved him because he was clever, he was a wonderful poet, and those girls, those friends of hers who were in love with pop stars, live pop stars, they did not think whether those pop stars were clever or not. She could not see what was there to love about pop stars, pop stars who were trivial and so she thought her friends were trivial like their pop stars, that is what she thought, she said, and that is what she still thinks, she said. Her classmates wanted to know what their pop star liked for breakfast, what kind of shoelaces their pop star wore or how their pop star cut his bread, and that was trivia, she thought, and she still thinks like that, and those were not the things that ever mattered to her. But her poet was a good writer, a good poet, a good translator from French, a man who knew his Baudelaire and his Henri Becque, and that mattered to her and that continued to matter to her and that is why she loved him and that is why when she was thirteen she walked to his grave every week, red roses in hand, and that is why she talked to him. He was clever, and clever with words, which was more important than any other kind of cleverness, and that is why she loved him and being clever with words was what she looked for in everyone she loved later in life. One day a friend made a joke and asked whether before she slept with a person she tended to ask to see their PhD and she laughed because the friend laughed, and she laughed because she could tell that the friend was making a joke, and she laughed to be friendly but she knew that the joke was silly and that it was no joke to her, that it was not funny to her. Education was important to her and there were people who had it and there were people who did not have it, and that was as simple as that. She could not love those without education, and sometimes she wondered how could anyone love those without education? She knew that in the eyes of other people she was silly, she was a joke, she had heard someone say once, that joke woman, she had heard that more than once, and that is why they laughed at her, they laughed at her behind her back, she knew that, but that is how she is, that is how she has always been, interested in clever people—and yes, those she thought clever—falling in love with those who were good writers, with those who talked about what interested her, with those to whom poetry mattered, for that was what mattered to her—poetry has always mattered to her. *Catch them when they are young*, she heard her mother say more than once and she certainly was caught when she was young. How could she who had to kneel in a corner of her mother's kitchen and face a blank wall for ten or fifteen minutes at the time when she was not-yet-four years old and because she failed to recite a poem by heart without stumbling and without prompting, how could she who learnt that if she were not clever, if she could not recite a poem by heart without stumbling and without prompting no one would love her, how could she possibly fall in love with some teenage idol, with some pop star or the like? She had read her poet, she had read everything that he had written, all his poems, all his essays, all his stories, all his journalistic pieces and it was his writing that made her love him and so she did love him, and she carried on reading his poems every day, and she recited his poems now that she could read herself, now that she did not have to rely on her auditory memory of her mother's voice reading to her, now that she could use her visual memory and now that she had no difficulty reciting poems by heart without stumbling and without prompting. His poems were beautiful, so beautiful that no one has ever written anything as good as that in the language of that country and so she had to love him. It was irrelevant that he was dead; taking that into account would have been petty. Had she told any of her friends about her love, they might have pointed out that she could not have had long walks with her lover, but that was only true in one, a rather ordinary sense, in the sense of those people who loved pop stars, in the sense of those grown-up street urchins, for that is what they were, but in the sense that she looked at such things at the age of thirteen and in the sense that she still considers such things, her poet was with her all the time and she talked to him on her long walks to his grave, red roses in hand and, yes, she knows the red roses were a cliché but a good cliché because, she said, because she was in love and she wanted to give him presents and a bouquet of red roses was a present she could give him and there were not many presents she could give him and she knew he liked red roses for he had written a sonnet about them, and what an exquisite sonnet it was. That poet was her first love and it was a love that never went away, the love that stayed with her when she loved others. It was a special love, a love that could not be tainted by the trivia of daily life; it was a love that was protected from the outside world. But once a friend said to her that she had seen a photograph of her poet, a photograph published in one of the biographies on his life and on that photograph, a photograph from his childhood, her poet, her love, was playing in the dirt with three other children, all in short trousers with dirty knees and two of them were barefoot, that friend said and she said it all in one breath as if she could not utter the words fast enough and that friend said that the photograph showed that the poet was a street urchin—only she did not use that word—and the friend made a face as if she was about to laugh but she did not and so the face stayed in the position as if asking, What can you say to that?

Nothing, there was nothing to say to that. Why should she say anything to such a preposterous idea? How could her poet have been a street urchin? That was not possible. As if that photograph proved anything, for who knows what the circumstances behind it were: he was a child and might have been passing by and someone took a photograph just as someone could have taken a photograph of her when she was running around with that pot of cherries and street urchins followed her and that someone might have concluded that she too was a street urchin and that would have been wrong, that would have been completely wrong. She loved her poet and that love survived all her other loves, it stayed with her when all other loves, short and transient loves, all other loves had gone.

Her love for the poet was a lasting love and that would not have been the case had her poet been a street urchin. She could not love someone who was not focused on self-improvement, who was not focused on their learning, she could not love those street urchins unless by some miracle they changed, and some of them did, she was sure of that, for she has heard of such miracles, for they were miracles and as such very rare, and once she even married one of them, and had a friend who was a former street urchin, a reformed street urchin, she said, a very reformed, truly reformed street urchin but still remembered her days of street-urchinhood. That was all right but that was rare, very rare indeed, she said. That was all right because that friend was no longer a street urchin and that was commendable, very commendable but sometimes, though no often, she wondered whether a tiny bit of street-urchinhood remained—even though it was not immediately obvious—and whether it might be the case of that well-known saying being true, that well-known saying: Once a street urchin always a street urchin. She kept an open mind on that, she said.

One evening when she was seventeen she went to an art exhibition but it is not right to say that she went for that suggests an intention on her part and she had no such intention that evening, as she had no particular intention to do anything on many evenings, and on many mornings, when she was seventeen except to be left alone to read and go for long walks alone, always alone. It would be better to say that she drifted into a gallery space after walking around the city for an hour or so, alone with her thoughts and at some point when she looked up and saw a poster for the opening of a new exhibition, she stepped in without giving it much thought whether it was a good idea or not to go in that night which was an opening night and such nights tended to be crowded and crowded with people who she saw as not very interested in art but people who were hangers about, all those fashionable women who liked to be seen with artists, all those fashionable women who talked a lot, and laughed, all those fashionable women who walked around with a smile on their face and she had nothing to say to such women. She had nothing to say to most people when she was seventeen and that evening when she had gone to that exhibition she had just spent a week alone at home and she liked that, she liked when her parents were away and so she could read for hours, read undisturbed and that was important, that was very important to her for it was around that time that she had discovered how much there was to know, how much she wanted to know and how little she knew. After being alone for a week and a week of not speaking to anyone at all and she carried that strange feeling in her mouth, that slightly metallic taste on her tongue, that unearthly sensation of lightness in her head, the feeling that comes from not having spoken at all for a week, from not hearing a single voice addressing her for a week, that strange feeling that made her feel on high, that sense of satisfaction of not having wasted words on daily living and on small talk, and she liked that lightness in her head, that feeling of slight dizziness, that impression of intoxication that made her think that she could soar above everything and above everyone who did not matter, that sense of intensity, that sense of sharpened perception that comes from not speaking at all for days and that sensation that comes from eating little and not feeling the weight of her body and so she walked into the gallery without thinking, she slipped in and she drifted around, looking at the paintings and she felt she wanted to write a poem and she wanted to write it there and then. She was standing in a corner, wearing her navy blue coat, a smart coat but a coat that was plain, a coat that was not fashionable, not fashionable at all for it was not a colour that was fashionable that season, and standing alone in a corner of the elegant gallery space with its glistening hardwood floors and groups of people chattering loudly, chattering happily, groups of people holding champagne flutes that sparkled as the people moved around, that evening in a gallery full of fashionably dressed women, she was aware that the navy blue of her winter coat was not in fashion because everyone else, all other women, wore camel-coloured coats and their coats were belted and her coat was not belted, her coat was loosely cut, it was a comfortable, simple, plain coat. But that was not the thought that preoccupied her mind when she entered the gallery or after she had looked at the paintings and after she had felt that she had to write a poem, that thought about her unfashionable coat came to her only later, after she had left the gallery and was looking back, that thought might have even come to her days or months later. It was not only the coat that made her stand out, and it was not only that she was alone while everyone else was with other people, and it was not only that she was not drinking and that was not because she did not like champagne or did not want champagne, it was because when a waiter appeared in front of her and proffered a tray in her direction, she was already bent over a small notebook, writing her poem. She would have wanted to take a champagne flute but the waiter had glided away from her without waiting for her to finish writing the words she had to write. When she finished her poem, a man spoke to her and later thinking about that moment, it occurred to her that she did not remember seeing the man walk towards her and although the gallery was crowded as such places usually are on such nights, the space around her, the space in front of the corner where she had positioned herself—perhaps to have a buffer of relative quiet from the din in the gallery, that space around her was empty and so later that evening she wondered whether the man who had approached her had been watching her while she was writing. That might have well been the case and that would not have been something she would have minded, she was only thinking about it because she wanted to ascertain whether there was intention on his part, whether he had been watching her and wondered whether he should talk to her or whether he had acted on the spur of the moment and that distinction, as it is to become clear, as it is to become clear she hopes, that distinction was important to her, she said. She does not remember what his first words were but it was most likely that he said something about her writing. When she thought about that after she had left the gallery and was alone at home, she was pleased that he would have noticed her because she was writing and writing a poem. She was pleased with that idea because it said something about him, something that she liked. He was not a street urchin, no grown-up man who had been a child street urchin would have approached a woman writing a poem, a woman who was alone, a woman who wore plain clothes at a fashionable exhibition where everyone else was chatting, where everyone else was laughing, where everyone else had a friend, where everyone else was sipping champagne. That realization also confirmed something else that she had sensed after talking to the man for only a couple of minutes. He was a person from whom she could learn, in fact that was the first thought on her mind while they talked and later, when she thought about their first meeting, it appeared to her that he had approached her, that he had started talking to her at that exhibition opening precisely with that purpose in mind: he had selected her, he had chosen her so that he could teach her. While they talked, that idea began to crystallize in her mind and by the time she left the gallery she was sure that theirs was going to be a relationship marked by mutual learning, marked by mutual self-improvement and that feeling was confirmed when she met him again, that feeling that he would teach her and that she would teach him and by that she meant teaching in the real sense of the word, teaching as sharing love, the love of learning and for her the word love is crucial because, for her teaching, genuine teaching, has always been about sharing love for the same interests, for the same passions, love for the same ideas and it is this erotic element that some vulgar souls might frown at, that some vulgar souls might consider inappropriate and how little they understand about real teaching, how little they understand about real learning, about real sharing of love for what is being taught, how little they understand in this day and age when learning is all about passing exams and acquiring tricks on how to finish schooling with best grades possible without caring whether one is learning anything, whether one is improving oneself and there is no shared love for what is being taught, and teaching has become a matter of some vulgar, commercial market exchange and there is no love, there is no love at all and the erotic element of teaching, that erotic element that has nothing to do with some vulgar sexuality, that erotic element that Roland Barthes writes about, that element to these people appears risqué and unacceptable and she can only think of such people as base, clearly they are former street urchins, grown-up street urchins, that element to such people means some disgusting exploitation, some paedophilic sexuality, she said. She recalls that after that first meeting in the gallery she told a friend at school about the artist and she told the friend that she was going to visit the artist in his studio. He has invited me to come to see his work, she said. The friend gasped. You should not go, the friend said. But why not? I am interested in seeing his painting, his drawings, his sculptures, she said. You have to be careful with men like him, the friend said. Men like him, what did men like him mean? Men who are older, so much older than you, the friend said. She went to see him, of course she went. She could not take note of such silly ideas, such base ideas, such street-urchin ideas. That is not what Barthes would have had in mind and that is not what she could possibly think because for her teaching has always been about sharing the love for what is being taught, that is what she knew when her mother was teaching her and she understood that kneeling in a corner of the kitchen and facing a blank wall when she could not recite a poem by heart without prompting and without stumbling, that was about love. And when her mother said that if she could not recite a poem without prompting and without stumbling that no one would love her, that too was about love, about love and learning. Her mother said those words because she loved her and her mother wished her to be clever so that she would be loved.

As for the artist, she was right, she said, and her school friend was wrong. She was always learning with him, and it was not only about poetry, it was not only about art or philosophy, it was also about working on herself, about making herself and that was real education. He told her that when she became a writer, as he was sure she would be, she would have to make sure that there was nothing else, and no one else, standing in the way of her art. She would have to be serious, always serious, serious about writing and being serious about writing meant being serious about life. But at seventeen she did not know how to be serious and so she listened to what he had to say. You must never have a child, he said. But some writers, some artists are serious about their work and they have children, she said. No, they are not serious enough, then, he said. One could always be more serious than one already is. There are no limits to seriousness about one's art. There is no such thing as enough of seriousness, enough of effort, enough of hard work for an artist, he said and then he took her to see *Andrei Rublev*, a beautiful Russian film that she would see many times later in life and that still captivates her. The artist said that she should aim to be as serious about her writing as Rublev was about his painting. Yes, Rublev was serious, she said, but he was a monk. Proves my point, he said, you have to live as seriously as if you were a monk. She was only seventeen and perhaps she wanted to be a monk one day but at seventeen, she did not know whether that would come to pass. She said that she did not want to give up living. But what did she mean by living, the artist asked. She did not know what she meant and she did not know why she said it, she did not know where the words had come from. Being an artist is living, being a writer is living, but living properly means being serious, he said and so they left it at that.

A few days later, she went to his studio wearing fashionable platform shoes and when the artist saw them, he laughed at her. He laughed at her, and it was a mocking laugh, an unkind laugh and he said: Is that what you call living? Wearing shoes that everyone else wears? He stopped laughing and he told her off: You are not serious about preparing yourself to be a writer. Your shoes are frivolous, your interest in such things is frivolous and that interest dissipates your energy, that interest destroys your effort, that interest kills your concentration, that frivolity stops you from being serious. You cannot allow that, he said, she said. But she was serious, she said, wearing platform shoes had nothing to do with being serious, she said. It was frivolous to wear fashionable shoes, he said. It was frivolous to notice what is fashionable, she said but he did not hear her. He had already walked away. She thought that perhaps he was right, but only a bit right for she did spend time looking for those shoes but that did not mean she had not enough time to think about being a writer. But what was enough? Was there anything that was enough for an artist, for a writer, was there anything that was enough for creativity? The artist was right about that. Soon after that discussion about fashionable shoes, she stopped seeing the artist for some time, a few months at least, and she missed their conversations but she had decided that she could only go back when she knew how to ignore his comments about her shoes, she could only go back when she knew what to say to him. She could only go back when she was confident enough not to hear his laughter. There was no question of her not going back to him. He had a place inside her and that was to remain for good. It was only a question of time, a question of her growing up a bit more before she could see him again. But what was that laughter about, she wondered years later. He was laughing at her. It was an unkind laughter but it was not laughter entirely directed at her, it could have also been a laughter born out of fear, a laughter born out of fear of his own omissions, of his own failings, of his own frivolity. But that thought did not cross her mind at the time, at the time when she was learning from him, at the time when learning was about love, at the time when she needed to learn, when she needed to better herself so that she would be loved. That was important to her in those days and that was important to her for a long time: she needed love, she always needed love. She thought about getting love when she was not-yet-four years old and pleasing her mother was a way of getting love and she thought about the stories that brought her love from the friends of her parents, and those stories came from that part of herself, that secret part she kept to herself when she was facing a blank wall, kneeling in a corner of her mother's kitchen on a clean, white, A4-size sheet of paper, the paper on which she would one day write her stories, the stories that came from that part of herself, that secret part that she kept while the girl who was her afternoon babysitter held her hand and she pretended to be asleep and it occurred to her that she needed a secret part of herself, that she needed a secret part of herself so that she could write, she needed a part of herself, a part kept secret from the artist. The artist had started teaching her when she was seventeen and receptive and malleable like his clay, receptive and malleable like his metal that he could beat into shape, into the shape that he had dreamt of, into the shape that he had dreamt of. But one day the time had come for her to dream of what she wanted to be, to dream of what she wanted to be without listening to him, without allowing him to play the role of Pygmalion, that patriarchal

sculptor, that control freak who breathed life into his creation—
oh, how she disliked the myth! She had to make herself without
the help from anyone else but how, how could she do that? Where
was her vision of who she wanted to be? All she knew was that every
day she wanted to be someone else and she always wanted to be
somewhere else. She was lost, she was weak, or so she thought, and
so she needed him—or so she thought—she needed the artist but
she also needed her secret part kept secret. When she stayed away,
she stayed away from the artist, she stayed away until she was
strong enough and knew what kind of shoes she wanted to wear,
and she stayed away until it did not matter to her whether the artist
disapproved of her shoes. It occurred to her years later that perhaps
theirs was an archetypal teaching situation with the pupil becoming
independent from the teacher, the teacher who was a very special
teacher, an extraordinary teacher, for only an extraordinary teacher
could have a pupil who becomes capable of opposing the teacher,
a pupil who becomes independent, a pupil who can walk away from
the teacher. She was strong, strong enough to be herself, strong
enough not to let the artist take over her thoughts and that was a
tribute, she realized that later, many years later, that was a tribute
to the artist and above all, to her first teacher, to her mother who
was teaching her to recite poetry by heart and when she could not
without stumbling and prompting, her mother asked her to kneel
in a corner of the kitchen on a clean white sheet of A4-size paper,
and that was teaching, that was very good teaching, that taught her
to push herself, to try harder, to make more effort, that taught her
that life was all about improving herself and improving herself so
she could be loved. And her strength, her ability to walk away from
the artist, from his love, from his love that was giving, too giving,
that strength of hers was a tribute to the artist, to the hours they
had spent in discussion, to the hours that made her think for herself, to the hours of discussion that made her learn that to be a

writer she would have to think for herself, she could not be a writer if she adopted the thinking of her artist friend, of her artist teacher, of her artist lover.

On some days when she visited the artist in his studio, she saw a young man drawing at the table or working on graphics. The young man, who she thought was a couple of years older than her, never said anything to her beyond an acknowledgement and a greeting. She would have liked to have been able to talk to him because he seemed studious, he seemed different from other young men she knew, other young men who were not interested in art, other young men who were loud, other young men who she thought were grown-up street urchins. And although she does not remember thinking about it at the time, now it occurs to her that she might have been attracted to that young man, and she would have liked to have been able to talk to him but from the expression on his face, the expression which was always straight, with no trace of smile or interest in her, the expression which was not so much distant, detached, as disinterested, she could not tell whether he was shy or absorbed in his work and any one of those possibilities would have given him extra points in her book. At first she thought that the young man, whose name in the language of the country meant peace, was the artist's assistant, but after being introduced to him, she learnt that he was a student of painting at the arts academy. The artist said that he had *rescued* him from the street, yes, I rescued him in every sense of the word, that is what he said to her, rescued him from sleeping with the homeless and rescued him from being nobody, the artist said to her. The young man whose name meant peace, had neither a job nor training and seemed to have been drifting around, in between being put up by friends, because the young man, whose name meant peace and she thought that meaning was interesting, that meaning was signifi-cant, as it marked the young man in her eyes, and perhaps in the eyes of others, perhaps the artist thought of him as peaceful and perhaps that is why the artist had rescued him, that is why the artist had selected the young man. The young man whose name meant peace, had no family, no one to occupy the time that the young man could spend in the artist's studio, no one to prevent him from dedicating himself to his work in the artist's studio. The artist had trained him to pass the entrance exam at the academy and now the artist was giving him further teaching, setting him tasks and commenting on his work. I will make a painter, and a good painter, out of him. Miro has talent and he works hard and he takes it all in when I talk to him, the artist said. Something about the young man, something that she could not quite define—and at the time she did not think about it but tried to define it many years later— something about the young man, perhaps it was what she knew of the young man's background or perhaps it was the air that surrounded him, the air of loneliness, the air of commitment to his art and perhaps something about his demeanour, something that suggested his helplessness, his helplessness about his life, the helplessness that might have been apparent only to her, something about the young man endeared the young man to her at the time and when later in life she found herself in similar situations, situations that involved a serious person, usually a male, a serious person who was focused on self-improvement, a serious person who wanted to learn, when she met someone like that, something stirred in her, something akin to a maternal instinct, some urge to protect the person and to love them. But in the days when she used to visit the artist in his studio, she was not aware of anything like that, she did not think about it beyond feeling a sense of attraction, an undefined attraction, for the young man and even that only became clear to her later. At the time it was not something she thought about although she might have felt it, she certainly felt something like attraction, something that she was not sure what it was and each time she saw the young man, she resolved to talk to him but each time as soon as she arrived, and the young man nodded in her direction, immediately to bend his head over his work, the artist would give him some brief instruction or the artist would comment on his work and with that the artist would leave the young man alone for the duration of her visit and often the artist would lead her to another room, usually to a galleried space that served as the artist's bedroom, the space where he kept his writing and his books and the space where they talked, where they always talked and where he showed her his books, and where he read her his poems. He would close the door and at the time she liked that the artist did that, she liked being alone with the artist and she liked the idea of him taking her seriously, taking her to his space, as if he had preferred her over the other young person, the other young person who was abandoned downstairs while she was being taken to a special room upstairs, a room with a big terrace, a room from which she and the artist looked out over the city's red-tiled roofs, the red-tiled roofs that were beautiful but their sight always made her feel melancholy and stirred some kind of longing for her to go away to a place where she would be whoever she wanted to be and where she would shake off the chains of expectation from her parents and everyone else, including the artist. Ever since, at the sight of any city's red-tiled roofs, she has experienced a feeling of melancholy mixed with restlessness.

A few times it happened that she ran into the young man somewhere in town and on those occasions the young man talked to her, but he talked slowly and cautiously, as if weighing every word, as if thinking that she would tell the artist about their conversation. Sometimes it occurred to her that the artist had in a way adopted her, as he had adopted the young man, the artist who was childless and who believed an artist should not have a family, certainly not children, if they wanted to be serious about their art, the artist had adopted them so that he could fashion them in his image and while the young man seemed obliging and perhaps it was that obliging attitude of the young man that stirred certain feelings in her, certain desires to protect him, and it was that willingness of the young man to be moulded, to be moulded in the image chosen by the artist that made her watch out, that made her oppose the artist. She wanted to show that she was not really the artist's pupil, the artist's material to be moulded into a shape that he had dreamt. She does not know why she wanted to do that and she still cannot tell whether that desire came from her protective wish to somehow warn the young man against letting himself be moulded in the image chosen by the artist, the artist who had assumed the archetypal father figure, or who might have dreamt of being her Pygmalion (no chance, she always disliked the myth) or whether that desire to show the young man that, unlike him, she was not the artist's material that waited to be moulded, or whether that desire came from her own interest in the young man. She wanted him to know that she was free, that she was free for him to talk to her, that she was free for him to see her outside the artist's studio. Whichever it was, and it might have been a combination of the two, she was not really the artist's material and she was not the artist's woman even when a year later, she and the artist became lovers and she was not his woman when she loved him and she was not his woman even when she knew that he was a man she would always love even though she would not see him for many years. She was not really his woman, she was never his woman, whatever that gesture of taking her up to the galleried room upstairs from where she and the artist could look out to the city's red-tiled roofs, whatever that gesture in front of the young man was designed to mean, she was never the artist's woman. She read the books the artist gave her to read, she made notes on those books, she thought about what he gave her to read, she listened carefully when he explained anything to her, she watched the films the artist recommended, she looked at the art the artist talked about, she was learning from him but sometimes she did not agree with him and as time passed, she learnt to tell him that. He was teaching her and that was love and she was grateful for that, just as she has been grateful and will always be grateful to her mother for all those mornings of learning, for all those years of love. And just as she kept her secrets from her mother when she was not-yet-four years old, she kept a secret, a big secret from the artist and it was because she kept a secret that she managed never to become his woman or his anything. At the time she worried about keeping a secret and such an important secret from him, but when she saw the young man, the quiet young man whose name meant peace, she knew that she had to keep her secret. And when the artist said that she should become a writer, that was fine, that was an idea, that was one of the ideas she too had had and perhaps he said it because he might have understood that that is what she wanted, he might have understood that about her. But the artist would never make her into a painter, the artist would never make her into a sculptor, for how could he do that without knowing that secret part of her, the painting and drawing part, she kept that part of herself so secret that she erased that part of herself and after she had met him in that gallery when she was wearing her simple, unfashionable coat, after that evening, never again did she take up a pencil, or a charcoal, or a brush to draw or paint and after that evening in the gallery, after she started spending her learning time, and her learning time was most of her time, after she started spending her learning time in the artist's studio, she could not paint, she could not draw, because she knew that she could not be so close to the artist and become an artist herself. But a writer, becoming a writer, that was different, that was very different, that was open to her, that was open to her to dream about.

But there were moments, there were moments when she wondered whether she could have continued doing her drawings, doing her paintings in secret, away from the artist, there were moments when she wondered whether she could have carried on drawing hands, her hand and other people's hands without ever telling the artist. There were moments when she thought it was a pity that she had given it up because hands, drawing hands was special to her, drawing hands that told a story, that was what she liked, single hands, touching hands, waving hands, loving hands, creating hands. Most of the time she used to draw her hand, her left hand from above and from below, relaxed or clenched, her hand in so many positions, her hand telling different stories, her hand being different people, her hand living a life. But sometimes, sometimes when she had a friend, a willing friend, or a lover, a willing lover, she drew two hands together, two hands touching, the friend's hands, the lover's hands touching, or the friend's hand touching her hand or the lover's hand touching her hand. The touching hands were living hands, always living hands, the touching hands were loving hands, the hands telling stories, just like those specks of dried-up paint that she had watched when she was not-yet-four years old and that she would connect into shapes, the shapes that told stories and those stories led to love, to her getting love. And hands, touching hands were about love, or that is what she thought when making those drawings. Even the hands that were not touching, such as her hand when she was alone and there was no other hand to touch her hand, it was still a hand about love, it was a hand looking for love, it was a hand wanting to give love, it was a hand reaching out to the world, reaching out to other hands. But when she met the artist, she stopped drawing, she stopped drawing hands, she stopped drawing altogether and so that part of her, that part that could have got her love, that part disappeared, she knew that only her stories were left to help her get love, the love that she always dreamt about getting. But the hands stayed with her, haunting her when she was awake and when she was asleep and the hands that haunted her, shouted at her, laughed at her, the hands that haunted her were reaching out to her but that reaching was not about love, it was about pushing her away so that she would fall, like those hands that had pushed her in the paddling pool when she was not-yet-five years old, the hands that haunted her were reaching out to her only to scratch her, to hurt her, the hands that haunted her were about hate and she wondered how could those hands, the hands that she used to draw, the hands that were about love, how could those hands turn out to be about hate? That was the question that used to bother her but not any more, not now when she no longer wants love, when she no longer wants anything.

She had lots of dreams, lots of different dreams in those days, many different dreams about being someone else and many different dreams about going somewhere else. (There was always this elsewhere in her life.) At first that somewhere else was the artist's studio, his bohemian house on a hill, and she liked that, she liked having to climb to reach his place, and she liked standing on his terrace and looking down at the town, at the town where her parents lived, where her other life was and she remembered the first time she went to his studio and he took her upstairs to the galleried room that led to the terrace and looked over the red roofs of the town and she remembered standing there and looking out and feeling separate from her life down there, from her life with her parents and from her life with her friends and while she was on that terrace, she was someone else, someone new, someone she had not been before. And even when she went back, each time she went back to her other life, to the life with her parents and with her friends, even then she carried that new self from the artist's terrace, she carried that new self as a memory within her and she remembered that neither of those selves belonged to the worlds of her daily life and so when she was in the world of her parents and her friends, she felt different from them, too different to be comfortable and when she was with the artist and his friends, again she felt too different to be entirely comfortable. And sometimes she wondered who was that real her and where was that place where she would not be different. She lived her life, and she would continue living it, as if she was always walking on the wrong side of the road, as if she was always looking in the wrong direction—except that at the time she did not know that—and she would continue living her life as a stranger, a stranger who moved from one place to another, and moved with a relative ease, more ease than others would have managed, others who could not move from one place to another, the others who did not have to move since they were fine where they were. For a while, for a year or two or three even, being on that terrace in the artist's galleried room and looking down at the red-tiled roofs, that was very much elsewhere, that was her secret place where she could go and be someone else, someone else different from that else that her parents knew.

His studio was surrounded by an unkempt, overgrown garden and next to his house there were other bohemian houses with studios from artists he knew, the artists he took her to see, and being only a seventeen-year-old woman, a precocious seventeen-year-old woman introduced to middle-aged artists who were mostly men, the men whose work she had admired from afar, she felt flattered with their attention and she liked that, she liked that she could talk to them about what interested her, she could talk to them about art, she could talk to them about writing and they listened and they asked questions and they commented on her ideas and they were interested in her as if she had been one of them and not a seventeen-year-old schoolgirl and they seemed to like what she had to say and their attention felt like the love she was given for her stories when she was younger, and that made her happy and it made her look forward to seeing them. But later, years later she wondered whether they were interested in what she had to say or whether they liked what she had to say because they liked her, because they liked her because she was young and she was a woman, and they were middle-aged and they were men. That question came to her only years later, years later when she was in one of her more cynical moods. At the time, she was happy to have the attention of the artists who were friends of her artist friend, the attention that she felt was directed towards what she had to say. She felt loved by the artist and loved by his friends. Sometimes she talked to them about her dreams, she could talk to them about her passions and they had similar dreams, they had similar passions and so they listened, they never laughed at her, they never laughed at her in the way her friends at school laughed at her. With the artist and with his artist friends she was learning, she was always learning and that made her alive, that made her happy because she was improving herself and that was what life was about, learning and improving herself, that is what her mother used to say to her and she remembered that time with the artist and his friends as happy time, as the time when it seemed to her that nothing was beyond her reach, that there was nothing that she could not do and she felt that one day she would do something special, something creative, something that would make her happy because she would be happy with it. And that was good, that was a very good feeling, she said, that feeling that every-thing was possible, that everything was possible one day.

And when she says that now, when she thinks of that now, she remembers an afternoon when one of her artist's friends, an elderly sculptor, a sculptor whose work she admired, a sculptor whose work made her stop and think, a sculptor whose images she carried around in her head when she walked around town, that sculptor, who at the time was more than sixty years old, that sculptor said:

Your face has an interesting shape, the shape that says that you will never be happy. That is what he said. Just like that. And then silence through which he continued to stare at her, sitting completely still, as if he did not wish anything to detract attention from his words, his heavy words, and as if he wanted his words to stick as much as possible, as if the weight of the words needed to settle, as if their freshness had to dry, to harden, so that the words would become indelible. She remembered the silence, she remembered it clearly as a confusing silence, as an embarrassing silence, a shameful silence, a silence that ate her thoughts, a silence that ate her words. When the silence was broken, all that came out of her mouth was a giggle, a loud giggle, as if she could laugh off his words and make them disappear. She remembered the scene clearly, for it was a scene, a dramatic scene with five characters sitting on benches around a wooden table in the sculptor's garden, with two bottles of red wine on the table and five tumblers. Whenever she thought about that moment of silence which was more than a moment, of eating silence, devouring silence, the silence that swallowed her, and that silence was gorging itself on her future, all of her future possibilities of happiness. She knew that it was not so much the words he had said that erased her thoughts, that halted her own words but it was the casual tone that he used that arrested the time, it was not so much the words the sculptor had said but the tone, the casual, flippant tone that belied the seriousness of the sculptor's words, as if they were words of no consequence. But those words were to be of consequence. She knew that they would be of consequence and she feared the consequence. She did not giggle straightaway, and when she did, it was not spontaneous. It was a giggle, loud giggle that she forced herself to produce, to break the silence, to assuage the impact of those words, to dispel their threat. Neither she nor her artist friend said anything. And the other two painters kept quiet as if their words had been eaten, too. There was only her giggle. And while she could hear her giggle and her eyes travelled from one face to another, she noticed how old they were, those four people around the table and there was a hunger in their aged bodies and then suddenly she too felt old, as old as them, as if with those words her future had been erased and all those possibilities of doing something special had ceased to exist. Suddenly she was old, as old as someone with no future, as someone to whom nothing important could happen any more. And yet she giggled, she giggled as if she had no care in the world and her giggle echoed around the heads of others sitting at the table and her giggle echoed around the garden and her giggle echoed beyond the garden and even after they had left the garden she could hear her giggle, she could hear it as they walked home and she could hear it when she was at home, far from that sculptor's garden, she could still hear it. But it was an ineffective giggle despite its loudness, despite its duration and despite its reach. No one said anything. No one dared say anything. They sat there dumbfounded as if the old sculptor's words had eaten their voices.

Years later she thought that they should have said something, they should have acted, they should have said something to abolish the sculptor's words, to annul them with some prophecy of happiness. But now she knows that such attempts would have been in vain, would have been empty, would have been meaningless. Nothing could erase the sculptor's words. She still wondered why they did not speak and if the two painters did not care. What about her artist, her lover, why did he not speak? She does not think they were shocked, or scared or offended, they were only surprised, she said, they would have been wondering why would someone say such words, such heavy words, why would someone say anything like that even if you had such power to predict someone's future state of happiness or unhappiness, why would someone, and that someone was a friend of a friend, a friend of her lover, someone she liked and someone she had met before, why would someone who liked her and she had evidence of that, plenty of evidence that he liked her, why would someone like that assume the role of an evil fairy and spoil the occasion, and more than the occasion, her life perhaps. Her life perhaps? But he, that someone, that sculptor, that old friend of her artist friend had no power to determine her life, no one had such power. Who was he to know what her life would be like? A crystal-ball holder, an evil fairy? No, no, she would forget his words, she would never think about his words, she did not want his words to come true, they will never come true if she forgot them. But he was a sculptor, he knew about shapes, he knew what they meant, and she liked his work, she liked him, she did not want to dismiss what he had said, his words scared her with their possibility, his words scared her, his words shamed her but she did not want the words to stay in her mind, so she giggled, she giggled and then her artist friend laughed but not as forcefully as she giggled, he laughed a short laugh and the two painters grimaced a quick smile.

But despite her giggle, the words of the old sculptor stayed with her for the rest of her life and in years to come whenever she was unhappy, which was often, she thought of that summer afternoon sitting in the garden of the old sculptor around a table on wooden benches with two bottles of red wine and five tumblers in front of them and she wished she could laugh at the absurdity of her fear but unlike that day when she did giggle and giggle loudly, she felt angry at the thought that those words were prophetic and that they had come true and she did not want to believe in that, she did not want to believe that those words could have been a curse. But did it really matter where her unhappiness had come from for she did not believe that it could have been avoided and therefore the old sculptor was simply putting into words what was there anyway. She came to believe that she had to be unhappy, except for those brief moments, those brief flashes of creativity when something inside her made her alive and almost happy—for she could never be sure that it was happiness—and even if it was happiness, it was so brief, so transitory, so elusive that it was always a memory, never of now, never in the present. All her happiness was past happiness. And she knew she had to be unhappy because she was a thinking person, and thinking people are unhappy and that is what the old sculptor must have meant, it was only that being a sculptor, he was thinking about shapes and the shape of her face must have told him that she was a thinking person. In the end, what he said did not matter for as time passed and she grew older, happiness or unhappiness, whichever it was, did not matter, and she hardly noticed the difference between the two for there was only one thing that mattered, only one thing she cared about, apart from her children, that is, apart from caring for her children, and that one thing was her writing. All she wanted was to be a writer, all she wanted was to write one good piece, one piece that would be truly good, one piece that would make it all worthwhile, one piece would be enough. But sometimes, sometimes even that did not matter and sometimes the room stayed too dark even when she remembered to switch on the light and even when she bothered to open the shutters and afterwards all she could think was that writing, her writing, and all writing, was to have it done with and there is no question of a good piece or a bad piece. But that is not true, she would say now. There are many bad pieces and her pieces are bad, usually bad when she looks at them for the second or third time but that is all right for she continues to write and perhaps one day, perhaps one day she may hope to write a good piece, a piece that will look good when she looks at it for the second and third time, a piece that will look good no matter how many times she looks at it and perhaps that is what keeps her going, keeps her going in part, that hope, that desire that she could write a good piece, one good piece. As to whether that old sculptor knew about shapes and their meaning, his prophecy, even if there are such words that are prophetic, his words had nothing to do with the shape of her face and with her unhappiness.

Her poet, the poet who was dead, was her first love and the sculptor was her second love and both loves stayed with her for the rest of her life and there were many loves after that but they were not loves that stayed with her for the rest of her life, they were loves that came and went, leaving a trace as everything leaves a trace on her life but that was all, a trace, a trace of memory. And always, with each love, what she really cared about was the person's improving self, their drawings, their prints, their sculptures, their writing, and it was this improving self, this committed self, this passionate self, this learning self that made her fall in love with different people again and again, and for her there was nothing more attractive than cleverness and she knew that she could not love someone who was not focused on self-improvement. She loved the artist because he knew things that he could teach her and that ability of others to teach her has always been important in her life, that is why she was always loving someone who could teach her, just like her mother used to teach her, and her mother loved her, and she loved her mother and she loved the sculptor and she loved the dead poet for teaching her, just as she loved her mother, loved her for wanting the best for her, for reading her poems and stories and making her kneel in a corner of her kitchen when she could not recite a poem by heart without stumbling and without prompting, for that was good for her, for that made her want to try harder and she loved the poet, the dead poet, loved him for showing her what language can do, loved him for making her think in ways that were different from the ways everyone else she knew thought and she loved the artist because he taught her to be serious about her writing and she always needed to be taught, she always needed to improve, so that she would be clever and so that she would be loved. It used to be all about love. Everything in her life used to be about getting love, giving love. Love. She always wanted to be loved, but not any more, not these days, she said, these days she does not expect love, she does not long for love and even when it comes to friendship, she is very careful not to fall prey to friendship.

At the time when she met the artist, she was dreaming of places that were elsewhere, of places where she could be someone else, be many different elses. For a while her artist friend's studio, despite being only a walking distance from her parents' home, her artist friend's studio was the elsewhere, her artist friend's studio was another country to that of her parents'. Her parents' home was the place of linen serviettes, each embroidered with a name of a family member and it was a place where all saucers, all cups, all plates, all glasses, everything was part of a set, part of a matching set and it was a place presided over by the rules set by her mother, her mother who cared so much about her education, her mother who would have been shocked had she known that her daughter was visiting an artist who was bohemian, whose housekeeping resembled someone camping, her mother who would have dismissed the idea that the artist was clever and that visiting him her daughter was improving herself. But places, no matter how different, do not stay elsewhere for ever, and when they become familiar, they are no longer elsewhere.

One day she told the artist she was leaving, she was leaving to go on improving herself in the country of Shakespeare. She could not do that, he said. She had to be a writer and how could she be a writer in a country of Shakespeare where the language was different from her own. Besides, in the country of Shakespeare, the weather was so bad that only a masochist would move there, he said. She did not care about the weather, that was irrelevant, she thought. He said some other words, made some other objections to her leaving, thinking that he could make her reconsider, but she did not hear them and if she did, she did not think about them. She was leaving and nothing could change her mind. And when she was in the country of Shakespeare, her artist friend was sending her cards with poems he had written for her, they were courtly love sonnets, old-fashioned and formal and she was his unattainable lady and he was the ever-hopeful suitor. That was nice but that was art, that was poetry, his poetry, that was his life and he was part of the life she had left behind, of the life she did not want. She read each poem, turned it over, looked at the picture on the card and pinned it on her notice board. Soon the notice board was full and every day she saw the pictures on the cards he had sent her but she did not pause to think about them. In the country of Shakespeare, she wanted to choose her thoughts without him.

After a year, when she was visiting the country of her birth, she went to see him and he placed a box, a shoe box on her lap and when she opened it, inside were dozens and dozens of black-and-white photographic index sheets, each filled with tiny, thumb-size photographs, photographs of her, close ups of her, pictures of her moving around, tucking her hair behind her ears, thousands of photographs. He was looking at her as she took each sheet out of the box and she could tell he was waiting for her to say something, it was her turn to speak for he did not need to say anything. She had too many questions, too many questions fighting for space in her head to be able to ask anything and so they sat in silence with her peering at the tiny pictures on each sheet in the pile and him keeping his eyes on her, looking at her closely, scrutinizing her as if she were his model and he was painting her and she knew she should ask her questions and she knew she should tell him how amazed she was but something was stopping her as if all these images of her have taken her voice away, as if she was no more than those images, those silent images that he had created of her, those fixed images. Later, years later, when she thought about that afternoon when she was looking at the sheets of pictures in that shoe box and wondering why she could not speak while she was looking at them and she remembered that the rug on which she was sitting was entirely covered with her images, tiny images of herself as if the world were populated by women who were copies of her and she remembered that she could not take her eyes off those tiny images, those tiny images that fascinated her, those tiny images that scared her with their numbers, those images that had taken her voice away. And later, years later she remembered that she was scared to see so many images, so many images of herself, so many images that she could not tell where they had come from and she was scared thinking that she had been observed, that she had been captured, and captured by this man she loved, by this man she would always love, the man whose love would stay with her for the rest of her life and yet this man had tried to fix her, to shoot her and she was not even aware that he was doing it and she felt nauseous at the thought that she had been observed, that she had been captured, that she had been shot, even though it was by a man she loved, she felt nauseous thinking that he had shot her, that he had observed, that he had captured her without her not knowing that he was doing it. That was scary and now here she was, fixed and voiceless and numerous, much too numerous and that was all she could think about. And perhaps even more than that, perhaps something else was happening to her because suddenly she wanted to run away, she wanted to abandon the images, she wanted to abandon this man who had shot her and captured her, but she could not, the images held her still, the images held her captive and she could not move. And then this man, this man whom she loved and this man who loved her, this man saw her fear and he spoke: They are not pictures of you. Not of me? She wanted to laugh. Of course they were. No, they are not of you. But whose are they, then?

They are of another woman, your double, a double I had found and befriended on a summer holiday. But it was not possible that anyone could look so much like me, that anyone would move as I do, that anyone would make faces in the same way that I do. Perhaps not, perhaps it was not possible, but he had looked hard, he was a sculptor, he knew about shapes and he wanted to find her double and here she was, the pictures were the proof. But where is this woman, this double of mine? I would like to meet her. The woman had the same voice as you, the woman laughed in the same way as you did. This woman was your double, he said. Where was she then? I would like to meet her, she said again. She wanted to see her, she was excited about seeing her double, a woman who was like her, perhaps a part of her that was lost, a woman she could love. She remembered that her first thought was that she could get love from that woman and she could give love to her. But she did not say that because she could tell that the artist wanted the double for himself. He said that he did not know where her double was, her double had disappeared, he said, and once they had parted he had not heard from her and had not been able to trace her. I missed you so much, he said and so I had to find a double, a woman who looked just like you, a woman who moved like you, a woman whose voice was similar to yours. She wished she could see her, she said again, her double, she wanted to see her double for if she had a double, a double who was like her, a double who moved like her, a double who sounded like her, she would not stand out so much—she did not want to say anything about love—please trace her, she said. No, he could not find her, he has tried everything, he said, official and unofficial channels: her double had disappeared. He had been to her home address and no one there had ever heard of her. And yet he had sent letters to the address and he had had letters from the woman from that address, and then they stopped. What if he had dreamt her? She did not say that. What if had made her up? She did not say that either but he guessed her thoughts. What about the pictures, he asked. What about the pictures? They are the proof, he said, he has her photographs. But that was no proof. Those pictures were pictures of her and she had no double. She had no double because no one had a double; everyone was alone. She had only wanted to meet her double because she wondered whether when you had a double, a double who looked like you, a double who moved like you, a double whose voice sounded like yours (she had to take his word for that), whether that meant that the double thought like you, whether that meant that if you had a double, a double with the same outside and whether that meant that the inside of the double was the same as your inside, and if that were so and if the double thought like you, would it mean that you would not stand out in the crowd? That is the question but even a better question is whether the double would wear the same shades, the same coloured lenses as hers. She will never know that and that is fine for it is not a real question, it is again one of those imagined questions, one of those amusing questions, one of those questions that she asks to pass the time, not a question that matters. There are no questions that matter, she learnt years later.

There are no more questions that matter and yet they keep coming, they keep coming to her, all those matterless questions about what could have been and why did something not happen and why did something happen. And why is she as she is and could she have been different had it not been for this or that, had she taken that chance or missed that chance, had she crossed someone or not crossed someone, had she crossed someone's path, had she loved or not loved someone and that someone introduced her to someone else whom she loved or not and that someone introduced her to someone else whom she loved or not and could she have been different had she had different parents, had she had different grandparents and different great-grandparents and had those great-grandparents had different parents and had those parents of her great-grandparents had different parents and different this and that and had she not read this or that book or loved this or that poem and all she can conclude is that her life is a chance, a missed chance and a taken chance, full of chances and nothing but chances.

Now at the end of her life, where she has arrived with all the resignation that there is no more to wait for, that there is no more to hope for, and yet she is not resigned to all the failures of her life, she wonders whether it means that she still hopes, despite knowing that there is nothing to hope for and what does she hope for, what is there to hope for? But one does not arrive at the end of one's life overnight, one travels to the end of one's life slowly and one travels painfully and one travels in that direction every day, every day another step, every day more shedding of hopes and she has always been rushing even though she has known that there is nowhere to rush to. And sometimes that rushing, that travelling to nowhere makes her laugh but sometimes that scares her too and the times of frightening inaction come thicker and faster as the time passes and then inaction is followed by anguish, the anguish that makes the room dark even if she remembers to switch on the light and even if she bothers to open the shutters. When the anguish eases a little, she wonders whether her life would have been different had her mother not insisted on things that were for her own good and had there not been that corner in her mother's kitchen and had there not been all those poems that she had to memorize and could not recite by heart without stumbling and without prompting. But that is a silly if-question, that is a silly suppose this or that question and all such questions are irrelevant because her past, like all past, has gone and her past cannot be changed and she wants to stress, she said, that even if she could change her past, she is not sure that she would want to do so because what would she change and what difference would it make, what difference would it make to her life as it is now, she said, and what difference would it have made to her life that was, she said. Besides, when she looks back on her life she wonders whether her life has really been as she remembered it, has it happened as she recalls it? For a long time her mother read to her and that she remembered clearly and she remembered it as love, as the beginning of love that was to last all her life. Nor does she question that her mother used to slip a clean sheet of A4-size white paper under her knees as she asked her to kneel down in a corner of the kitchen when she was not-yet-four years old because that memory too is so clear in her mind, not fuzzy or vague, not distant as if it had happened to someone else and she is sure that she was pushed into a paddling pool that winter when she was not-yet-five years old and she clearly remembered that brown duffle coat dripping wet and forming a puddle under her feet when her mother opened the door but she is not so sure of other memories and she wonders whether she really was as scared as she remembered when her mother had said that no one would love her if she was not clever, and there was no indication, as her mother said, that she could possibly be clever since she could not recite poems by heart without stumbling and without prompting and sometimes she wonders whether that fear came later, whether that fear formed itself much later, much later when she could find words for her feelings, when she could articulate her feelings, and when that fear might have become more prominent under the effect of other events in her life, and she wonders about the street urchins and she wonders whether she could ever be sure of what she had really thought of them at the time, for despite her mother making her attitude towards them clear, she feels, she said, that even at the age of not-yet-four years old, she did not always accept what her mother said and being a lone child, though not necessarily lonely— but how could she ever be sure of that either, for even taking into account her precociousness, she may not have been aware of the difference at the time—she would allow for the possibility of the street urchins being attractive to her, even if that attraction was a repugnant attraction, such as when one is drawn to look at something disgusting, a squashed pigeon on the road, for example; and so there is no certain way of telling what she had really thought about the street urchins at the time when she was not-yet-four years old and perhaps, perhaps it is just possible that her feelings of revulsion for them were not that strong when she was not-yet-four years old and that such feelings only became pronounced in the light of other, later experiences. Our present always casts a light on our past and therefore the past is constantly reshaped and if she were to tell her story tomorrow, she said, that story would be a different story and with the memories from her childhood, as must be the case with such memories from other people's childhoods, the question of what happened, let alone how anyone felt about it, is even more complicated, she said. For how could she be sure that the image of her kneeling in the corner of her mother's kitchen would have survived in her memory and survived in the shape it has, had her mother, and in the case of other memories, her father and her grandparents, and sometimes their friends, too, had all of them not talked to her reminiscing about her when she was not-yet-four or not-yet-five years old and how could she tell which part of the story comes from whose memory and besides, these individual memories are coloured by the personality of each teller, not to mention that people tend to embellish a detail or two—such as that uncle of hers who used to be annoyed because as a child she did not like to play with jigsaw puzzles that he had given her and who would then repeat that she had ignored his gift and he would repeat that every time he saw her and so everyone started saying that she had never liked jigsaw puzzles when it really could have been one jigsaw puzzle that that uncle had even given her and only one jigsaw puzzle that she did not like doing—and the next time when they repeat the story, the embellishment is upgraded to the status of a fact and other details become embellished and so on it goes and then stories are weaved and something comes out of nothing. Something always comes out of nothing.

When she was eight years old, her best friend was a boy in her class, a very amicable, kind boy, a boy who was chubby and a boy who moved slowly, a boy who was teased by other boys and a boy who did not play with other boys. She liked him, she said, because he was gentle, because he wanted to talk to her while other boys were always running around, just like those street urchins she remembered when she was much younger. And that boy, who was chubby and who moved slowly and who was teased by other boys, that boy was always next to her as soon as the bell rang and they were released for a break or to go home. Sometimes he would tell her about a film he had seen, or a story he had read and she would tell him about a poem she liked but most of the time they talked about something they had heard on the news, and what they liked about the world and what they did not like about the world. When she was eight she developed a habit of listening to the news on the radio and this boy was the only child she knew who listened to the news too. Those conversations made her feel grown up because they were serious conversations, serious conversations about the world, the world that was beyond her family and her school, and the world that was beyond her friends and beyond everything she knew. She remembered talking to this boy, this boy who was chubby and who moved slowly, she remembered talking to him about an African leader who was removed from power in a *coup d'état*—but that was not the word she would have used at the time—and this boy agreed with her, this boy knew of the case, this boy did not have to ask who this African leader was, and this boy said that it was a terrible thing that all the family, even the children of that African leader were murdered by the man who had deposed the African leader and when he said that, other children from their class overheard it and they started asking questions but neither she nor the boy wanted to tell them and instead she and the boy walked away from the others. Sometimes the two of them would think that one day when they grew up, they would like to stop such things as what had happened to that African leader and they would try to do something to prevent awful things happening to little children, little children being murdered, or little children starving, as they did in many African countries. This boy who was chubby and who moved slowly and who had brown hair and straight-cut fringe across his forehead, this boy always agreed with her but sometimes, only sometimes, they fought, but they fought playfully and they never stopped being friends, not even for a day. Once, this playful fighting, this banter between them, and it most certainly was not about something that either she or the boy would have heard on the news, although she does not remember what it was that they fought about, fought playfully, but she remembered that they started hitting each other and his hitting was very gentle, his hand barely touched her and there was no force coming from him and although she was much more forceful in hitting him than he was in hitting her, he did not say that her hitting hurt him, and although they were both laughing, and the fighting was playful, a playful banter between friends, she started hitting the boy with her umbrella, a child's umbrella, and he did not complain, he was hitting her back with his hands but still very gently—you could hardly call it hitting—and he stopped laughing but he was not angry, definitely not. She could see his face, his chubby face and he did not complain, and he did not run away, he stayed and exposed himself to her blows and that must have indicated to her that he liked that she was hitting him and for her there was something pleasant in hitting him—she could not understand it then and she could not understand it later: she liked him, he was her friend, one of the very few friends she had and so why was she hitting him?—and she carried on hitting him and only stopped when her umbrella broke, when its spokes fell out because the spokes were bent from her hitting him. The boy stopped hitting her too, and he helped her pick up the spokes of the umbrella from the ground and they tried to fix them by strengthening them and pushing them back into the frame of the umbrella but they could not do it. After that umbrella fight, they stayed friends but soon her family moved house and so she went to a different school and she lost touch with the boy and she never thought of him, she never remembered him. But one day, almost thirty years after that umbrella fight, thirty years later and at the time when she was living outside the country of her birth and she was on a brief visit to the country of her birth and the visit was only a few days after the end of the war in the country of her birth and she was reading a paper, a national paper and there was a death notice for the boy, the chubby boy, the boy she had been hitting with an umbrella so much and so hard that the umbrella broke. The death notice said that he had died on the front in the last days of the war that was waged in the country in which she was born and after reading the death notice she thought about him a lot, she thought her sentimental thoughts and she felt guilty to have hit him so hard, so hard that her umbrella broke. And she wondered as she thought more sentimental thoughts whether he had ever remembered that fight, that umbrella fight and whether perhaps when he lay dying—if he did lie dying, and if he did lie wounded and knew that he might not live and his life flashed past his eyes—she wondered whether he had remembered how hard she was hitting him, so hard with the umbrella, so hard that the spokes broke and fell out and could not be put back, she wondered whether that chubby boy who was to grow into a man who would die on the front, whether he ever thought about her and she wondered whether he ever thought about making the world a better place as the two of them used to plan in those days, in those days when they were eight-years old. And it was at that time when she saw the death notice for the boy, the chubby boy who would no longer have been a boy and perhaps no longer chubby, it was then for the first time that she felt sorry to have been hitting him and hitting him so hard that the spokes on her umbrella broke and fell out and that hard hitting must have meant that he would have been hurting because she, who was his friend, she would have been hurting him and in her sentimental way, which has always been her way and the way she dislikes, in her usual sentimental way she wished she could undo the past and go back to that day when she was eight years old and if that could be done, she would not be hitting him, or at least she would not be hitting him that hard that the spokes on her umbrella bent and fell out. And she knew it was silly to think like that, to be so sentimental and to regret hitting him so hard with her umbrella only because he died and he died young on the front. But is it not silly to think that had she not been hitting him so hard, it might have made a difference to that poor chubby boy in the longer run and that it would have prevented him from dying on the front in the last days of the war in the country where she was born. But even that idea is not as absurd as it may at first appear and perhaps that episode of her hitting him had contributed to something in him, had perhaps made him lack confidence, had perhaps made him used to receiving blows and had he not been used to receiving blows, and had he not been lacking in confidence, he might have been better prepared for the front and he might have survived and he might have survived had she not been hitting him and hitting him so hard with her umbrella that the umbrella broke and spokes fell out and could not be put back again.

And as she is thinking that she might have caused the death of the chubby boy with the straight-cut brown fringe, she remembered that he is not the only one and there is at least one more man who might have lived had she been different. If only she had been friendlier and if only she had been more forthcoming on that day when as an undergraduate she went to the offices of the student paper and spoke to the editor, the editor who was a nice young man, another undergraduate but a few years older than she was and that nice young man asked her to write for the student paper. And that nice young man fetched past issues of the paper from the adjoining office because he said he wanted her to look at the reviews pages and compare how they had changed over the years, and he said he wanted to hear her views and he wanted to know what contribution she wished to make and even though she said she could look at past issues in a library or even in one of the offices down the corridor from him and although she said that she did not wish to bother him and waste his time, the nice young man was hanging around and sitting next to her and he was talking to her about books he had read and some of them she had read but others were new to her and the old copies of the student paper were lying on the table in front of them as if they had wilted from the lack of attention. And that nice young man was asking her about the seminars she was attending in Comparative Literature, which was the same department where he had studied except that he had not as yet taken his finals and, as it was to happen, he never would take those finals. And then he brought them coffee and she remembered that he offered her chocolate wafers and the chocolate wafers were in a box that he had fetched from a kitchenette of the offices of the student paper and she remembered that having no plates to offer her, he placed a clean white A4-size sheet of paper in front of her and in order to do that he had to free the space on the table and so he pushed away the old copies of the student paper, the old copies that were wilting from the lack of attention and some of them fell on the floor and she remembered that she made a move to pick them up but the nice young man told her not to worry. But she did worry because the copies of the paper made a crashing noise as they fell on the floor and that noise, that crashing noise made her uncomfortable and she found it difficult to talk to the nice young man afterwards because she kept hearing that noise while the nice young man talked to her. The nice young man offered her the chocolate wafers and she took one and placed it on the clean white A4-size paper that was in front of her on the table and the nice young man took a chocolate wafer himself and placed it on the same paper, some distance from her chocolate wafer. He looked at her for a moment without saying anything and she felt it was a moment too long of looking at her without saying anything and so she started talking about a book, a book she was reading at the time and the mention of that book was out of place but the nice young man then said something in response and soon the conversation flowed and there were no more too long moments of looking at her without saying anything. They drank their coffee and ate the chocolate wafers, one each, and as they lifted them off the clean white sheet of A4-size paper, she noticed that the sheet of paper, A4-size, was no longer clean because the two chocolate wafers had left chocolate marks on the paper and she remembered looking at those chocolate marks, two strips lying in parallel and the nice young man noticed her looking at the marks and so he looked at the marks and smiled. I wonder what that could mean he said and when she did not say anything, he added, well, instead of one of those people who tell fortune from coffee dregs, perhaps someone could read our fortune from the marks left by our chocolate wafers. She had nothing to say in response to such a silly idea and so there was another long silence between them and the young man started busying himself with some files, as if he was looking for something, but she did not mind the silence and she did not care what he was doing because she was thinking of the clean white sheet,

A4-size, that her mother used to slip under her knees when her mother asked her to kneel on the floor in a corner of their kitchen when she could not recite a poem by heart without stumbling and without prompting and she liked the clean white sheet because in her mind that sheet was there with her when she was writing her stories and so it was a good sheet, a clean sheet, a blank sheet, it was a sheet carrying many stories, many stories that she had made up and many stories that she would make up one day. But the sheet with chocolate smudges was a used up sheet, a sheet with only one story—although you could interpret it in many different ways, but that is not what she was thinking at the time, that is something that she came to think only years later—and so it was not a good sheet, it was a sheet that was smeared, it was a sheet with few possibilities, and it was the editor, who might have been kind, but who was responsible for destroying the sheet. It was a sheet that was finished, a sheet that carried no possibilities, except those of a palimpsest (but that thought too came to her many years later, many years later when she learnt that all sheets, smudged or not smudged, carried stories, and that it was only a matter of finding them, just like that figure in the carpet that a critic writes about). The nice young man seemed to have finished shuffling the files and he made a comment about her wafer leaving a smudgier mark than his, than his wafer that had left a straight line and he wondered what she made of that. She ignored the question, if that was a question. This nice young man was a poet—she had been to his readings, she had read his poems in journals—this nice young man was editing a student paper and this nice young man had a reputation for being very clever, and she admired his critical position, she took note of his reviews and yet this nice young man was talking of telling their fortune from marks left by chocolate wafers on a clean A4-size sheet of paper and she did not wish to be part of that. She had thought she might like him but this talk of the meaning of the marks left by chocolate wafers made her think that he was silly and that she was wasting her time with him in the office of the student paper. How silly his comments were compared to the beauty, compared to the potential of the clean white sheet and how bad that he has not noticed that. What could she learn from someone like him? She had to go. He said she should come again and look through old copies of the student paper and he said that he hoped she would write a review of a book or of a play for the paper. That would have been good, that would have been what she had come for but she could not make herself go back, she could not make herself go back to see the man who destroyed clean white sheets of paper, clean white sheets of paper that she loved so much. A few months after her visit, her first and only visit to the offices of the student paper, the nice young man who was editing the student paper met a friend of hers and that friend became his girlfriend and then within the next two years the nice man from the student paper became very ill and so both of his kidneys failed and he needed a transplant and he waited but there was no one to help him and so the nice young man died and she saw a death notice in a national paper and she was shocked to see it and she thought that had she not been so unforthcoming, had she been friendlier and had she gone to see him and had they started going out, the man would not have died. The man would not have died because she was a caring person and because she would have done everything possible to save him, everything possible to find him another kidney and she would have asked her father to help, her father who by that time was a successful doctor, a well-known doctor, her father who had very good connections, and her father would have done everything for her and her father would have fixed something—she knew that then and she was sure of that later—her father was always good at sorting out medical issues and he loved fixing medical issues and he would have loved to have helped her and who knows but she feels that is how it would have happened, that is how the nice young man editing the student paper might have been saved. But he was not saved and he was not saved because she did not go back to the editorial office of that student paper and so she never saw that young man again and she never wanted to see that nice young man because he did not notice that he was responsible for smearing a clean white sheet of paper, a clean white sheet of paper that could have carried stories.

That means that there at least two deaths on her conscience, two deaths that might have been avoided had she been different. But she would not have wanted to have been different and she would not question whether it matters, whether it matters at all that she can now recite poetry by heart without stumbling and without prompting and whether it matters that when she was not-yet-four years old, she could not recite poems without stumbling and without prompting and so she had to kneel in a corner of her mother's kitchen facing a blank wall for ten or fifteen minutes at a time, she would not question that. And what does it matter that she and that chubby boy with straight-cut brown fringe used to listen to the news on the radio when he never had a chance to do anything about the awful things that they had talked about? And how come that he, of all her friends was the only one who used to listen to the news on the radio when they were only eight years old? And perhaps had he not been listening to the news on the radio when he was only eight years old, he might not have had anything to talk to her about and he might not have been her friend and therefore she would not have been hitting him with the umbrella, hitting him so hard until the umbrella broke and he might not have lost his self-confidence, and he might not have become used to being hit and he might have been able to save his life. So she was not the only one responsible for his death, there must have been someone else, someone in his home who would have listened to the news on the radio and so the chubby boy would have listened with them because at the age of eight, children do not listen to the news on the radio of their own initiative. And there would have been other people who could have helped that editor of the student paper, there would have been his brothers to start with, for he had three brothers and could not one of them, just one of them, had given a kidney, could not one of them had given just one kidney to their ailing brother, to the editor of the student paper? But why did she not go back to see the editor of the student paper, (what's the point of all these ifs and mights and all these questions?) why did she not wish to talk more of her possible contribution that she could have made to the student paper? She has thought about that question many times since she had seen the death notice of the editor of the student paper, the death notice that she had seen in a national paper and she was sure that at the time of not going back she had not made a deliberate decision not to go back, it was simply one of those instinctive feelings that she did not wish to see the kind young man again and that might have puzzled her over the years, for he was a nice man and he was a man who wrote well and he was a man who knew about poetry, and she might have learnt from him, she might have improved being with him, so why did she have that instinctive feeling that she should not see him again?

That question might have puzzled her but it did not because each time she thought about that instinctive feeling that she should not go back to see the nice editor, she experienced a new fear, a fear that was to last for many years and that was the fear that he could be the person giving her love and preventing her from travelling elsewhere. She feared that love might stop her from going to that elsewhere. Going to that elsewhere and the clean A4-size white sheet of paper were more important than anything else, more important than getting love, more important than giving love. But what about the life, saving the life of the kind editor of the student paper? She might have been able to do that but at the time that was not a choice presented to her, that was not something she could have known was needed, let alone possible. But her guilt persists and perhaps the whole story with the wafers and chocolate marks is only a story she tells herself to assuage her guilt, to justify to herself why she didn't go back to see the kind editor of the student paper. She always remembers those chocolate marks left by two chocolate wafers and the words of the nice young man about the meaning of those marks and sometimes she wonders whether those marks and that moment, that second moment of silence, when the nice young man was busying himself with the files, whether that was really significant or whether she made it significant in her memory because she needed to find a reason, an excuse, a justification for not going back to the offices of the student paper. And perhaps the only reason was her fear of getting love, of getting love from that young man who was a poet and the editor of the student paper. Many years later when she started writing in earnest, when writing became the most important preoccupation in her life, she looked back on all those times in her life when she avoided giving love and getting love because it could have meant staying in one place, staying in one place literally or metaphorically, or both even, and that was something she felt, she must have felt without being able to explain it even to herself, she felt it would have made it more difficult, if not impossible to write.

As for that chubby boy with the straight-cut fringe, and the possibility that there was someone else in his family, someone who had started him on the habit of listening to the news on the radio, someone whom the chubby boy liked and whom he wanted to imitate and someone who could be seen as responsible for that chubby boy's death, because it had to be someone, someone in his family who would have introduced him to listening to the news on the radio. She had started when she was six years old because her

Grandfather Francis listened to the news on the radio, and he listened regularly, several times a day, and it was very important to him to know what was happening in the world and so she came to think that listening to the news on the radio and knowing what was happening in the world was important, and it was important because her Grandfather Francis said so and she loved her grandfather, and she wanted to do the same as her grandfather. She also wanted to do some of the things that he did in his life and she thought like that then and she thought like that for a long time throughout her life.

When she was six, they had already been back in the capital for a year and for a while they stayed with the grandparents. She loved that year because she saw her grandparents every day, her grandfather walked her to school and her grandmother collected her from school and there was something about them, something about her Grandmother Maria and something about her Grandfather Francis that made them special to her when she was six and for many years later. They never asked her to kneel on the floor and face a blank wall and it was not only because they usually did not read poetry to her, or not on a regular basis, but because they loved her in different ways and because they had other ways of helping her improve. Her mother was not her only teacher outside school, her mother was her first teacher but not her only teacher in the family. Her other teachers, and very good teachers, teachers who taught her in ways that were not like her mother's ways, but ways no less effective, her other teachers were her Grandmother Maria, her Grandfather Francis and her absent grandfather of two names, her grandfather whom she had never known.

Before Francis became her grandpa, he had worked as a typesetter for a big publisher but he did not use that word, he never called himself a typesetter, he called himself a purveyor of words and he told her that the best aspect of his job was that he always had books around him, the books that he was about to set into print, the books that he had set into print and the books that had been printed and there were always free copies of those books to be taken home and she imagined that anyone like that would have accumulated a large library over a lifetime and she asked her grandpa where those books were, where those free copies of those books that he had set to print were and he pointed to his head. All stored in there, he said. What is the point of keeping them on the shelves at home, what is the point of keeping them for me and those who know me? I read them and I gave them away, I gave them to those who wanted to read them. People want books; there is always someone who will love a book, any book. There is no book that would not be liked by at least one reader. I have read those books and I liked some of them, some more than others but none so much that I would want to read it all the time for the rest of my life and it was better to pass them on to those who might like them more, who might like to read them all the time. Books are like lovers, some are satisfactory, some are more satisfactory than others, but there is only one book, there is only one lover that is made for us, only one that exists for us alone and most people never find that one, no matter how long and hard they search, that one lover, that one book, her Grandfather Francis said, she said. At best you can hope to find a lover or a book that is closest to the book or the lover that was made for you. I could have kept those books but I wanted to give them a chance, I wanted to give them a chance to meet their ideal reader, the reader they have been written for, Grandfather Francis said, Grandfather Francis who was a typesetter but called himself a purveyor of words. And to show her what he meant about keeping those books in his head, he would recite poetry to her. His was a reasonable view to take, she could see that then and she could see that now but that view was not something she could learn from her grandfather, that was not something she could learn even though it came from her grandfather, the grandfather she loved. She had to possess books, she had to possess them physically, she had to surround herself with books, she had to have books next to her, or at least some of them, those that she liked more than others, those that were not written for her but came close to what she imagined was the book written for her and because she could never be sure—because books, like lovers, changed, or she changed and so the books she loved and the lovers she loved changed—if a book that came close to what she imagined was the book written for her, or might become such a book over time, she had to keep them all, she had to keep them just in case one day she realized that that book was her book, or close to her book, to a book written for her. And when she travelled from one country to another, she always took a big box of her books, the books selected as the ones that came closer than others to what she imagined was the book that would have been written for her and as long as she had that box with her, she had a home, as long as she had that box with her, even if she never opened it, she had a home anywhere in the world. Her library was her country, or that is what it would have been, that is what she could have called it had she thought in those terms, in terms of mother countries, father countries, his countries, her countries, their countries, in those terms used by all those people, all those people in different countries, all those people young and old, all those people who wanted to know whether she missed her country. And she began to think of her books, she began to think of her library as her country only because her books, her library was important to her, as important as mother countries, father countries, aunt countries, uncle countries were to all those people.

When she thinks about the story of her life, she wonders whether anything from her past, from the past as she knows it, as she remembers it, really happened, or has come from someone's story, someone's story that they have presented as their memory of her past, or perhaps it might have come from someone else's story that she had read about and perhaps it was someone else who was kneeling in the corner of their mother's kitchen as part of their constructive punishment. She doesn't always trust herself, she said, she has learnt not to trust herself, she said. And even though there are pictures and objects that have survived, and that will probably survive her, such as that photo of her and her mother, the two of them smartly dressed and wearing white gloves in the middle of a summer, or that pair of white gloves, the pair that fitted her perfectly when she was not-yet-four years old, the pair that she still has. These objects have not been made up, no one has imagined them. She can fetch them and show them even now or she could put a picture here of those gloves, except who can trust images and why trust images more than memory and who can say that the gloves, or the image of the gloves is the proof of some of those memories but then who is not to say that her mother was not taking her to some special event on that day, perhaps even a fancy dress party? She knows—how does she know that?—that is not the case, that would not have been the case because there were no parties in that provincial town where they lived in the days when she was not-yet-four years old and even if there had been, her mother would not have wanted to mix and mingle with the locals and while that is so, she is only mentioning this as an example, she said, as an example of how the so-called documentary evidence, objects and photographs can be interpreted as one wishes, as it suits one's memory, as it suits one's story, she said and this is her story, let that be known, this is her story, her story to love her. She has been telling her story to herself, she said, and her story is of no concern to anyone else, and when she started telling her story, and she had been telling her story as long as she remembered—remembered, she

said, memory again, is there no way of existing outside of memory?
—and at first she wanted to tell her story because she thought there
was something to tell, something worth telling, and when that
began to seem not such a good reason to tell one's story, she
thought of telling her story so that she—sometimes she thought
that there may be someone else, but what a silly thought that was
that there may be someone else—who could read it that someone
else may want to see how she came to be as she came to be, so that
she and anyone else who reads it could see why she thinks whatever
she thinks of those grown-up street urchins, so that she and everyone else could tell the origins of her views, the origins of her likes,
the origins of her dislikes but that reason for telling her story no
longer interests her and besides, why would the origin of her views
interest anyone? She has written the story, her story, for herself and
not for anyone else. Why would anyone else be interested in her
story? And she is not worried, she is not worried at all, if she had
been mistaken about anything in her story. There was a time when
she had qualms about not putting order in her story, but those days
are gone and she is not striving to put order where there is no order
and her life has been anything but orderly and so she no longer
looks for patterns but if patterns emerge in her story, if patterns
emerge on their own, with no effort on her part, they emerge by
chance, by accident, by coincidence and one should not read much
into that. She has given up looking for form, even if that form
would come from no form, even if that form would come from the
repetition of her days, and so she has given up looking for that
something that would make her story a story, that would make her
story—if not her life—have a meaning, even just so to amuse her,
to entertain her, even just so to be a joke, yes, that would be funny
if her story and her life were to have a meaning, a meaning that
would be purely accidental, purely chance, purely a mistake. Having
a meaning has to be a joke for anyone who takes life seriously.

Perhaps she should have written a story that recounts what she has not done and what she has not thought. Perhaps she should have started her story *ab ovo*, like Tristram Shandy, and not with that image of her kneeling in a corner of her mother's kitchen and perhaps that beginning might have allowed for a pattern, for a meaning, to emerge. But how could she tell her story, how could anyone tell their story, how could anyone expect their story to have a meaning, to have a pattern, while that story is not finished, while the subject of the story lives? And anyway, who is this *she* who has been telling the story, her story, someone may ask. How does she see that *she*, what is the image of herself that she recognizes from that story? Is it the image of herself kneeling on a floor in the corner of her mother's kitchen, facing a blank wall and making up stories while the street urchins were running around or is it the image of her pretending to be asleep and holding the hand of a young girl her mother had hired to babysit while the street urchins were shouting down below or is it the image of her standing outside the front door of their flat in a wet brown duffle coat and a puddle forming around her feet and her worrying that her mother might think she has had an accident or is it the image of her thirteen-year-old self, red roses in hand, walking in a cemetery on the way to the grave of her poet lover, of her dead poet lover, or is it the image of her visiting her artist friend, or meeting him in that gallery wearing her navy blue coat that was not fashionable and writing a poem or is it the image of her on a night flight to Nigeria and hoping that her heart would miss a beat, or is it the image of her as a Jewish mother, a proverbial, not-real Jewish mother, always baking, always cooking, always educating her children? Whichever it is, she is always different, she is always different from the street urchins, small or grown-up street urchins, and she is always alone, never fitting in, always clumsy, always the odd one out, always the one with shades, with a pair of coloured lenses permanently stuck in front of her eyes, always the one kneeling down in a corner and facing the blank wall while others are running around, laughing and playing together and that is her abiding image, that is how she sees herself: kneeling in a corner, alone and silent, facing a blank wall. She has nothing more to say, she said.

Except, except perhaps to ask who is that *she*, who is that *she* that this story is about, who are those *shes* that have been made up here? Is that *she* who could not recite poetry by heart without stumbling and prompting, that *she* who had to kneel in a corner of her mother's kitchen when she was not-yet-four years old, is that the same *she* as that *she* who was pushed in a paddling pool in a nursery or is that the same *she* who fell in love with a dead poet or is that the same *she* who became a Jewish mother and who loved baking? And if there is no answer to that question who is the *she* that writes and the *she* that asks, if she has no answer to that, *she*—and that is yet another unknown *she*—*she* will have to admit that her project has failed, that her story, a story that once upon a time *she* might have hoped would bring her love, that story that could not do that—what a vain hope that was—that story could not even tell her who *she* is. But hang on, the point of her writing was not to bring love—that was a catchy phrase that an editor might use on a blurb but not her serious intention—nor was her writing about a quest for a *she*, all those *shes*, lost and reconstructed from her fallible and cheating memory, from her devious memory, from her storytelling memory, but her writing was about going on for there was nothing else to help her go on except to confabulate, except to confabulate. And now, towards the end of her life, *she* is even less sure who those *shes* were and remembering them, remembering all those *shes*, now that more than the year is dying and more than the leaves are falling and only the wind, the lascivious, promiscuous wind—*she* will allow herself the metaphor, at her age *she* has the right to that—is as strong as ever, *she* remembers that a writer, a writer *she* loved, wrote about the impalpable and protecting mist of memory and *she* remembers that another writer, talking in his old age said that he could no longer remember most of his life and when a friend visiting the writer in an old people's home where the writer spent the last years of his life expressed sympathy, the writer said that there was no need for that because not remembering his life was a good thing, a very good thing—a silver lining.

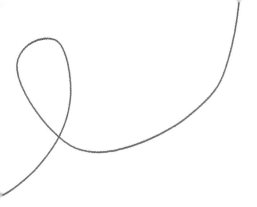

CHAPTER TWO

The Acrobat

We flew above the city.
He said, hold tight. Hold tight, Marie.
I looked at him and wondered how he managed to keep his top
    hat on.

We weaved in and out of the clouds.
The wind played with my hair and unfurled my scarf.
His top hat stayed on.

Grandma, how did he manage to keep his top hat on?
I don't know.
Didn't you ask him?
No.
Why not?
It was his secret. Everyone should have a secret.

Fantasies. Damn fantasies.

My mother's?

Yes. She's filling her head with fantasies.

No harm in fantasies.

Plenty of harm.

What harm?

She needs to keep her feet firmly on the ground. The old woman's gaga.

Do you have a secret, Grandma?

Yes.

I don't have a secret.

I will tell you my secret.

It was a hazy sort of day.

In summer?

No. Late spring. I was sitting on the grass, my back pressed against the trunk of a solitary poplar. I felt its bark cutting into my back. A shadow fell on the pages of the book in my lap.

What kind of shadow?

Elongated. Like El Greco's figures.

What did you do?

I rubbed my back where the bark had made itself felt.

And then?

I closed the book and looked up.

What did you see?

Black tails of a coat.

What else?

Polished shoes. Immaculate. No creases or scuffs. They looked as if they had never been worn, as if they had been put on for the first time, moments before I saw them. I marvelled how clean they were despite the wet grass.

Had he hovered above the ground?

I wondered the same.

Grandma, are shoes important to you?

You can trust a person who looks after their shoes.

What else did you see?

A top hat. A black top hat.

And what happened then?

He raised his hat and bowed.

Did he say anything?

First, he slipped off a glove from his right hand.

He wore gloves?

Yes, white gloves. Like a magician. He extended the hand and said: My name is Fabrizzio.

Fabrizzio?

Yes.

An unusual name.

To my teenage ears, it sounded magical. That name smelt of foreign lands. When I said it, my mouth filled with delectable pleasure. It was a name to make you dream.

Like the first word of a new language.

Yes, like the first word of a new language.

Mother says people cannot fly.

They can fly if they want to.

Father says people cannot fly.

Most of them cannot.

Where did the trapeze artist come from?

From elsewhere.

Elsewhere. I want to travel to elsewhere.

Grandma, how did you manage to fly?

Fabrizzio helped me.

How could he fly?

He said: *Solo la mente piu vincere la forza di gravita.*

What does that mean?

Only the mind can conquer gravity.

Solo la mente piu vincere la forza di gravita—I shall remember that.

I wish I had been a poet.

Why Grandma, why would you have wanted to be a poet?

A poet would have the words to describe what it was like to fly
    above the city.

Grandma, I want to fly.

Why do you want to fly?

So that I can see the world from above.

You will.

When will I be able to fly?

When your wish is strong enough.

Sit on the bed, my little one.

Will the nurses mind?

No. I'll prop myself up with pillows and we can talk about Fabrizzio.

The man who could fly?

Yes. He was an acrobat.

In a circus?

In Il Circo del Mondo.

Grandma, I have never been to a circus.

Circuses come and go as they will. You cannot plan to go to
a circus.

Stef says we used to play together, Maria and I, when we were children. They lived in a smaller house then, opposite us, Stef says. I
think I remember her but those days seem like a dream. We played
hopscotch, this beautiful rich girl and I. How could I have played
with such a rich girl, I ask Stef. Francis, don't be silly, my sister says,
she was a child then and they were not rich. Maria, this beautiful
girl and I, we played together. Sometimes we went to the park
together. Fish Pond Park. Does she ever think of me now?

My Grandpa Francis used to take me to play on the swings in Fish
Pond Park down the road. He said it was his favourite park. In
spring we chased butterflies.

We flew over the city and beyond.

High above the roofs?

Yes.

How did you lift yourself so high?

Fabrizzio used the power of his mind.

What did it feel like to fly?

Like dreaming.

Did you flap your arms like birds?

No.

How did you move through the air?

Fabrizzio guided us. The invisible force of his willpower made us
travel. He stretched out his right arm and placed his left arm
around my shoulders. Sometimes we weaved over and sometimes we weaved under the clouds and sometimes we weaved
in and out of the clouds. The cathedral steeples swayed as we
passed over them. The wind danced through my hair, swishing
and trying to unfurl my scarf. I wondered how Fabrizzio managed to keep his top hat on.

Grandma said she had flown above the city in her young days.

You didn't believe her.

I did.

She shouldn't be filling your head with such nonsense.

It may be best if she doesn't visit again. Not alone, certainly not
alone.

You haven't been around for a few days.

No.

I missed you.

I missed you, too.

And yet you didn't come to see me.

But I wanted to.

They didn't let you.

No.

They think I have lost my mind.

They didn't say that.

But they thought so.

I would like to fly above the city.

You will, my little one.

When?

Soon. It is difficult to live without having flown above the city.

Does everyone fly above the city?

No.

Why not?

They don't get a chance.

How do they live then? You said it was difficult to live without having flown.

Only strangers want to fly.

Who are strangers?

Those who want to fly.

Like you?

Yes. And you. Non-strangers do not think of flying above the city. They like to stay below. On the ground. You and I, we need to fly. You and I, we were born to want to fly. We are strangers.

Strangers? Do they come from different countries? Countries we don't know.

They come from here and nowhere.

But which country?

Any country or no country. A country does not make a stranger or a non-stranger.

How did you meet Fabrizzio?

In the meadow above the promontory, next to the old town.

I often walk in the old town.

You are like me.

That's what they say.

I see the dimples on your chin.

They come out when I smile.

And in summer freckles speckle your nose.

Is that the same with you?

Dimples and freckles. In the whole family only you and I have them.

Why did you go to the meadow?

To watch the horizon.

Was that the first time you went?

No. I used to go as often as I could, usually after school.

Why did you want to watch the horizon?

Beyond the horizon there was a world I dreamt about.

Was Fabrizzio already there when you arrived?

No. As usual, the meadow was deserted. I thought of it as my place. People didn't venture above the promontory. I went to be alone. That afternoon, I took a book out of my bag but I didn't start reading straightaway. The air was fuzzy with dreams and for an hour I sat looking into the distance over the horizon.

You waited for the sunset?

No. I think I was lost in wonder at the sight of a rainbow. It had stopped raining as I was climbing the steps next to the funicular and the sun came out. I remembered a short story about a girl who believed that running under a rainbow would turn her into a boy and then she would be able to do all those things that were forbidden to girls. She ran and ran to reach the place under the rainbow.

Did she become a boy?

No.

Why not?

She ran across the marshes. She ran and ran until she drowned.

A sad story. A sad ending to a dream.

No. It's a beautiful story. She had ambition. Seeking a rainbow is beautiful.

But she died.

She died full of hope. She died running. She died looking, looking at the rainbow. She died seeing beauty. She did not see the mud around her feet. That is all most people see. She died believing she would reach the place under the rainbow. She had a fulfilling life.

Has she been spinning more silly stories?

No.

Are you sure?

Yes.

No more talk of flying?

No.

Good.

How does one become a stranger?

Strangers are born.

I saved her. I saved her from a muddy boot, a peasant's muddy boot that would have crushed her on the floor of the tram. Francis, you have to return the tram pass, Stef says. If you don't want to do it yourself, Violet can take it, she could say she found it herself, Stef says. Maria will be missing her pass. Pity to drop it like that. My sisters always want to do things for me. I know I should return it but, how can I? This beautiful object. Perhaps I could unglue the photo and tell her it was not there when I found it. But how can I lie to the woman I love?

What was the book on your lap when Fabrizzio arrived?

Poetry.

Who was it by?

Antun Gustav Matoš. A sonnet.

Which one?

'The Consolation of the Hair'.

Tell me about it.

The narrator watches the hearse of his beloved in a morgue. He is in awe of death and muses on its beauty as it rules the atmosphere. At the same time, he is devastated by the loss of his beloved and wishes to die but then he hears a voice—the voice of the hair of the dead woman—telling him that death is only a dream.

Not much of a consolation.

You're right. But it is not what the poem says that matters but what it does to you, what thoughts it provokes in you.

The light, oh, the light on her face. When I am working, I want to look at her face but I dare not touch the tram pass with my hands smeared with lead. A printer's hands are always dirty. I have to clean them, wipe off every black smudge and then I can take this object of beauty out of my pocket and open it. Her face shines bright. She is my happiness.

Did you speak Italian with Fabrizzio?

I cannot remember.

What did you talk about?

We did not exchange many words.

Why not?

He sat down next to me on the grass and most of the time we remained silent.

You stayed silent?

That is the way of the best conversations.

Where did Fabrizzio come from?

He came from elsewhere.

How long did Il Circo del Mondo stay in the town?

One day and one night.

Why not longer?

They never stayed longer in any place.

Why not?

They had lots of ground to cover.

What do you mean?

They had to give a chance to more people.

The chance of what?

The chance to dream.

Did you see Il Circo del Mondo perform?

Yes. Before he left the meadow, Fabrizzio gave me three tickets.

Who were they for?

For me and my little brothers.

Why did you take them with you?

My parents wouldn't have let me go alone.

Did your brothers like the show?

They liked the clowns and the woman on stilts.

And you? Did you like the clowns and the woman on stilts?

I had eyes for no one but the trapeze artist. The acrobat.

Fabrizzio?

Yes.

I stood on the pavement opposite her house today. I held the tram pass in my hand, hidden in my pocket. I told myself, Francis, you have to ring the bell but I knew that I lacked the will. How could I part with something so beautiful? Maria. My luminous happiness. Each man and woman seeks beauty. Now that I have found it, how could I part with it? I waited outside and watched the closed door.

Have Mummy and Daddy flown above the city?

No.

Don't they miss it?

You cannot miss what you have never wanted.

Grandma is not well. When people are dying, they turn to god. She has never been a believer but she needs something now. She has created this fantasy. We hope it helps her. That's all. It is hard to face death. You have to understand what is happening to Grandma.

A shadow fell over the pages in my lap.

Did it startle you?

No.

Why not?

I was expecting him.

Did you think she looked smaller today?

Smaller than what?

Smaller than yesterday.

No.

Every day she looks smaller.

Francis, that's not kind. Why haven't you returned her tram pass? All these months you've kept it under your pillow, Stef said. Why did she have to look in my bed? Mother asked her to change the sheets, she said. All right, Stef. I will return it. If only I could copy the photo. I must have that photo. I tried to draw it but I am not good at art. I could ask Charlie, but he's always coughing, always ill. My poor brother.

Was she asleep when you visited?

No.

No? She is always asleep when we come in.

She must be tired.

Tired from what? She is lying in bed whole days and nights.

I don't know what she is tired from.

What do you talk about?

This and that.

What do you mean this and that?

Nothing important.

Has she been telling you more silly stories?

No.

So what do you talk about?

We talk about school.

You don't like talking about school. You never talk about school
   to us.

It was my lucky day. It rained buckets, the tram crowded, people
complaining. A peasant stepped on my shoes. I looked down and
saw that he was about to press his muddy boot on her face. The
angelic face framed by her long plait. The white embroidered collar
of her blouse. All that beauty was about to be soiled. I screamed and
pushed him back. He swore at me, raised his hand as if he were
about to hit me. I could see that he held a basket with two hens
stuffed into it. I had time to pick up Maria's tram pass. The picture
was untouched. All that beauty on the floor of the tramway in the
middle of the ugliness of the world. I saved her from a coarse stamp
of a muddy boot.

When Fabrizzio came to the meadow, was that the first time you
   had met him?
Yes.
But you had heard of him before?
No.
How could you have been expecting him then?
Because I have dreamt of elsewhere and he was a person from
   elsewhere.

Remember.
Yes, Grandma.
Remember. Sometimes you have to dream in spite of the world.

She looked smaller today. No doubt about it.
Yes, I thought so too. She's disappearing.
Always asleep and always smaller, your mother.

Do you think she looks smaller to her?

Let's ask her. Did Grandma look smaller when you visited today?

Smaller than what?

Smaller than yesterday. Or the day before.

No.

Are you sure?

Yes.

And she wasn't asleep when you were with her?

No.

She's always asleep when we visit.

I was thinking of you flying above the city.

And?

What I saw in my mind's eye was a painting by Chagall.

Oh, Chagall. He must have seen us.

Grandma, tell me, how did Fabrizzio manage to keep his top hat on
    when you were flying above the city?

I don't know.

How could he do that, flying high up in the air and the wind
    blowing?

I wondered that myself.

Didn't you ask him?

No.

Why not?

Because it was his secret. You don't ask about secrets.

Violet, sweet Violet, my lovely little sister. Thank you, thank you
so much. Stef is hard but you understand. You understand why I

have to keep the photo. It makes me happy to look at it. Luminously happy.

Did he wear a tie?
Yes.
A bow tie?
No. It looked like a cravat, but it was not as wide.
What was his face like?
Serene.
And his body.
Gaunt. He was thin. Tall and thin.
Like Grandpa.
Taller and thinner.
Tell me, how tall and thin?
Many years later, when your grandpa and I visited Paris, I saw a
    Picasso sketch of Don Quixote and I thought that Fabrizzio
    could have modelled for it.
You sent me a postcard with that picture.

Our latest order is for a pamphlet saying that one day we shall have
a just society with everyone contributing according to their ability
and taking only according to their need. I prefer typesetting poetry
but such ideas intrigue me. I take the pamphlet home and when I
have read it, I pass it to Ivo and other apprentices. One of them asks:
But when will that society happen? I don't know the answer but I
tell them that we can try to speed it up. We can work together, all
of us—printers and typesetters. Why us, Ivo asks. Because we have
books, we have pamphlets, we have ideas and we can help others.
You are a dreamer, Francis, Ivo says.

Did you fly above the city before or after the circus show?

I took my brothers home. At midnight, when everyone in the house
was asleep, I slipped out and made my way to the promontory.
The moon was shining and as I was climbing up, I could see his
silhouette. He looked like a puppet in a shadow theatre. When
I approached, he bowed, lifted his top hat in greeting and we
were off.

How long did you stay up in the air?

We watched the dawn break.

And before that, at night, did you see the stars?

Yes, they flickered in the distance but sometimes when I put my
hand out, I thought I could touch them.

What did it feel like?

It made my head spin.

Touching the stars?

No, the music we heard up in the sky.

What was it like?

In a foreign town, a woman sang.

Violet says Maria is ill, Joe has told her. He said, his sister thinks
she had flown over the city. A doctor has arrived from Vienna. Papa
would not allow anything deleterious, Joe said. *Deleterious?* Francis,
what does that mean, Violet asks. Francis, you're a typographer,
you bring books in, you read them, you know strange words.
Tongues wagging, that's what they fear, those posh people.

What did the doctor say?

The same as before.

What about the test results?

Inconclusive.

Will they repeat the tests?

No. No one knows what is making her shrink so visibly from day to day.

Remember.

What should I remember?

You have to dream in spite of the world.

Was she asleep when you visited?

No.

What did you do?

We talked.

What about?

School.

Not about her life?

No.

Don't ask her too many questions. Best not to speak. Don't stay too long. It tires her out.

I won't speak. I won't stay too long.

You must have noticed how much smaller she is.

No, I haven't.

Don't pretend. You are hiding something from your parents.

I am not.

Grandma, how did you manage to lift yourself above the ground and fly higher and higher?

When Fabrizzio arrived, a curious lightness, the lightness of my whole being took hold of me.

I walked outside the house thinking of her lying ill in bed. I hoped someone would come out and their face would tell me how she was. But no one came out. I watched the closed door.

What happened when you landed?

We lay in the grass, side by side.

Did you talk?

I can't remember.

Try to remember.

We talked silently.

Silently?

The way of the best conversations.

And then?

We watched the sun come out. I thought I could hear a woman sing in a foreign town.

How did you part?

We walked away in opposite directions.

Were you sad?

Sad? No. I was happy. I had been fortunate to have the most wonderful experience.

But it was over. The wonderful experience was over.

I had the memory. The impalpable and protecting mist of memory is more powerful than any experience. A memory lasts as long as we do. A memory is for ever.

What happened to Fabrizzio?

He left with the circus.

Did you think of joining the circus?

Yes.

Why didn't you?

In the morning I set off for the field where the circus wagons were about to drive away when I saw my father in the distance. He walked slowly towards me, with his cane touching the soft ground as if testing it before he made each step. I stopped. I could tell he knew I had made arrangements—

With Fabrizzio?

No. The owners of the circus said, Come with us and you will see the world.

Was your father cross?

No. As a young man he had come from a land far away and he understood my wish.

But he stopped you.

No, he did not. He said: Maria, I'm pleased to see that you're taking fresh air in the morning. It is good for your health.

Was that all?

Yes.

He didn't mention the circus?

No.

I was minding the shop over lunch and those young apprentices took so long, on a different day I might have been annoyed with them. I still had to finish setting the type for the evening paper. Had they got back on time I wouldn't have been minding the shop when she came in. She asked to see the designs for visiting cards. We keep the book of samples under the counter but I pretended I had to fetch it from the back. I needed to collect myself. I took a moment or two taking deep breaths in the storeroom. Maria, beautiful Maria came to my master's shop. When she spoke, I thought she was more beautiful than the picture in the tram pass.

What do they think?

No one has ever seen anything like it.

How are they going to treat her?

No one knows.

What is the prognosis?

They have no idea.

Don't they have something to give her?

What do you mean? She is not complaining.

There must be medication to deal with this.

No one knows what it is.

She is shrinking before our eyes. Your poor mother. She has always
   been strange.

She is shrinking but has no pain, no pain at all.

And so that was that?

What do you mean?

You never saw Fabrizzio again or heard from him?

No.

And you never flew above the city after that?

No, people cannot fly.

But you did.

That was special. That was exceptional. It was my good fortune it
   happened once. I could not expect it to happen again. And for
   the rest of my life I have had the impalpable and protecting
   mist of memory.

Don't leave me yet. I need more time to talk to you.

I didn't want you to tire you.

Is that what they told you?

Yes.

My son and his wife, they told you not to tire me out.

Yes.

I have a lot to tell you. And time passes quickly. Time passes too quickly when you have a story to tell.

She hesitated over what we had on offer. I said she could order a bespoke set. I would like that, she said. She is coming tomorrow with her own drawings. I have to make sure to mind the shop. Ivo will be happy to be let off.

They told her, come with us and you will see the world. She said she wanted to see the world beyond her street, the world beyond her town, the world beyond her country, she wanted to see a world with no end. The world beneath a rainbow.

The world of elsewhere.

I was twelve when she told me her story. I did not know what to think but I knew better than to tell my parents what we talked about. She said I was like her. Dimples and freckles. Dimples when we smile. Freckles in summer. She said I was like her. Other people said the same, I remember. It made me happy to hear them say I was like her. She too wanted to hear we were alike. Dimples and freckles is all they see, she said. There is more that we have in common, she said. They can't see that. Most people can't see that.

She flew above the city. Will I ever fly above the city?

She knew exactly what she wanted. She spoke with precision. I asked if I could keep the drawings once we had used them. I said I wanted to show them to Mr Kemfer, the owner. He might want to make them part of our regular offer. Really, she said, they are nothing special. We do such sketches all the time. Well, to me they are more special than anything else. But I couldn't tell her that. And then before she left, she said: Francis, may I call you Francis? We used to play together when we were children. In Fish Pond park across the road from your house. I blushed.

She remembered. She remembered we played as children in Fish Pond park.

Their platitudes bore me. Their cards and their flowers. But the girl is different. Who will recognize her difference once I am gone? Francis? No. He does not see anything. He has his own world. The world of trade unions. I have to help her with the fragility of beginning.

She came in to collect the cards. At the door, she paused and said, as if she had just remembered: My year is holding an exhibition. Our work, we are showing our final projects. Textile and fashion designs. If you want to come, I could take you around. But it may not interest you. I thought I should mention it. And Violet may wish to come with you. I would like to see Violet, she said. I feared I might blush again. Six more days, six more days before the exhibition opens.

My back was pressed against the trunk of a solitary poplar when a shadow fell over the pages in the book in my lap. It obscured 'The Consolation of Hair'.

And you looked up?

Yes, after I had rubbed my back where the bark of the tree had made itself felt.

What did you see when you looked up?

A man who was tall and thin like Don Quixote in Picasso's drawing.

Violet accompanied me. Stef said she had no interest in those posh girls making fashion, playing with fabrics. Rich people have nothing better to do. Dear, sweet Violet. I couldn't have hung around without her. She can chat easily even to those she doesn't know. I am not shy but in that big hall full of well-dressed people, I did not know where to turn. Maria waved to me, and cast a smile once or twice in my direction but her parents were near and I did not dare approach. I noticed her two brothers and aunts and uncles. Too many friends, too many girls giggling. I stood no chance of having a word. Joe came over to talk to Violet. He spoke about him and his younger brother training to take over the business one day. People will always need upholstery, he said. People will always need books and pamphlets and newspapers, I thought. I amused myself thinking of a good upholstered, comfortable chair and a book. They go together. She sent a note, someone gave it to Violet. This is for you, Francis, Violet said. I will meet you at the bottom of the steps, main entrance, at six, the note said.

He was tall and thin like Don Quixote in Picasso's drawing.

We took the funicular. To the top. We stopped at Schwartz's and looked at chestnut cakes. She didn't want any. I bought a bag of chocolates. There were ten pieces inside a paper bag but she had only one; she said I should take them to my sisters. Violet may like them, she said. She couldn't remember Stef's name. We strolled up the promontory parade. There must have been other couples around us but I did not see them. At the end, she leant over the stone banister. It was her favourite spot, and she said she never tired of looking down at the city. I wished I had known that before. Some people look at the roofs and think of all the human dramas that evolve under them. But I think of shapes and textures, patterns and colours as they change with light. Without turning to me she said, the patterns of the red-tiled roofs are beautiful. She wanted to create beauty, she said.

When I am with her, all I want is for the time to stop. Last year I set *Amores* to print and kept a copy. As the poet says: *Lente lente currite noctis equi.*

I lay in bed for three months.
Were you ill after Il Circo del Mondo had left the city?
I was not ill. I lay in bed. I had to be alone to dream. I said I wanted to
    relive the experience. They asked what experience I was talking
    about. I flew above the city, I said. What did you say, they asked
    and shook their heads. It didn't matter. I didn't insist. I had the
    impalpable and protecting mist of memory.

Stef says the girl is ill. Everyone knows she would marry a rich man. They think they know who it is. A friend of her father's. Mr Gustav Wagner. She should not be going for walks with you, Francis.

I love an acrobat, I told the voice in my dream.

Acrobats and trapeze artists, they are nobodies. They have no identity. They leap from one to another like grasshoppers. No one should love them.

I love an acrobat, I told the voice in my dreams.

Grandma, I want to love an acrobat.

Why do you want to love an acrobat?

So that I can become an acrobat myself.

You do not need to love an acrobat to become one.

I slept and dreamt. The doctor from Vienna said they had to leave me in peace. Your daughter is a sensitive young woman and she is growing up. It is a phase. It will pass. No need to worry, he told my father, Joe told me years later and added, Mama and Papa were worried when you said you had flown above the city. I knew he meant they didn't believe me. But I could prove it: I had the memory.

That voice, that voice spoke again. And other voices joined in. A cornucopia of voices, in harmony with each other: Acrobats are like globetrotters; they are nothing. They have no identity. They do not belong.

I do not want to belong, I said. I love an acrobat.

Rubbish. You are too young to know what matters. You need to belong. Everyone needs to belong. Everyone needs a firm footing.

But I love an acrobat. I want to be an acrobat.

What kind of acrobat, they asked.

A trapeze artist.

A trapeze artist? That's not a proper job. Who needs trapeze artists?

I also want to be a tightrope walker.

What good is that, they asked. Tightrope walkers lose their footing and fall down sooner or later.

I thought everyone should learn to be a tightrope walker, but I didn't say it.

What's wrong with us? What wrong with being like us? Feet firmly on the ground. What's wrong with belonging to us?

I don't want to belong to you or to anyone else.

You will learn one day that you need us. Without belonging you are nobody.

The voices shouted in my ears and I shouted back. And I travelled. Time and again I travelled and dreamt. I visited places I had never known existed and I spoke to people I had never heard of.

I spoke to people of my spirit.

I spoke to people from elsewhere.

I spoke to strangers.

I do not know what to make of this tale. But I do not want to question Grandma. I listen and I remember. I am only twelve.

The dream of the acrobat kept me sane. It kept me sane for years to come. Francis was a good, kind man—

You mean Francis the Grandpa?

Yes, Francis was a good man but he had his own world. His world of trade unions and his women. And the drink. Lots of it, Grandma says.

Walks on the promontory, next to the old town, when the horse chestnuts were in full bloom, a few hiking trips with her friends up the mountain on Sundays and she said: Francis, I would like us to be married. Did I blush? I told Violet and she said Maria was beautiful and I was a lucky man but Stef was sceptical. I thought she was supposed to marry Gustav Otto Wagner, she said. A friend of her father's, a man who has known her since she was a little girl. Gustav Otto Wagner is an old man, I said. So what, Stef said. Rich girls like her marry rich, old men. Watch it, Francis, Stef said. You are only a replacement. A replacement to annoy her parents. No, Francis, do not worry, Violet said. Maria loves you, I know. Joe told me. Maria told him.

You will see the world resonated in my ears.

Today when I came in, Grandma was reading, or perhaps not reading but a large folio-size book was open on her lap. She showed it to me: *The Art of Tightrope Walking* by Fabrizzio Rossi. She stared at me. I felt ashamed. There were moments when I had thought he might have existed only in her imagination.

In a foreign town a woman sang.

The wedding was small. That is what she wanted. I am the luckiest man in the world.

Today she says: My little one, have a look at *Las Meninas*, a painting by Diego Velazquez. Take down one of the art books I gave you for your birthday. Have a long look at it and when you know, tell me what you think. If you do not know what to think, look again. Some time may pass but one day you will recognize it as the most wonderful painting in the world. Do not read about it. All those words about illusion and reality—who needs those? Look at it until you know. We saw it in Madrid. One day you will have to go to the Prado. There is no other way. That painting made me think that if I had to lose all my senses but one, it would be the sense of vision I would want to keep. As long as I could set my eyes on it, my life would be worth living.

She draws. She draws every day. She does not hide her drawings but she does not offer me to look at them. You have to respect her privacy, Francis, I tell myself. I have my own poems. I never show them to her.

At home, I look at the painting but I am not sure what to think. She never mentions it again.

In a foreign town a woman sang.

The boy is hers. He looks like her and he talks to her. She did not say a word to me. Someone whispered to Violet. She said: Francis, I am sorry but she went to see a doctor. Don't tell anyone. You know what kind of doctor. I thought you wanted another child. I am sorry, Francis. Oh, Violet why did you tell me? I ask myself, I don't say anything to Violet. It might have been a girl. A daughter. I might have had a daughter. I say nothing to Maria. I say nothing to any-one. Because there is no one I can speak to about this.

Is it better to die with an unrealized dream or with a shattered illusion? Who asked that? Was it Grandma? Or was it Grandpa?

When I brought no money home, she said nothing. She didn't ask what happened. It wouldn't have mattered to her to know that I have been inviting all the workers out every night and the drinks were on me. Nothing ever matters to her. I don't like her equanim-ity. I wanted her to say something. I wanted her to complain. Shout. Show me that she does not want me to do it. Any response would have made me alive. Instead she spoke to Joe and he started sending orders. Curtains, armchair covers, valances. The beautiful rich girl having to earn money for the family. People talked. Was our life deleterious, as someone once said? What is deleterious? Being too rich when others are poor, that's what I call deleterious. People talked of her Singer. The bloody sewing machine is always open. Why can't she put it away? Her feet like those of a mechanical doll, up and down, up and down. Bloody Singer. And she always so smart with her white collars. White lace or white embroidery. Some called it her indomitable spirit.

They say she is disappearing. No one knows what's wrong with her. I cannot tell that she is disappearing. But he says so, my son the doctor. Mum is very ill, he says. We have to be prepared for the worst. Doctors are used to saying that. She is disappearing steadily, he says. But she has always been disappearing, disappearing behind the closed door. Disappearing behind that equanimity of hers. Perhaps that is why I cannot see it now.

She is on a quest. I feel the weight of her longing but I do not know what it is for. I ask, I ask every day but she doesn't tell me. Perhaps she does not know it. Is it love you need, Maria, I ask. I love you and I can try to love you more but I am not sure that it is possible to love you more than I do. No, I do not need love, Francis, she says. You are a good husband to me, she adds, looking away. You have my love, you have all my love, I say. I know, she says. And yet she goes in and I watch the closed door.

I cry for my lost daughter. I imagine she could have been the only person to whom I would show my poetry. From now on, everything I write is for her, the daughter I never had. And when I set other poets' work to print, my tears for her, for the daughter I never had, fall on their words.

Did she fly or not? It's a riddle that I do not care to solve. Nor did I care when I was twelve years old. She believed she flew over the city in the arms of her trapeze artist. She believed. No one could deny that. She possessed the impalpable and protecting mist of memory.

She was an acrobat. My grandma was an acrobat. My grandma was a tightrope walker.

She lives from day to day, bent over her sewing machine, working with that absent-minded precision, that excluding self-sufficiency. A less tolerant man would have gone insane. She does not see me. I watch the closed door.

Could we begin again? Could we begin again in a slow, more fragile and hesitant way?

Remember, my little one, you have to dream in spite of the world, Grandma says.

All that remains are her dresses, her meticulously cut dresses. Navy polka dots with white V-neck collars, chocolate browns with tiny stripes, always white collars, lace or embroidery. My sisters never paid that much attention to their dresses. Nor did other women I knew. Your wife is the most elegant woman I know, someone once said to me. And the shoes, the sandals, solid medium heels, always a strap across. Her exquisite ankles. Oh, her exquisite ankles.

She draws a trapeze artist. All her drawings are of a trapeze artist. She has a large box full of drawings.

I want to travel to elsewhere.
Who said that?
I said that.

I took out her hair combs. I looked for a hair, a lost hair, hiding between the teeth of the combs. Nothing. I wiped the bottom of the glass bowl where she kept her hairpins and combs; I wiped it with the tips of my fingers, hoping that a hair or two was lying there, her white hair, hiding away from me. But nothing sticks to my fingers. No consolation of the hair. Where else can I look? One, only one hair would be enough. A closed door. Always a closed door. I thought I loved her. I thought I could make the world a better place by loving her and by loving others. I persuaded them and we got together. They had to take note of us, our printing workers union, the largest and best-supported workers' organization.

I persuaded them, my mates and we got together. United we stand. But I could do nothing for her. My love did nothing.

I remember the evening after the exhibition when we walked to the old town and I bought her a paper bag with ten chocolates and she only had one and sent the rest to Violet, my dear little sister, and I remember looking at Maria when she said she was seeking beauty.

She wanted her life to be a quest for beauty. So did I. When she came to me, I thought I had found it. But what happened to her quest? And what happened to the beauty of my love? Why does she not want my love? Her slim body bent over the sewing machine with that absent-minded precision. The interminable noise of the Singer, the foot pedal clicketing and clacketing up and down, up and down, the clicketing and clacketing into the night that shuts me out.

He never stops looking at me. When you are being looked at, you cannot look yourself. I have to close the door. I cannot dream with his eyes boring into me. I cannot feel my impalpable and protecting mist of memory if he is around.

There must be more to life than casting slugs and dissing type.

They said she was filling my head with nonsense. They said that there wasn't much to it except a story of a sixteen-year-old girl who arranged to run away with a visiting circus, bringing shame on the family. They said there probably was a man who persuaded her to come with him. What for? A life in a horse-driven wagon? Like a gipsy, they said. What shame, their daughter a gipsy. Her parents got wind of what was brewing and stopped her. She didn't protest or argue but something happened to her. She withdrew into herself. Three years later, she was married to a man she had known since childhood. That's all there was to it, they said.

I tiptoe to the hall and listen to the clickety-clack of her sewing machine. Bloody Singer. I dare not go in. I watch the closed door.

We flew over the city, the wind swished through my hair, unfurling my scarf, gliding over my stockings. I wondered how Fabrizzio managed to keep his top hat on.

What does she want? I asked her. What does she want from me? Nothing. I have everything, Francis, she said. Now, I need to finish this order. Joe is sending a boy from the workshop to collect it tonight. More curtains. More damned curtains. Why do people need so many curtains? To close themselves off. Open your windows, push away your shutters, lift your blinds, pull back your curtains, I wanted to shout. I watched the closed door.

Her last drawings of a trapeze artist had no figure in them. Only a tightrope.

In a foreign city a woman sang. The air glided over my stockings and tickled my neck.

I am like a word that has been missed out by a compositor. But there is no proofreader to notice my absence and write OUT in the margins. There is no one to notice my presence or my absence. You're nothing, Francis, I say.

When they are both gone I find a photograph of my grandparents at a group outing to the countryside, probably organized by the printers' union of which Grandpa Francis was the president. Twenty men and women and several children, all dressed in their Sunday best, are sitting or standing in three rows. Francis is right in the middle of the front row, looking straight ahead. He is a tall, attractive man with glasses, the kind of man I wish I had loved. (Is this an incestuous thought?) Maria, in a dark dress with a V-neck and a white starched collar, is looking down towards her son, my father (the date on the back tells me that he is six). Most of the people are serious but the expression on the face of my grandfather is more than that. He is lost, he is unhappy. Maria's downcast eyes isolate them from the rest of the group. They are surrounded by the people with whom they share values and aspirations, and yet they appear isolated from the rest of the group, alone in their own worlds.

Before my parents, too, are gone, I learn that Francis had a reputation for drinking. Drinking and womanizing. In my parents' documents, I find photographs of parties, with people sitting at long tables covered with food and drink. Francis is invariably slouching, and in some pictures he and a few others are sitting on the floor, his arm around a woman and a hand holding a bottle.

People say no one can tell what happens to a couple. Grandma believed you needed to fly to live. Meeting Fabrizzio made it possible for her to endure what followed. But perhaps that flight, the memory of that flight, the memory of what might be possible but not outside the realm of a dream, that memory kept her in her own world and hindered other relationships. I am being silly saying that. Why do I want to explain things?

I thought I showed her I loved her. I thought I could make her happy. I thought I would make the world a better place. But all I did was spend my life watching a closed door.

He is always looking at me. When you are being looked at, you cannot look back. Nor can you dream. I have to close the door. I have to close the door to live.

What is it that I can do for you, I asked again. Nothing, I have everything, Francis, she said. But why do you close the door, I asked. I need to remember. Remember what? She did not answer. What is the purpose of memory, I asked. We live now. I need memory to dream, she said. There is no need to dream of the past, I said. We cannot change it, I said. I do not want to change it, she said. I like to dream of the future, I thought but I did not say it. I watched the closed door.

You will see the world. The sentence resonated in my ears. You will see the world with no end. In a foreign country a woman will sing. I am coming, I said.

Some people go to church, others to poetry. I have my trade-union work and yes, there is drink and yes, there are women, but I would give it all up if she did not close the door.

They said she filled my head with nonsense. *Las Meninas*, she said. Don't forget *Las Meninas*. And books. They are our friends and lovers, our children and parents. They are all we need. I took to heart her words.

Some people go to church, others to poetry. Where does she go? Clickety-clack, clickety-clack.

My head remains filled with such nonsense.

Best not to leave any traces behind, she said.

When my parents are gone, among their documents I find a newspaper cutting:

> *A woman, 69, died yesterday of a mysterious illness. Doctors at the Central Medical Research Institute could offer no explanation for her condition which made her visibly diminish in size over a period of the three weeks that she spent in hospital, following a stroke. The woman, originally of tall stature, 173 cm, gradually shrank to 2 cm before eventually disappearing. She did not complain of any pain or discomfort, apart from having to deal with the family and medical staff whose reactions to her changing physical shape she found, as she put it just before she disappeared, 'thoroughly annoying'.*

In a foreign town a woman sang. The breeze tickled my neck. Air glided over my silk stockings.

The way she had looked at me before she closed the door. I was drunk but how could I not be after watching her closed door for years? How does she bear the pressure of solitude? The interminable clickety-clack of her Singer.

Most people's lives are ridiculous, she said. What does she mean, I thought but I didn't ask. That is why they never think of flying over the city. And another time she said, we should make death ridiculous, laugh at it. I listened and asked no questions.

Perhaps she never loved me because I did not deserve to be loved by her. How could I deserve to be loved by her when I had not returned her tram pass, when I never owned up I had it? The picture of her at sixteen with her long hair in a plait, wearing a dark blouse with a white lace collar. That was all the beauty I needed.

Who are strangers?
You and I are strangers.
Is Grandpa a stranger?
Maybe. I don't know.

Today I took out her coats and jackets. I ran my hand over the shoulders of each. How is it possible that not a single hair is stuck in the fabric? Why hasn't a single hair survived her? Everything's taken from me. No, Francis, a voice tells me, the voice of Stef ? The voice tells me, Francis you're lying. Francis, you still haven't returned the tram pass. You've kept it for sixty years. Don't make me feel guilty, Stef. You're dead. And so is she. Who can I return it to? It's mine now. My wife's tram pass is mine because she is dead. I am not a thief any more. I am not holding on to something that is not mine. I wish I could tell Stef. But she is long gone.

We circled around the city, weaving between the clouds. We flew over the steeples of the cathedral, toy-like in their importance. The moon shone on the red brick of the roofs, the roofs I loved, the artistic roofs with their red-tile patterns but now I wished to look further away. I was excited when Fabrizzio led us in ever-wider circles. The world was there, down below and all around and it existed for me to dream about.

In a foreign city a woman sang.

I have looked everywhere for the box of drawings. Where could it have disappeared? Her last drawings of a trapeze artist had no figure in them. Only a tightrope. Where had he gone?

The consolation of the hair. Empty like everything else.

She has left no trace of herself. Francis, all you have is a memory of her. A memory of the ever-closed door.

I listened. I didn't question. Why should I have? I was too impressed and I believed her. I believed her because I loved her. I believed her because I wanted to believe her. I believed every word she said and I still do. I could see that, despite her apparent melancholy, she possessed a richer happiness than anyone else: hers was the happiness that comes from things imagined. Besides, I wanted to fly myself. Grandma had said that as long as I wanted to fly, I would. When it didn't happen, I wondered whether I hadn't wanted it enough; perhaps with years passing I lost that clear focus of my desire—there were lovers and there were children and they take time and they take effort—the desire that, it seemed to me, had sustained my grandma. But who can tell? After all, life is nothing but adventitious. Or perhaps there is still time for me to try to want harder.

Serendipity. That's the word I learnt with my English. The word I love. She never knew it. Was her meeting with Fabrizzio serendipity?

Death, in its furious envy of the strength of my love has taken all of her, snatched every hair from a side comb. Greedy death has swallowed everything of hers.

Sometimes I wonder where my desire has come from. Has she passed it on to me or has she awoken a longing that lay dormant, a longing that I had inherited together with dimples and freckles? Perhaps that longing could be recognized and awoken only by a person who shared it.

She is dead and all her hair is gone. There is none left in combs or in collars; I have stroked white embroidered ones; I have searched in white lace ones. She is dead and yet the sun rose on time.

Before he dies, Francis gives me his books and Maria's tram pass from her schooldays. The date of issue tells me that Maria was sixteen at the time. The document looks like a tiny notebook, small enough to fit into the palm of my hand. The outside is made of cardboard and covered in grey cloth, its edges frayed after so many years. Inside, my grandmother's name, date of birth and the name of her school are written in long hand. But the most wonderful part is the picture: a black-and-white photograph of my grandmother as a young girl. Her long brown hair tied in a plait pulled to the front over the right shoulder. She is wearing a dark blouse with a white V-neck collar. Her eyes are looking straight out but her stare is both intense and aloof. Her expression is serious. When I look at her, I sense her single-mindedness and determination to live her own life; I can see the woman who was about to meet Fabrizzio and fly over the city. I cannot help thinking that the experience was inevitable; such is the strength of her longing. I know that's nonsense. Serendipity, that's all there was to it. If there is a pattern or meaning in what happens to us, it is the one we impart. Circuses, at least in those days, used to travel around the world and stop in cities as it suited them, often on the whim of the moment, and their trapeze artists went for constitutionals, choosing random paths in unknown places.

I work my way through the pages of her books. I open them carefully, lest I disturb anything that might be stored there, and look in the middle where the pages are bound. Somewhere in-between those white sheets of paper, hiding among words, must lie a single hair of my love. When I finish, I shall look through her sewing box. There must be a hair, a single hair left somewhere. Maria, my love, tell me, is there a hair left for me?

I remember Grandmother telling me about Fabrizzio. Grandmother described flying over the city with him. It was her memory she imparted to me. Now it is my memory. What is the purpose of memories?

The tram pass is beautiful. But that is not the reason I carry it with me, and every now and then look inside. What drives me is the sensation the picture brings about, the sensation of the strength of my grandmother's desire, or was it a dream?—no matter which, sometimes one cannot tell them apart—the sensation that makes me feel as if I too could be flying one day, as if everything were possible.

I seek the consolation of the hair.

I carry the tram pass in my purse and one day on the way to a theatre in Islington, while I am standing on an escalator, a man opens my shoulder bag and snatches the purse. Somebody shouts, 'a thief, a thief', and my companion runs after the snatcher. We report the theft and a few weeks later my credit cards—cancelled by then—are recovered. There is no mention of the twenty-pound note or Grandmother's tram pass. The former is irrelevant and the thief is welcomed to it but what happened to the tram pass? Perhaps, he too was drawn to its beauty and as he looked at the photograph, the strength of my grandmother's longing for the unknown, for the unreachable, made an impression on him and he abandoned his life as a tube thief. I imagine him sitting in his room and looking at the picture of my grandmother, taken almost a hundred years earlier, and mesmerized by its beauty, he dreams and the dream transforms him into a seeker of beauty.

When my parents are dead and my brother is sorting out their possessions, I ask him to keep for me a box of Grandma's drawings. She told me I should have it one day. My brother never refers to the box and ignores my request. Instead, he says: I have found a white porcelain tray that was Grandma's. It is very delicate. Would you like to have it? You can keep salt and pepper mills on it.

Is that all that is left of the palimpsest of her life?

My grandmother's story is a story of joy and triumph and not some nostalgic Mitteleuropa tale of loss.

In a foreign town a woman sings, I remember.
In a foreign town a woman flies through the air, I remember.
In a foreign town a man flies through the air and keeps his top hat on despite the wind, she remembers.
In a foreign town a man looks at a picture of a girl in an old tram pass, I remember.
She is beautiful, he thinks, I remember.

CHAPTER THREE

The Dead

There are many difficulties to be reckoned with in the
recollection and recounting of things.
W. G. Sebald

Those four ancestors, my forebears, who were they? Parts of them must have passed on to me. I wonder which feature of Maria survives? Or Francis? Fanny? As for Pavel, my grandfather . . . who was he? What I have inherited from him may be even harder to discern.

When I was growing up, I was told—but was it by a credible voice? —that he had been conscripted in 1943. Six months after he had left, Fanny, my future maternal grandmother, received a telegram with the news that her husband had died of typhus and had been buried in an unmarked grave. There was nothing remarkable about that. At the time, Fanny was about to give birth to their fourth child, my mother's youngest brother. Fanny was an unsentimental woman and took whatever befell her without complaint. She laughed a lot, and laughed more loudly than anyone I knew. That made her appear easy-going and relaxed. But even as a child I sensed that her soft exterior belied a hard and opinionated mind that brooked no discussion or dissent. She brought up her children on her own while working full-time in a brick factory (probably in the office; nevertheless, it showed her indomitable spirit, as she had never had a job before). Once the children were off her hands, she married again. When her second husband died, she married a third and survived him, too, by a few years. I remember her as strict, far too strict for a granny, but also as a woman who, when retired, enjoyed tea dances, took regular spa trips, where she relished the social life and would return with stories of parties and excursions. An outsider seeing her with us might have attributed Grandmother's laughter to happiness at being with her grandchildren but my brother and I could tell that it was joyless—an exaggerated amusement. When she laughed, she performed. Her short, corpulent frame shook amiably but we knew her joviality was no more than a protective screen, another way of holding us at a distance, as much as her insistence that we, and my parents, too, should address her in the formal, second-person plural. None of my friends had such grannies. I could never tell what she thought nor relax in her presence. She spoke in trite clichés and made statements that left no room for questions. Each opinion was sealed by laughter as if the merriment asserted the truth of what she said. These days, people might call it 'passive confrontation'. To me, Fanny remains an enigma; I will never know her story. I do not think she wanted anyone to know her story. I could not imagine her calling me to her hospital bed and telling me about a rendezvous with a trapeze artist and how she wanted to run away with the circus. She was too proper, too conventional, mentally and physically the polar opposite to Maria. When I dreamt of Fanny a few years ago, it was a nightmare that made me wake up screaming. I saw her in the back garden of her house with a large peacock on the patio. She laughed loudly as she said it was her husband, the third, a man I remember as ancient, fragile and silent, a man who sat quietly on the sofa in the corner of the kitchen while she busied herself at the stove and talked to us. The peacock in my dream, I am sure, had nothing to do with him but was an image of my granny—an image that puzzles me. I do not know how to interpret it unless there is a clue in the fact that peacocks terrify me. I find their celebrated beauty disgusting. The thought fills me with terror that even a single feather of this huge bird might touch me. More than twenty-five years after Fanny's death, that nightmare-peacock strutting menacingly on the patio, accompanied by her loud guffaws, is the most vivid memory I have of my maternal grandmother.

As for Pavel, his life unfolded gradually when I came to think he might not have died in the war after all. I pieced his story together, filling in the gaps between what was passed to me by witnesses whose accounts I found believable and material from the Croatian National Library in Zagreb. That act of writing it down, more than anything else, helped me understand his life and perhaps even his part in who I am.

Pavel's narrative started in May 1945 when he walked for a week through fields and forests from the front to his family's home in a small town outside the capital. A couple of days before his unit was disbanded and the soldiers were given their remaining rations for the journey, he might have learnt of the telegram. I imagine that in the turmoil of the war, with armies on the move and poor communication, such mistakes were not uncommon. But wait. Before I proceed, I must say that at the time his name is Victor; the man married to Fanny and the father of my mother is Victor; the man walking home is not Pavel but Victor. Once Victor learns that the person responsible for informing families of the death of their nearest and dearest had sent a telegram to his wife rather than to another soldier's wife, the wife of a soldier who did die of typhus and was buried in an unmarked grave, Victor is anxious to return home as quickly as possible, to assuage Fanny's grief and help her with the children. He would not have responded in any other way. My mother, his oldest child and his only daughter, remembered that her father liked order, planned his days, hated to be late and had a strong sense of duty. An anxious type, he feared that a tragedy of some kind was just around the corner. He expected the worst so that if his fears were realized, he would be prepared. But would that not make him permanently unhappy? With the years passing, Victor, or Pavel as he is by then, acquires two vertical worry lines between his eyebrows which make him look severe, even angry. But I am jumping ahead.

For now, with the war over, we see him walking through the countryside, day and night, on the way to his provincial town, hardly taking any rest, desperate to reach home. His boots are falling apart; both soles are holed and he stuffs them with dry leaves and old bandages. Keen not to waste time, he ignores his bleeding feet but, as he approaches the small town near the capital, a different kind of pain, a more debilitating pain which he cannot ignore, takes hold of him: he worries that he might meet someone who knows him and that they would be shocked by the abominable state of the footwear of a proud master cobbler, well known in the area and beyond for his exquisite, handmade shoes. He is not sure he could bear the embarrassment and shame. (As my mother did throughout her life, Victor cares deeply about other people's opinions and makes every effort to present a carefully honed image to the outside world.) Poorly shod and faced with the possibility of being recognized, he thinks that although he has survived the war, the journey home might undo him, strip him of his identity. He chooses remote paths even though that means a longer journey, and stays alert to sights and sounds, determined to avoid chance encounters. His cap is pulled down over his forehead, hiding his eyes. He reaches his destination on the evening of 8 May, after eight o'clock; under the cover of darkness, he staggers stealthily through the small town, forever glancing over his shoulder like a thief. He is standing on the edge of the road, opposite his house, when he sees a light switched on in one of the bedrooms, his daughter's. He notes that the neighbour's house is empty. He remembers that the Levis had been taken away a month before he was called up. His children asked about Max but only his daughter understood. I cannot tell what else goes through his mind. I cannot see his face but I know that he doesn't wait for the silhouette of the figure that had entered the room to become visible behind the net curtains. He turns away and hurries in the direction of the capital.

You may ask why, after walking for a week with nothing else on his mind but the wish to reach his family as quickly as possible, Victor turns away. It is a question which—I would imagine—to Pavel's irritation, assails him throughout his life but he can never find an answer. There isn't one. In a fictional story, one would invent something that Pavel overheard as he was crossing the town, some gossip about Fanny having a new man; or we could speculate that he might have remembered an incident, an old argument from his marriage, or that he was traumatized by what he had witnessed in the war and was unable to face his old life. Stories require such plausible, psychologically coherent motivations. But here it is pointless to guess what might have caused him to turn away. There are times in our lives when we make a decision without knowing why. With no rhyme or reason. An arbitrary decision. A decision that makes no sense and which, even we may see as out of character. A decision that makes no sense or follows anything that preceded it. But that is life, rough and meaningless, full of contradictions, unlike stories where ordered narratives establish direct links between cause and effect.

And why wouldn't he have walked out on his past life? Given the chance to cover our tracks and reinvent ourselves, how many of us would not take the opportunity? Imagine drawing a line under your past and being given a second chance. Imagine all those unfulfilled dreams and ambitions you would be able to realize, correct your mistakes, address your regrets. For most of us that remains an unattainable fantasy. But it was a reality for Pavel.

At some point, he hitches a lift from a military lorry and I can see him sitting in the back, silent and inconspicuous among whatever cargo the lorry is transporting. The asphalt is broken, the route bumpy and as they reach the outskirts of the capital, cheering crowds line both sides of the road, welcoming returning soldiers. We can imagine, a carnation hitting Victor in the face and the sergeant, sitting in front, next to the driver, laughing. He turns towards Victor and starts a conversation. He wants to know the soldier's name. Victor is at a loss what to say. Who is he? The noise of the crowd and the racket from the lorry hurtling along, dodging the potholes, buy him time and he pretends he hasn't heard the question. The sergeant repeats it. On the back of the sergeant's metal seat someone has scratched the name Pavel. That is his answer. He is Pavel. The sergeant is chatty, overwhelmed by the general sense of jubilation.

'You've got a sweetheart waiting for you, Pavel?'

Pavel looks down. What can he say? He has a family, three or possibly four children. But no, that was Victor. Victorious? Hardly. Poor Victor who died of typhus. What an inappropriate name. Victor who is no more. He is Pavel.

'I see,' the sergeant laughs. 'No need to be shy. I bet she's ready and waiting for you.'

Pavel nods, and the sergeant winks at him. As soon as the lorry stops, jammed by other vehicles trying to move through the narrow streets, Pavel jumps off and is lost in the crowd.

The next time I picture Pavel, five years have passed and he is teaching history in a secondary school in the capital. He has made use of the scholarships that were on offer to anyone who wanted to study and who passed the university entrance exam. The funds came from American foundations and charities. The American help, particularly after 1948, was part of the effort to prevent this mostly agricultural country with hardly any industry from falling under the Soviet sphere of influence. The country needed to rebuild its infrastructure; there was an urgent need to raise the low literacy levels of its population and generate a professional class. People were encouraged to study. Those who lived at the time tell me that after the destruction and chaos of the war, young people who presented themselves without papers, encountered no obstacles if they wished to finish their schooling and go to university. Many people would have been in the position to fashion a new identity. Few questions were asked and no eyebrows were raised if you claimed that your papers were buried under the rubble after your house had been destroyed by a bomb.

The archives of the University Library in Zagreb contain a Latin copy of Pavel Horvat's (a clever move on Pavel's part to choose the most common surname in the country) degree certificate. The date is 26 June 1950 and, considering that the course lasted four years with an additional year for exams and dissertation, after which a student formally graduates (the year of being an *absolvent*), we can say for certain that Pavel completed his studies in good time.

He teaches history at a grammar school, known as the Fifth, a few paces from the Croatian National Theatre. He is a dedicated teacher, thought of as well read and knowledgeable but also reserved and unapproachable. We could speculate whether his reserve is a mask that reassures him and allows him to rewrite Victor into Pavel. His colleagues complain he is unsociable. After a few years, he is promoted to deputy head. His colleagues wonder why he has no wife and no family. Rumours circulate that he could be one of those men, one of those, they say without finishing the sentence, as they nudge each other and wink. Homosexuality is frowned upon, seen as unnatural and unacceptable by most people. Pavel is not gay but he has no interest in relationships either. He has had a family, he abandoned them and he does not need another; even if he does, he reasons, he doesn't deserve one. He is careful to reveal nothing about his lifestyle, despite the repeated efforts of his colleagues, particularly the female ones, to find out. None of his fellow teachers—in fact, no one except a plumber on two or three occasions—has ever been inside his home. He does not accept invitations to lunches, dinners or parties and on only one occasion did he find himself inside a colleague's flat. He has regretted it ever since.

Myra, the geography teacher, had made no secret of her interest in him and he blamed himself for not being more careful; he should not have allowed himself to be taken in by her charade. He was about to drive home when he saw her limping across the staff car park, calling his name. A few students passed by and he could not ignore her. She claimed to have twisted her ankle and needed help to reach her car. She leant much too heavily on his arm but at least there was not far to go, he thought. When her car wouldn't start, he wondered whether it was a coincidence. He hated to think badly of her but with hindsight, knowing how she pursued him for months afterwards, he would not have put it beyond her to have disabled the battery. That late afternoon after school it rained heavily and he had no choice but to offer her a lift. On the way to her place, he was prepared to help her up the stairs and that would be it. He would depart as soon as they reached the flat. But the stylishly minimalist decor of the entrance hall, something he had not expected, threw him off his guard. What followed was entirely his fault but who could have anticipated such elegance from a woman who didn't bother to have the heels on her shoes repaired? For carelessness when it comes to shoes, Pavel thinks, is an attitude of the soul. It affects everything about the person.

As you might guess, Pavel has strong views on the state of people's footwear. In fact, my mother, his only daughter and by her account, Victor's favourite child, inherited that trait. She would recall her father saying, 'You can't trust a man who doesn't look after his shoes.' The pride in her voice left no room to doubt that she agreed with the sentiment. And although Pavel wasn't Victor, whenever he met someone new, he would check the state of their shoes. This survival of a trait from Victor was immensely irritating. How could he rid himself of it? He was a man who believed in self-control and the power of the will, and yet no matter how hard he tried, in the presence of others his gaze inevitably dropped to the floor. If the shoes were scuffed, or the heels were worn, Pavel could not help but be wary of the owner whom he judged unreliable, untidy, unpunctual and possessing who knows what other moral deficiencies. You couldn't display insouciance about your shoes without being inadequate in at least one, and usually more than one, area of your professional or private life. Once Pavel had reached an opinion about someone— usually an opinion based on an instantaneous assessment, and allowing no room for mitigation —he made sure to avoid, if at all possible, any contact with that person. I don't think we should judge Pavel too harshly in this respect. We all have our quirks and prejudices but, unlike most people, at least Pavel was aware of his and, to compensate for what was usually and inevitably a negative judgement, he tended to go out of his way to be kind to the wearers of badly kept shoes, albeit in a formal, superficial way. It wasn't because he wanted to give them the benefit of the doubt, a second chance to prove themselves, but if he couldn't avoid having contact with them, he thought it best to keep his views to himself and put on a kind face in their presence. Ultimately, they stood no chance with him. Not that anyone did.

I might have made too much of this prejudice but it helps us understand the blow that Pavel's view of the world would have suffered when presented with the sight of Myra's hall. All his experience —and he had never been wrong—told him that her home should have been an untidy, cluttered space, full of cheap *objets d'art*. In a state of confusion, if not shock, he accepted a cup of coffee, in thanks for being helpful, as she said. While Myra disappeared into the kitchen, he sat in her lounge, and even though he was reassured to see the mantelpiece unencumbered by trinkets—such a rare thing, would have been the thought going through his mind—his anxiety resurfaced and he planned to make his excuses. He must have vacillated for a second too many and Myra appeared with a tray just as he was about to stand up. Another surprise: the coffee was as good as in Italy and, damn, she served it with a glass of brandy, an exquisite Armagnac. He knew he shouldn't have taken it, let alone done what he did afterwards.

For the rest of his life he shuddered at the memory of her misshapen buttocks with puckered skin like the peel of a juiceless orange. Despite the brandy clouding his mind, the sight of her veined, blotchy breasts made him think of the disgust Gulliver feels in the land of giants when his size offers him a microscopic view of a young girl's nipple. Pavel knew it was unpardonable to have lost control and he paid for it with months of persecution at work.

There was no end to her insinuations, often in front of colleagues; even after he had pleaded with her to forget what had happened, she wouldn't shut up. When she was killed by a bus that skidded and mounted the pavement, he felt the accusing stares in the staff room as if he had been the driver. He wasn't a hypocrite and admitted to himself that he was relieved she was out of his life. Cruel, no doubt, but accidents happen and there are always winner and losers. The episode taught him a lesson and he never slipped again. That's not quite true. I ought to say that he never slipped in such a manner (more on that later).

A likely reason why he protects his privacy is not so much because he fears revelation of his past but because spending time with the people he knows would be, if not a complete waste, nowhere near as beneficial for his self-improvement as it is to be on his own. Life is short and most people squander it on small talk and inconsequential gossip when they could be learning a new language. He has taught himself Latin, ancient Greek, Italian, French and English and is now working on Spanish; he also maintains his German, a remnant from his previous existence. He lives the life of the mind. He is an exile into his internal world. A voracious reader, for many years he has entertained the thought that he might write something of value. (My mother remembered her father saying that there was no one he admired more than writers. They were the only people he envied.) He has not abandoned the ambition but as time passes and his writing, despite his daily efforts—*nulla dies sine linea*—fails to correspond to the idea of what his writing should be, it falls short of the idea he has in his head, and he fears he is approaching the time when he will have to accept that he will not succeed. He writes a book after book to bring closure to his life, to make it meaningful, but destroys each one in turn. He can never find the right expression. Nor can he think of the end to his stories. He longs to write a book that would signal possibilities of life. But all his stories are too closed. His solitude is both productive and creative and he does not miss what others would call a social life. He is far too busy with self-improvement. That's what living is about. There is nothing but self-improvement, *creative self-improvement*. According to my mother, those were Victor's exact words. Alas, as she used to add, his life didn't allow him to put them into practice. Pavel, however, was different.

For a person who values self-improvement, holidays provide a wonderful opportunity to focus on their aim: meticulous planning is essential. Pavel is keen to make the most of his time and money to broaden his knowledge of the arts and practice his linguistic skills. Despite making detailed advance arrangements, he is open to chance. I have a simple explanation: Pavel is a linguist. He loves words. He loves words as objects, not merely as signs. He loves their sound, their smell (yes, he says, he can smell them), their form, their sensuality, their tactility. During his first trip to London, in 1960, he visited Horace Walpole's gothic castle in Strawberry Hill where, in a large oak-panelled room, the guide said that the writer and politician had coined the word 'serendipity' in that very room. Pavel remembers being charmed by the music of the word and instantly falling in love with it; he had to say it aloud there and then, like a child who cannot wait to open a packet of sweets. The feeling left in his mouth was as if he had experienced the most passionate kiss of his life. While some people may reach for a box of chocolates or a glass of wine, Pavel's morsel of instant pleasure comes when he says *serendipity*. It is a perfect word. The English are lucky to have it, he believes. Other languages either have to use a clumsy phrase—like his own first language—or resort to borrowing the English word—which Pavel judged a much better solution—adapting it to their own rules and forms. Portuguese uses *serendipicidade* or *serendipidade*; French has *sérendipicité* or *sérendipité*; Italian goes for *serendipità*; Dutch *serendipiteit*; German *Serendipität*. How could he not then believe in serendipity? How could he not, from time to time, depart from his schedule to act on the spur of the moment, allowing his instincts to take control?

After London, he wondered how he had managed to live without the word for more than half a century. There were examples of serendipity in his life but until he heard those beautiful syllables, he had not realized that. Horace Walpole had made it possible for him to see his life in a new light. Things fell into place. He would not try to explain what happened at the moment he stood opposite his house (Did he think of it as his house? No, it was Victor's house.) and turned away—the moment he had returned to many times— but sometimes he wondered, I am sure he did, whether it was serendipity seeing the light switched on in his daughter's bedroom when he stood outside, opposite the house, that moment before he walked away from his old life. One day, he hoped, he could find out. He did not doubt the role that serendipity had played in his life.

Years later, serial serendipity led him to acquire two photo albums that have since lain deposited in the bottom drawer of his desk. And who knows, the albums might be part of some future serendipity. That particular series of happy, chance events started with him replacing, at the last minute, a teacher who, because of his wife's nervous breakdown (it could have been something else but for the purposes of this story that is not important) had to drop out from a student excursion to Paris. Visiting the Louvre, Pavel was taken by Ghirlandaio's *Ritratto di nonno con nipote*. He spent more time in front of that painting than all the other exhibits put together. He was puzzled by the ambivalence of his response to the point where he could not think about anything else. He was familiar with the painting from its reproductions. What intrigued him most was the juxtaposition of the old and the young. The theme has preoccupied him ever since he saw Leonardo's *Magi* in the Uffizi (a painting that he believed had nothing to do with Christianity and its stories, in fact, a painting that he considered unashamedly secular) and that interest we can attribute to Pavel's awareness of his own ageing. But seeing *Ritratto* in the Louvre, in the flesh, as it were, another question emerged. He admired the painter's brutal honesty, literally warts and all, but he could not decide whether Ghirlandaio had conformed to, or opposed, the physiognomic convention of the period which implied a connection between external appearance and moral truth. Most people would not be bothered by such a dilemma and would be happy to leave it unresolved but Pavel was a touch, or more than a touch, obsessive—a feature of his character I might have inherited—and so he returns home and decides to seek out other, earlier Ghirlandaios in order to resolve his dilemma.

That is why, a few months after the Louvre trip, Pavel travels to Italy to see Ghirlandaio's *Ultima Cena* in the cenacle of the abbey in Passignano, the Badia a Passignano. He stays in a *pensione* in a village near Tavarnelle in the Chianti region and the day after his arrival, he plans to set out on foot. But during his breakfast of homemade pastries, he is engaged in conversation with the owner of the *pensione*, an old *signora*, let's call her Signora Ucci. That sounds Italian but since the name is not important for the verification of my story, she could be called Mutti or Tutti, that would not change this account. As you would no doubt agree, I should be able to make up such details and then later I could always find something more authentic in a telephone directory online. The important thing is that Signora Ucci takes a liking to him and gives him a packed lunch, the sort, she claims, that pilgrims in the area used to take on their way to the Badia. The lunch consists of locally grown olives, sprigs of basil, miniature almond breads and dry figs. Pavel is more interested in the soft cardboard box holding the food. As soon as the *signora* places her gift in his hand, a powerful erotic sensation shoots through his body. Yes, erotic. Pavel is moved by such beauty. For the briefest of moments, he is perturbed by the beauty of the box and as soon as he collects himself, he comments on the sensuality of the soft cardboard. Signora Ucci says that it was made in her sister's workshop, a paper mill that uses centuries-old techniques.

'All handmade,' she adds.

'Where is the workshop?' Pavel asks.

She mentions the name of a village outside Sienna, situated to the west; he is about to walk east. Gently cupping both hands around the box, Pavel sets out towards the Badia. It is the end of April; his path is scented with the blossom of pear, apple and peach trees. He passes centuries-old vineyards, neatly pruned and waiting for the heat to make them spring into life. Olive trees stretch as far as his eyes can see—you can verify this by travelling to the region or even by checking guide books on Tuscany—but I think Pavel (I know, my mother told me that about Victor) is one of those rare people who are immune to the beauty of nature. I cannot imagine him making an effort to see a rare bird or visit a garden, no matter how perfect. Instead, he has cultivated an urban taste; he could not survive without opera, concerts, galleries. He walks through temperate Chianti valleys, ascends gentle hills, and soon after proceeding through the town of Sambuca—a settlement of white stucco buildings and red-tiled roofs that would normally impress him but not today—a view of the abbey unfolds before him. The pictures he has seen in travel brochures could not possibly prepare him for the magnificence and grandeur in front of him. But he is restless and does not pause; he hastens along the narrow mountain lane, edged by metre-high stone walls on each side. He doesn't have to hurry. This is a working abbey and the monks do not usually allow visitors into the cenacle but he had written to them, and after several requests—he does not give up easily on culture—Pavel was given permission to spend a day in front of the Ghirlandaio painting. He has plenty of time to take in the view. Only those who have seen the Badia a Passignano from the spot where Pavel stood could understand the power of his restlessness. And what was its cause? Yes, the soft cardboard box in his hand. He was attracted to the idea of a workshop producing handmade paper and it crossed his mind that it was Ghirlandaio who pointed him in that direction. Without the *Rittrato*, he would not have come to the region. The serendipity of a chain of events going back to . . . What was it? A teacher's wife's nervous breakdown?

The monks received him with gentle courtesy but he spent only two hours in the cenacle in front of the *Ultima Cena*. It was a calm and thought inspiring painting and in his usual, scholarly fashion Pavel made copious notes on the details of the picture, focusing on the fascinating dishes and still life. But his mind was elsewhere. He returned to the *pensione*. Signora Ucci wasn't there and the young woman who had taken her place could not tell him the way to the paper mill. She had never heard of it. Yes, she was brought up in the area, knew every village around. Besides, Signora Ucci had no sister. Pavel showed her the soft cardboard box. They must have more in the pantry, in a storeroom. Couldn't she look? She had never seen a box like that in the *pensione* or anywhere else. She had worked there for many years and knew the place inside out. All that made Pavel even more determined. His spirits were high; he marvelled at his good luck in meeting Signora Ucci and recalled that he had chosen her *pensione*—not the best value according to guide books—only because he had learnt that it stood on the spot where Galileo Galilei used to sit for his drawings while he lived in the area, teaching mathematics in the Badia. He could not explain why that trivia—was it true, he wondered?—had swayed him in his choice of accommodation since his interest in the 'Tuscan artist', as Milton called him—was because he was the only contemporary the great English poet mentions in *Paradise Lost*—one of Pavel's favourite poems—and the protagonist in Bertolt Brecht's play *Galileo Galilei*. As you no doubt realize, I am not privy to why Pavel chose the Ucci *pensione* and do not know whether it was the information about Galileo that was decisive. But Galileo did teach mathematics at the Badia—I've checked that—and if there had been a link between the *pensione* and the scientist, and Pavel had come across it, he would have been sufficiently impressed to book his stay there. That settled, let's move on.

The day after visiting the cenacle, I see Pavel making his way in the direction of Pistoia. He hitches a lift on a coach full of Japanese tourists. He sits next to an elderly man called Shoo, who speaks some English, and from him Pavel learns that the next stop on their sightseeing tour is a paper mill. A paper mill? Could it be Signora Ucci's sister's? Shoo is interested in calligraphy and he has made the trip especially to buy fine paper for his work. He talks excitedly about his calligraphy and says that he intends to leave his handiwork to his grandchildren.

'A gift to remember me by,' says Shoo. He asks Pavel if he has any grandchildren. Pavel looks out of the window, pretending that he doesn't hear. When the coach stops, Pavel exploits the momentary confusion caused by the people disembarking and he walks away without a word to Shoo. He strolls in the garden, waiting for the Japanese group to depart. By then, it is close to five o'clock and an elderly woman whose physique would suggest that she is Signora's Ucci sister but then, he thinks, most elderly Italian women look as if they have walked out of a Fellini film, appears on the gravel path, holding a set of keys and proceeds towards some double glass doors. (How do I know such details? I don't, but whether there were double glass doors or not does not change my story. It only adds to the atmosphere and the description of the scene; it makes it more plausible. You must allow me some poetic licence.) Next, this follows: the *signora* says they are closed for the day and that he should come back in the morning. And then something else happens, something that brings them together and makes *signora* repent and take Pavel around the workshop. I wasn't there to see it and Pavel left only scraps of notes, some of which recorded sketchy details of his travels but from what I know about him, this is not only what could have happened but what had to happen: When the *signora* says that the mill is closed, she fiddles with the keys and speaks without looking at him. He doesn't argue or try to persuade her to let him in; he is too disappointed and he sighs. Hearing the sigh, she looks at him and he feels that she might change her mind. He is wrong but, at that point, fate intervenes: a cat, a large but very thin, scraggy cat, runs in and stops between them. The cat is carrying a mangled, barely alive bird in its mouth. It insists on gifting it to the *signora* and her visitor. With the last vestiges of life, the big, black feathered creature flaps around in a desperate attempt to free itself. Feathers fly. The *signora* appears to panic; she wants him to put the dying creature out of its misery by twisting its neck or hitting it with a stone. He is horrified at the idea. He has never knowingly killed anything and, besides, Pavel has an aversion—this lineament of his character (if one can call it that) is not in doubt because he passed it on to my mother and then to me—to anything with feathers: he doesn't eat poultry, avoids feather pillows and is anxious when walking in cities, fearing that he might be touched by a pigeon. The *signora*, too, is scared of birds but she has no idea of Pavel's phobia as she has never come across anyone who shares her fright; in tears, she begs him to do something. He hesitates—he has always kept his fear secret—and hopes the cat will finish its deadly work herself or at least run away. The cat enjoys the attentions and redoubles its efforts in handing over the gift. In the meantime, the bird struggles to free itself, releasing a shower of feathers that frighten both the *signora* and Pavel. They jump away. The cat follows, more determined in its intention, and the bird continues to fight for its life. They try to shoo the cat away but it does not budge. The *signora* calls out the name Simone and a young child, probably a grandson, no more than five years old, appears out of nowhere. With no fuss, the boy takes the bird out of the cat's mouth—surprisingly, the cat does not seem to mind—and walks away cradling it in his arms. *Mi occuperò di esso. Andrà tutto bene*, he says in the direction of the *signora*.

Pavel is shaken and so is the *signora*; they are aware of each other's distress and unite in their fear. What follows may seem surprising but those who share phobias often feel affinity for one another, relieved that they have found someone who belongs to the same world of suffering, and so the *signora* offers him comfort in the shape of a glass of water and a slice of preserved lemon. That is what she finds helps her recover and dispels the taste of disgust in her mouth. (I learnt this from an Italian woman; she was Sicilian but she assured me that they use the same remedy in the north.) Perhaps she also includes a few almonds in a small bowl—that too is likely as the region is famous for its almonds. They sit down in the shade of a large olive tree. Neither mentions their shared phobia; they prefer to forget it. The *signora* has just returned from a visit to Milan where she saw *Rigoletto* at La Scala.

'How he loves Gilda,' she says, 'the love for his daughter always brings tears to my eyes.'

Pavel is not very musical and Verdi is not his favourite composer (I am not sure whom he likes; I cannot remember my mother mention any specific names of composers when she spoke of Victor). However, he likes opera as a spectacle and the conversation flows. She takes him on a guided tour of the workshop. I imagine they continue being embarrassed by their phobia, as sometimes I am of mine, and they make an effort to be more than usually communicative. The *signora* may be communicative anyway but Pavel, needless to say, is out of character. She talks him through each stage of the paper production; several of her employees—*Miei artisti*, she calls them—are still around in the early evening. She introduces them to Pavel and he is impressed by their knowledge and dedication.

The *signora* looks at him, places her hand on his arm, as if to stop him and says, 'La bottega e l'orto vogliono l'omo morto.' She shakes her head and laughs. Pavel does not comment. Maybe he doesn't even register what she says as he stares at the workers, admiring the meticulousness of their craft. For a fleeting moment, he is envious and feels a pang of nostalgia for his life as a master cobbler but he forces it out of his mind. Either fighting the memory of his past or on the spur of the moment, he buys two photo albums, exquisite objects, entirely crafted from the paper made in the workshop. He leaves by taxi to Sienna. In his hotel he hardly sleeps, taken by the beauty of the albums and the memory of what he saw earlier. He spends the night sitting at a small table, the back of his hand hovering across each page of the albums. Buying on impulse is not how he usually conducts himself but we can understand that if we remember his love of serendipity. But why would someone like him, someone who not only does not own any photographs but for whom photographs are reminders of death, chronicles of the past, and who thinks of himself as a man with no past, why would someone like him acquire an album, let alone two? That question puzzles me and as soon as he returns home, it comes to puzzle him, too. Perhaps, at this point, I need to digress and explain Pavel's attitude to family photographs.

He believes that taking pictures is a vain attempt to trap time and freeze our lives in the moment. Looking at a photograph is looking back, seeking confirmation of our past, corroborating our existence. As soon as you take a picture, he believes, it is obsolete. A photograph is not an image of who you are, not even of who you were; it hides by pretending to show. What's the point of taking pictures, he wonders. Ultimately, both processes, taking pictures and looking at them, try to assuage our fear of death. Most people use photographs to relive their memories. Pavel believes that is a false sensation, a self-delusion. (What might he make of the culture of taking selfies?) Besides, Pavel is a historian of the old school, one of those who believes in the unimpeachable value of facts. For him, photographs falsify our memories; that is why the grass is always greener in the past. Pavel is not interested in the past, greener or not. He lives for now and the only future he thinks about is that associated with his parcels. (I will come to those later). But why did he choose the albums? There were other objects he could have bought. Paper-mill workshops, similar to the one he visited, sell notebooks, stamp albums, covers for books, bags, cards, envelopes, writing sets, picture frames, bookmarks, boxes of all shapes and sizes, boxes for storage and boxes for presents, boxes for holding jewellery and boxes and trays for stationery, paper shades, magazine racks and who knows what else. He did not think of that at the time, he did not think of anything at the time as he was, influenced by the moment, much to his annoyance. But once he is back at home, it occurs to him that he bought the albums because they could perform no practical function in his life and, therefore, he could consider them solely as objects of beauty, exquisite to handle, pleasing to look at. He feels relieved that it was not a momentary loss of control. It was a moment of recognizing beauty.

I wanted to save this for later but perhaps now is the time to confess that I once saw Pavel. I feel this is the right time as the reader might be impatient with me and be wondering how I know what happened in his life. But if I tell you that I saw Pavel in person, not to mention that a lot of my information comes from analysing the choices he made for the books he gave me over the years—the mysterious or not-so-mysterious parcels—and that from observing him on that occasion I could tell what kind of character he was, that should reassure you. The date I saw him was 1 November but I cannot be certain of the year; I would have been ten or eleven, possibly twelve and therefore it had to be sometime in the late 1960s. Like most families in our part of the world, we regularly went to the main cemetery to lay flowers and light candles on the graves of family members. Usually those visits took place on the birthday of the deceased one or some other anniversary. The only fixed date was All Souls' Day. Like most families in the town, we never failed to visit the cemetery on that day. Smartly dressed, we drove uphill, parked and then walked to the grand, neoclassical arcades that surrounded the biggest and most elegant cemetery in the town, indeed, as I realized many years later, one of the most impressive final resting places in the world. We bought bouquets of flowers, sometimes small wreaths, and candles for each of the graves we were about to visit. The occasion was special to me and I looked forward to the day, but not because I had a need to pay my respects to the dead. That need was confined to my parents. They were atheists, did not believe in the afterlife or in the soul and had taught me that once the body is dead, there is nothing left except matter, dead matter: no consciousness, no memory, no sense of the I; dead matter is no different from the clay in which it is deposited and into which it turns. Despite that, my parents seemed to have absorbed some of the country's Catholic tradition—which may not be only Catholic if we think of Antigone and her conflict with Creon—including a belief in the need to look after the body of the departed by tending the grave, thereby allowing the soul to find peace. Later in life I began to understand my parents' attitude to visiting the graves or, rather, I began to see how their behaviour was part of the time and culture to which they belonged. As a child I did not seek any explanation for my parents' visits to the grave and I am sure that the Catholic, and not only Catholic, need to look after the body in order to show respect to the dead and allow their souls to reach peace did not occur to them and had anyone put it like that, my parents would have thought it absurd since they did not believe in the soul and they would have said that it had nothing to do with any religious ritual.

After laying flowers and lighting candles, my parents paused in front of the graves as if in silent communion with the dead. Sometimes my parents complained about cousins who lived abroad and who never visited their family graves, as if the cousins' behaviour was a sign of bad manners, an indifference to the memory of their departed relatives. Later, when I had left home and the country, and on my infrequent visits never asked to be taken to the cemetery, I knew that although they did not let it be known, my parents did not approve of my attitude and must have thought me uncaring and lacking in respect. But by that time they would have realized and accepted, with sadness probably, as all parents do and as I did when my own children had grown up, that I was to be my own person—as they were their own persons in the eyes of their own parents—my own person with my own ways that were not their ways and those ways did not involve the need to stand in front of a grave to remember its occupants and show them respect in that way. Even as a child I knew better than to point out that there was no way of showing anything to anyone who was dead, unless you were a believer and thought that the dead were looking down upon you. But visiting the graves was important to me in other ways. Throughout my childhood and adolescence, I looked forward to our trips to the cemetery and in particular to the annual pilgrimage on All Souls' Day, because those trips held the attraction of a strange, calm beauty; the beauty that was brought about by the atmosphere of the evening as we walked through the dusk giving way to night, our breath freezing in front of us, the November air crisp with cold, the ground crunching under our feet and the vistas blurred by fog, ubiquitous at that time of the year, through which flickered the lights from the candles lit on the graves stretching out all around us. Amid all this beauty, which was magical to me as a child and, in different but no less powerful ways, throughout my youth, there was the mystery of death, the mystery that was attractive. With each passing year it became increasingly associated with a longing for the unknown and distant, with the mystery that brought about a melancholy which in my teens I took to be the only desirable state of mind, the only state of mind that engendered profound thoughts in a world that seemed to me steeped in ceaseless trivia. In my teens, I believed that being melancholic, not to say gloomy, was to be deep and serious, perhaps even clever and creative, and that such moods helped in the search for beauty, the beauty that transcended the banal and ephemeral, which is how I saw my daily life. I believed that my visits to the cemetery allowed me to enter the presence of something elevated and elusive, something that I thought of as beauty, the kind of beauty I experienced when reading poetry or taking long, solitary walks in the deserted streets of the town's medieval quarter. It was that sensation which attracted my then romantic frame of mind, the frame of mind that, in those days when I was innocent of life and life's tragedy and the pain it brings; and when I lived through books, most of my experience was based on the role those books played in my thoughts, in those days I could see the world only through the prism of literature and art and there were many works that meant a lot to me but there are a few I remember as being particularly significant.

One of those texts was a sonnet called the 'Consolation of the Hair' by Antun Gustav Matoš, a Croatian modernist writer, a professional cello player, a translator of Baudelaire, a seeker of beauty. Matoš had lived a bohemian existence in Paris at the end of the nineteenth century; and his life, entirely dedicated to writing and music, ended at the age of forty-one when he died of throat cancer, diagnosed far too late to be cured. I lamented his early death and my teenage, naive and romantic self was convinced that, if only he had had someone to look after him, someone to love him, me for example, he would not have died so young and he would have written many more essays, many more plays and short stories and, above all, many more poems. When I look back on those days of my love for him, my first serious love, I do not think of it as purely teenage infatuation. I admired him for his work and I am pleased to say that my judgement from those days still stands and I believe what I believed then: Matoš is the greatest Croatian writer. His journalism and essays which address the political and cultural concerns of a nation on the frontier of the disintegrating Austro-Hungarian Empire, are brilliantly written in a style that is as fresh, elegant and relevant as the best of the genre. His short stories, with their imaginatively idiosyncratic use of language and quirky magical realism, compare well with the best of the twenty-first century narratives. Above all, Matoš excels as a poet, as the only voice that rose above the provincialism of Croatia and whose writing has not only stood the test of time but is comparable with the best French symbolist poetry. In the sonnet, which soon became one of my best-loved poems, a male narrator speaks to his dead lover in a morgue and when, full of despair, he wishes to give up his own life, the woman's hair tells him to stay calm because death is only a dream. But it was not the consolation that interested me, the words outside of their poetic context offer little comfort, rather, it was the heightened language conjuring the idyll of flowers, agony of candles, the passion of suffering, the morgue that is described as both fatal and malign and, above all, the death whose entrancing beauty fills the space. Texts like this sonnet were crucial to my development—or so I believed; they were the aspects of my life that mattered more than anything else. They shaped my mind, along with those walks in the cemetery.

Another artwork that I remember as being important to me at that time was Caspar David Friedrich's *A Wanderer* which came to my notice almost a year after the episode that I am about to describe, the episode that took place by the cross that is a memorial to the dead with no known graves. I first saw Friedrich's work in an art book I had been given as a present at the New Year Eve's celebration (later it will become clear why it is important to mention this book here—remember the parcels I mentioned earlier, the book came in one of them). It was a large, hardback volume, expensively produced with numerous coloured plates, charting the development of European art from medieval church paintings to Cubism. I remember leafing through the book, slowly turning its heavy glossy pages until I came to the nineteenth century and saw a figure, with its back turned to the viewer, on top of a hill, looking into the distance over a sea of rising fog and I could see myself in that figure, I wanted to be that solitary observer looking into the distance as if he had risen above the ordinary, pedestrian business of everyday life. Like him, I wanted to rise above the ordinary and, after seeing the Friedrich painting, I had little interest for the art that came later in the book. Since nothing in my life at the time, neither my family, my school nor my friends were helpful to my desired state of mind and to what I wanted to be, since none of them were as helpful as literature and art, the poetry of Matoš in particular, and the atmosphere of the cemetery, as soon as I was old enough to walk alone among the graves, I did so. It is possible that neither Matoš nor Friedrich might have entered my life at the time had it not been for my grandfather of two names and that is why I wish to return from this digression—which is not really a digression because that would imply that there is a correct, straightforward way of telling this story and I do not think that is the case—return to that moment when I stood in front of the old oak and while my brother and my father sat on a bench talking, my brother probably holding a Dinky car in his hand and attempting to play with it without making too much noise with his ninnoo-ninnoo sounds, and my father keen to prevent him from disturbing our mother. I watched her as she leant forward to place a candle on the ground, encased in a glass jar to protect the flame from the breeze, next to hundreds of other candles that people had left in memory of their own dead. I had seen my mother do the same every year after we had visited the three other graves of our relatives, starting with the one where my parents' baby son was buried. I knew that she lit the candle in memory of her father who had died of typhus during the war and whose body lay somewhere in an unknown communal grave. I knew that my mother had been six-teen, the oldest of the four children, when the telegram had arrived. She used to tell me how that news had changed her life and how a year or so later, she had to go out to work and help the family and she said how she had been her father's favourite and how they would read together and how after his death she had found it very hard to find time to read. Her mother discouraged her from burying her face in books: apparently those were her mother's exact words, *do not bury your face in books, what is that for?* My mother used to tell me that her mother had said those words many times; and I could hear Grandma Fanny's words, whenever my mother leant forward at the cross where people lit candles for those who had no known graves and I thought how it was right for my mother to think of her father since she had been his favourite.

On that particular occasion, as she leant forward, having placed the lit candle on the ground, I saw her lost in thought, more so than I had ever seen her, and I imagined she was thinking of her childhood and the days after the death of her father and perhaps she was hearing her dead father inviting her to read with him and

thinking how her life could have been different had he not died and she had not abandoned her education. I moved closer to the cross and to the people surrounding the area. I kept my eyes on my mother, drawn by the unusual expression on her face. It reminded me of the death mask of a poet that I had seen in a book, and I remember experiencing a moment of terror, fearing that my mother had disappeared and this woman who wore the same clothes as my mother was someone else, someone alien to me. Hundreds of candles flickered on the ground and I saw a tear sparkle as it slowly descended the cheek of the death mask, and another, and I remember thinking that she needed to wipe her cheeks and that my mother who was always so tidy and meticulous about her appearance, my mother who always kept her composure in public, and would have been ashamed to cry, would not have behaved like that. It was the mask that was crying. Then something unexpected happened. A carefully folded and ironed, white handkerchief appeared in front of her face. I followed the hand holding it as it became an arm inside a dark grey Crombie sleeve and I looked at the owner of the coat, an old man, or so I thought at the age of ten, or eleven or twelve, his eyes, small and grey, his lips thin, his whole face neat and focused under a trilby, trim and absorbed, as if there was nothing spare, neither skin nor expression. And I saw my mother look up and her eyes meet the eyes of the man. For a few moments they remained locked in this candle-illuminated tableau, both hardly breathing, but then someone pushed in front of me to place a candle on the ground and all I could see were the shoes of the man who had offered the clean white handkerchief to my mother, his brogues, shining black, as clean and new as if he had only just put them on. I remember staring at those beautiful shoes and thinking how was it possible for the man to have walked to that spot in the cemetery and not to have creased his shoes, not to have caused even the slightest line in the black leather. Then the shoes turned around and stepped away, at first slowly and then faster and faster, accidentally kicking small pebbles, rough pebbles that would have scuffed the leather, and soon the grey Crombie vanished into the dark, misty air, like a frightened ghost escaping the material world. By the time I looked back at my mother, she was upright and her cheeks were dry, the look in her eyes no longer distant. She was back with the face that I knew. I returned to the place in front of the old oak and waited for her to join us. My father and my brother were talking about the Dinky car, looking at the toy in my brother's hand, my father saying that one of his friends in Switzerland had driven him in the same model as my brother's toy and my brother was asking about the colour of the car of my father's friend from Switzerland. I saw my mother open her handbag and put something inside, and I could tell that she did not drop it in the bag; she placed it in a small, zipped pocket. When she rejoined us, her eyes were smiling and I wanted to ask her whether she knew the man and whether she had taken the handkerchief from him but I had a feeling that I had witnessed something that I should not have, perhaps even discovered something that should have remained a secret and that she would not like me to mention. I did not think she would have taken the handkerchief, she who was petrified of germs, other people's germs, she who shuddered at the thought of most people's lack of hygiene, and she who wore white cotton gloves in summer to prevent touching anyone. And when, in the car on the way home, not only did my mother not complain about what she would usually consider a vulgar gesture of offering one's handkerchief, no matter how immaculate, to someone else, not to mention the horror of horrors of offering one's handkerchief to anyone unknown, but she made no reference at all to the man with the impeccable shoes, I knew I had to keep quiet about the episode. After all, most people would think nothing unusual, if they saw an old man offer his handkerchief to a woman he saw crying. That was life, they would say, full of haphazard events, unconnected and meaningless, not a theatre play, where a gun on the table in the first act has to be fired by the end of the third. I have to agree with them and I would add that only a fool or a narrative pedant would insist on the coherence of a life story. And yet, and yet, I think the cemetery episode is crucial to what I am telling you.

I am sure Pavel would have been shaken by the cemetery episode. As my mother told me, Victor had believed in discipline, self-discipline above all, and Pavel had even more reason to exercise self-control in all areas of his life. As he rushed away from the cross, he would have been furious with himself to have let his guard slip so badly and to have let the moment of weakness risk the collapse

of the whole elaborate edifice of his life that he had carefully con-
structed. The cemetery encounter took place a couple of years
before Pavel's Chianti trip; in Italy his face and his mind still bore
the memory of that late afternoon in November. You can understand now why when Shoo mentioned his grandchildren, Pavel's
alarm bells rang and he stayed dumb. Similarly, with Signora Ucci's
sister describing Rigoletto's love for his daughter. Whenever he
thought about what had happened in the cemetery, which was every
day, Pavel shuddered at the thought of what the episode—*the careless
episode* as he called it—might have led to had he not collected himself in time and rushed away. But he had been pained by the
woman's distress, paralysed by her grief, and despite an inner voice
urging him to go away, he could not move. He had to summon all
his willpower to withdraw his hand. He hates sentimentality and
yet he had yielded to a bout of that shallow emotion. His inner voice
chided him. Sentimentality interferes with self-discipline and
without self-discipline there is no self-improvement. And without
self-improvement, what is life worth? Nothing.

'But there was my . . . ,' he ventured to answer.

'Your what?' the voice asked him.

Pavel couldn't say the word. It was easier to call her my *figlia
che piange*, it was easier to think of the memory as an image from
Eliot's poem. And to distract himself further, he thought how beautiful the words sound in Italian. No wonder the English poet chose
the language of Dante. He wondered if she, the woman kneeling by
the cross in the cemetery, would have read Eliot. Her daughter
might. Or her daughter's daughter one day. The thought tickled
him. Years earlier, he had sent a collection to the mother—that
word was fine—the woman kneeling by the cross in the cemetery.
Soon, it will be time to send one to her daughter; something to look
forward to (so far, he has sent her Matoš). One day, both copies

might be passed on to the daughter's daughter. One day, one day when he would have been gone for a long time. That will be his legacy, his immortality. Not something he has written—as he used to dream of—but the contents of his parcels and their effect on the generations to come. But let's not give in to sentimentality, Pavel, he warned himself. Now I would like to ask a question Pavel would not have dared entertain because by now he has regained his composure, his self-control: had he stayed, would she have thought he was a ghost, returned from the dead? She might have fainted and then if she had, would she have remembered what had happened when she came around? But would that have been such a disaster? A life unmasked as fake? Would they have been angry with him? Fanny would have seen it as a rejection of her, and she would have blamed him for the years of hardship as a single mother. She wouldn't have wanted to have had anything to do with him. The boys would have agreed with her, but not *la figlia che piange*. She would have understood. His, his . . . his *figlia*, she would have remembered their hours of reading together and she would have understood. But what was there to understand? The shame of a proud craftsman cobbler coming home from the war wearing footwear that would have been disgrace to anyone, let alone to him. The shame of a proud craftsman cobbler knowing that he was no longer a craftsman cobbler let alone proud.

'Don't lie to yourself, Pavel. You didn't care about the state of your boots at the time. No one did, not even you. It was not shame that stopped you.'

But what did? Was it a desire, a vague desire, to be someone else? Or perhaps—dare he think of that aspiration?—it was the urge to write, the urge that he could not satisfy as Victor, the master cobbler. Is that what spurred him on? The possibility that he could be more than a reader, that he could be someone who is read? He should have never entertained that idea. No guilt, no shame at abandoning Fanny—not that he feels any guilt or shame he tells himself, even if he were a person who harboured such emotions—none of that could be as big as his realization, the realization that grew as years passed by, the realization of his failure as a writer. He tells himself that he has accepted it now. But what he tells himself is not necessarily what he believes. He cannot escape the question of whether it was worth it. Was it worth it now that he knows it hasn't led to anything? Now that he knows, even if it is difficult to accept; now that he knows he will never write anything he can be proud of? But these are sterile questions.

'Come on, Victor, carry on with the parcels.'

'Who says Victor? I am not Victor! Pavel. I am Pavel.'

'No, you are Victor when you prepare, pack and send the parcels.'

'Who says that?'

'I say that and since we are talking about this, I want to ask why Pavel would send parcels? Pavel has no family. But Victor, that is a different story. And stop deceiving yourself that you feel no guilt, no shame.'

Voices speak to Pavel. Most of the time, he ignores them—but they do not stop.

Next time I see him, it is December 1970. He retired two years earlier but he is busier than ever; he has acquired Portuguese, Esperanto and Dutch. He organizes two cultural excursions for himself every year—the Prado most recently; the Rijksmuseum is next on the list—but the rest of his time is dedicated to the parcels; after all, at sixty-eight, tasks take longer to complete and he is not the sort of person to cut corners. In fact, he is meticulous to the point of obsession. I am looking at him as he stands by his dining table, four boxes in front of him, each containing ten books. All the books in a box and the wrapping paper, different for each box, are chosen according to the information Pavel has compiled on each recipient. He goes through the checklist of books; everything is in order and he is ready to close the boxes and write the names and addresses, four different names, one address. For many years, he typed the labels but last year—and he will do the same now—he used his own handwriting. Why not? It is not a serious risk and the idea of them seeing his large loops tickles him. Last year he made another departure from the ritual: he no longer includes a letter informing the recipients that they have been chosen in a lucky draw to receive the enclosed books as part of a promotional campaign. How he used to agonize over the composition of the letter, careful to phrase it as vaguely as possible, not mentioning any names. He won't bother with that any more. By now the family must be used to receiving them; they are much too busy to make enquiries. But the parcels can't go on for ever because he won't go on for ever. What will the family think when the parcels stop? He closes the flaps of the boxes; two of them have some space left and he stuffs in some paper to keep the books in place but as he is about to pull the sticky tape over the top, he hesitates. He stands still for a few moments, his eyes on the boxes. He opens the bottom drawer in his desk and pulls out two packages, each covered in white tissue. Slowly, he unfolds the paper. It is four years since his trip to Chianti. One for the girl. One for the boy. No. That is what the old Japanese man would have said. He is not like that man, he reminds himself. He doesn't wish to encourage them to keep photographs, to develop a dependence on those flimsy images that merely confirm their existence. He wouldn't want his grandchildren . . . did he say his grandchildren? Watch out, Pavel, or you will end up knocking on their door. The tears, the sentimentality. I am your long-lost grandpa. So, what? Really? Where have you been? How come? And then what? Listening to stories from the past; they would call it catching up, getting to know each other. What for? As if one could make good writing out of it. As if one could improve oneself by knowing about the daily lives of others even of the ones who are supposedly family. A waste, it would be a waste of everyone's time. But he must also remember: the girl and the boy are their own people. They are not like him. He shouldn't impose. If they like family photos, it's up to them. Is it? Is it up to them? A teacher is bound to impose, even if indirectly. He should know that well after years of teaching. The gifts he chooses, all the books he has sent in the past fifteen years, they have imposed—he hopes so—they have guided the recipients in the direction he has chosen.

Besides, if he includes the albums, he would be rid of them and that would put to rest his disturbing thoughts. What to do? What to do with them? What would Mary have done? Please Mary, help me, I never ask, I never bother you. Say something, Madam Carleton. But she remains silent. He takes out the notes he made in the British Library on her two autobiographies: *An Historical Narrative of the German Princess* and *The Case of Madam Mary Carleton* and looks for help. He reads the lines he copied from Mary's texts, wonders how her words could be interpreted to suit his purpose, how he could read them as metaphors for his dilemma, but alas, he learns nothing. He leafs through the notes again and pauses at her words: 'I trust in my own power'. He should trust his own power. But what is his own power? Instinct? Commitment, diligence, attention to detail? Fifteen years and fifteen ledgers filled out in his loopy handwriting. Two parts in each ledger: one for information gathering, spying, or field research as he likes to call it, and the second filled with columns and tables recording reviews throughout the year, making long lists, medium lists and short lists. And then the final one: ten books chosen for each recipient. That is his power. The power of data, the power of meticulous precision.

I must make another digression here: in 1960, Pavel spent a few days in London. On his first day, he called at a small antiquarian bookshop in Bloomsbury. Except for the owner, who seemed to be nailed to the chair at a desk in the back of the shop and who kept his head buried in a large leather-bound book, Pavel was the only person around. Undisturbed, he passed several hours browsing. He loved the silence of the place and its musty smell. Never in his life had he been surrounded by so many old books; it was paradise, worth the whole trip to London. As happens to a believer in serendipity, he was on his way out when his coat snagged on the corner of a table and, bending to disentangle the garment, Pavel knocked down a file that in turn hit a shelf and dislodged a 1663 copy of *The Case of Madam Mary Carleton*. Pavel apologized, the bookseller looked up and walked towards him. Having picked up the file and then the book, the bookseller said: 'I didn't know this was on display. I should be grateful to you. It is one of the most valuable items I have. It has to be behind lock and key.' They started a conversation and that is how Pavel was introduced to Mary Carleton, alias the German Princess, a lower-class seventeenth-century Canterbury woman who married a local man, had two children then left her husband after the children had died in infancy. She moved to Dover, assumed a different name and married someone else, a Dr Day. A few years later she left him to travel with a noblewoman across Europe, acquired high-society manners and became proficient in several European languages. Staying at an inn in London, she was taken for a German princess in disguise—which she didn't deny—and was courted by John Carleton, a young law student, the brother-in-law of the innkeeper. A few weeks after they were married, the Carletons, Mary's new in-laws, who went into debt to secure the marriage, hoping it would bring them fortune and social status, were tipped off that their daughter-in-law was a bigamist and a fraud. Mary was imprisoned at Newgate, where she held court as a celebrity (Samuel Pepys visited her and mentions the occasion in his *Diary*). At the trial, the prosecution produced neither witnesses nor documentary evidence (Mary had been careful never to sign a marriage certificate) and the defendant was acquitted. However, the Carletons and their supporters issued a series of pamphlets denouncing her. In response, Mary wrote an autobiography, where she described her German childhood, followed by a slightly rewritten version a year later. Both were best-sellers. Short of money, she starred in a play about her life. Always practical, ever-opportunistic, she did not mind the playwright's hostile presentation of her character. However, her luck eventually ran out and, in the manner of many an eighteenth-century rogue, she ended her life at the gallows, in her case, for stealing a silver tankard. Her fame survived her and Daniel Defoe used her life as a model for Moll Flanders. Years after Pavel's death, feminist scholars who wrote about the German Princess, celebrated Mary Carleton for her power of self-fashioning and her ability to lead the life of an independent woman, not tied by marriage or social class at a time when there was no divorce for ordinary people and no social mobility.

Her appeal for Pavel was obvious. She was the only figure in history he had ever come across in whose life he found a similarity to his own. She confirmed him in his belief that our life stories are ours to construct. Like him, she was good at languages and, like him, she moved up the social ladder. It was love at first sight and a love that deepened over the years. He looked up to her and on the rare occasions when he was stymied by life's demands, when plagued by unanswerable questions, he consulted her. After the Bloomsbury bookshop discovery—there was no way he could have afforded to buy the book—he managed to obtain a reader's ticket at the British library with the help of the antique bookseller who wrote him a reference in which he claimed to have known Pavel for many years as a distinguished scholar and even wrote down the titles of several of Pavel's book-length publications. When Pavel, embarrassed at the lie, protested, the bookseller, Mr Leonard Stein, explained that it was entirely appropriate to have counterfeit reference to consult Mary Carleton's autobiographies. They both laughed. Pavel spent the following two days copying Carleton's autobiographies by hand. She has been his rock ever since. He was no longer woken at night by voices telling him that he was a traitor to have abandoned his family, a failed father and husband, an unreliable human being who had no heart and deserved no love. When haunted by those nightmares, he reached for the notebooks he had filled in the British Library. He was comfortable with Mary because she was not a credible voice and he believed that credible voices were dangerous, the voices that never lie, the voices that claim authority. (I like to think the same and if you don't agree, you must reconsider what you are reading here.) Pavel agreed with Mary's that 'all the world was a cheat, along with everyone in it'. How he loved her maxim that 'it was better to make a splash than not; to have a glorious name, however obtained, than live by common fame'. But fame did not interest him, common or not. He used to dream of writing, of belonging to the *famille d'esprit* and he would have been glad to have had readers, appreciative readers, no matter how few, or just one, but really what would have mattered even more was to write something he was proud of, even if no one read it. But that was not to be, either. And as Mary never looked back— she was good at moving on—he tried to do the same but despite his discipline, the past encroached and there were times when it was difficult to banish it. One day he had to resort to repeating aloud: *I will never look back*—mechanically shouting as if to clear his head. That was the day of their only disagreement. Mary had asked him about the parcels.

'Aren't they a way of looking back? A way of atoning for your past, Pavel?'

He has nothing to atone for, he told her. He has nothing to be ashamed of. He could hear her giggle. She didn't believe him. But did he believe himself? He couldn't answer that.

Pavel knew that banishing the past is tough and shouting slogans didn't help but he could not think what else to do. How come he didn't learn that from Mary? She invented the past she required: when the Carletons questioned her identity as a German princess, she described her German, aristocratic childhood. Anyone can imagine the past they need and turn it into a story, preferably a written story because writing it down makes it real. Whether you have lived the past or not is irrelevant because unless the past becomes a story, it is forgotten. And what's forgotten has never existed. Writing makes it plausible and true (and unlike Pavel, most people want true stories); writing brings it into existence. But these are my thoughts, the thoughts that do not come to Pavel or perhaps they do but he banishes them. He thinks of himself as a failed writer and that deprives him of the ability to address his past creatively, in the way that Mary Carleton did. He wishes he could destroy it once and for all.

I am again looking at him on that afternoon in December 1970 as he is ready to close the parcels. He is sixty-eight years old. His hair is grey, but still full and wavy. He runs his hand across the flaps of the box on the table in front of him. He waits and then walks into a small room next to his lounge. The walls are covered with shelves holding boxes and ledgers, storing information from the past fifteen years on the recipients of his parcels. Each ledger carries a label with the month and year and the name of one of the four members of his *figlia*'s family. He stands in the middle of the room. This is his world, the world of ledgers. He brushes the back of his hand against them. The movement does not produce a sensual experience. Ledgers are dull. There is nothing creative about them. But this is him, this is what he is good at, gathering and recording information in columns and tables. This is his lifework. A historian by training and temperament. The irony doesn't escape him: a historian who wishes to erase his past. For a moment, he feels proud of the physical presence of his lifetime's work but then a sharp pain shoots through his body. A pain of loss. The ledgers repel him. He wanted to be a writer, an artist, a creator, not a compiler of data, a recorder of sightings and of other people's words, an analyst. But that is all he was good for. A historian who is a meticulous gatherer of information but lacks creativity is a failure. He knows that.

Seeing him surrounded by ledgers, I can confirm he is the kind of person who takes seriously the responsibility of introducing four people to new books and, by implication, new interests, new values, new ways of thinking. Besides, two of his recipients are what most people would call 'impressionable' youngsters. That is not a term Pavel would use. In his eyes, everyone is impressionable and swayed by what they are told by the authorities, the newspapers or advertising. As a history teacher, he took it upon himself to make his students question everything they were taught but after a couple of years he realized that his words fell largely on deaf ears. The majority wanted to know the truth and there was no point telling them that history is always written by victors, that every historian has to be taken *cum grano salis*. All the students cared about were the qualifications, the qualifications and the qualifications. The qualifications that would translate into income. It pained him to see how most students were lazy with no joy in learning and with an aversion to pushing themselves. At the beginning of his career, the realization was a blow and every subsequent year he considered leaving but he had no other means of supporting himself. Perhaps he started the parcels to give purpose to his life and he threw himself into the task with passion. Educating those four satisfied his pedagogical instinct. He began to think of the task of parcels, even the duty of parcels and the responsibility of parcels. Choosing the content required his full attention for eleven months. In the remaining few weeks he was occupied with wrapping individual items—in paper of a carefully selected design—and then posting the four parcels. As soon as he returned from the post office, he would check that all the information he had used for the year's decisions was in order and within days he would start preparations for the following year. Here, nothing was left to chance; the information weighed and assessed and only then did he make decisions on the content and the design of the wrapping paper. One half of his research involved monitoring the publishing industry, reading reviews and making lists of books suitable for each of the four recipients. But in order to make the lists, in order to be able to determine which titles were suitable, the other half of his research was absolutely essential: he needed to know not only the preferences, the tastes, the likes and dislikes of each of the four recipients and know them well so that he could satisfy their preferences but also, and this was the difficult part, the most difficult task, the task that carried more responsibility but it was an absolutely essential part of his enterprise, the part that required more effort from him than any other and naturally that part was more rewarding than all his other tasks and that part meant expanding the preferences of each of the four recipients, widening their horizons, pushing them in new directions, introducing them to the writing that was not the writing they would pick up on their own. Pavel saw it as his duty to expand their taste—he was a teacher after all, by training and by instinct, he liked to think—and to challenge their likes and their dislikes. What would have been the point of doling out the same stuff year in year out? What would have been the point of providing them with those novels about someone's adultery and how their partner coped with such a betrayal? What would have been the point of buying novels where a character faces a moral dilemma or a predicament that requires a decision or leads to a tragedy and then they overcome whatever has happened so that everyone can walk into the sunset and live happily ever after? He was not in the business of destroying trees only to dull the minds of the four recipients of his parcels. He was an educator, life was about learning, life was about improving oneself and he was there to help those four people do just that.

When I consider Pavel's views, I sometimes wonder whether someone else, definitely not me, but a stranger, might find him arrogant, sufficiently arrogant to feel that it was his right to make choices and impose his views, his values, his ways of thinking on others, even if there were only four of them, even if such decisions were based on the best of intentions and on information that was reliable and well researched. After all, they could say, only an arrogant man thinks it is his right to decide what others should learn, what others should read. I know they would be wrong. If he comes across as arrogant, that is my fault because of how I have represented him. Pavel was not an arrogant man, quite the contrary: he was modest, excessively modest, always questioning his decisions and his right to even make them. As a clever and well-educated person, he was aware of the gaps in his knowledge and that awareness bordered on fear that sooner or later he would be found out and then he would be ashamed of being ignorant, of being publicly exposed as ignorant. Those gaps were so huge that sometimes it seemed to him, as it does to any well-educated person, that their knowledge is nothing but gaps, that what they know is infinitesimally smaller and infinitesimally less significant than what they do not know. You have to trust me when I say that he was a modest person (I can hear your mumbling but please do not tell me that there is no reason to trust anything I say, please do not tell me that), and that is why he took the tasks of composing parcels so seriously. He was cautious, extra cautious about every decision relating to the content of those four parcels. After he had assessed his meticulously gathered and recorded data he would still spend considerable time hesitating and prevaricating about each choice, checking the date and assessing his decisions. He had to remind himself that he could back each of his decisions by the information in the ledgers. We have to remember how hard Pavel worked to know the recipients of his parcels, to know them as well as anyone could be known. I would venture to say that he knew each of them better than they knew themselves. Therefore, I have to accept that he could plan the directions of their learning, with all the meanderings, and there are always meanderings since the acquisition of knowledge is never straightforward, never linear, and it should not be straightforward or linear since learning is about trials and errors and blind alleys, and garden paths; and knowing all of that, we can say that Pavel was better versed in the necessary directions of cognitive development of each of the four recipients of his parcels than any one of them could be had they been entirely left to their own direction. And this would apply not only to the direction of their cognitive development but also artistic and emotional. No one could say that was an easy task, not an easy task at all, and it is to Pavel's credit that he was well aware of the enormity of his task, that he took it seriously, and it was to his further credit that he never underestimated the responsibility of his task, that he was aware of the consequence of his decisions even if those decisions turned out not to have been the best—that was unlikely to have been the case but we have to allow for such a possibility, no matter how theoretical. It should be obvious that he never cut corners or took an easy route to save time or effort; he never skimped on whatever he thought was required. He was meticulous and dedicated; someone unkind might call him a pedant, an obsessive pedant.

Pavel gathered information on the four recipients and called that part of the operation his fieldwork. He carried it out in parallel to what he saw as more traditional, desk-based research. For a person like Pavel, the fieldwork was the more difficult part of his task because Pavel, the researcher, Pavel the observer, Pavel the gatherer of information, really had to be Pavel the spy, and Pavel the detective. As such, he had to remain anonymous, unobtrusive, inconspicuous, discreet, low-key and subtle. And that would have been easy for a man who was always quiet, a man who never said a word in vain, a man who never drew attention to himself and yet, to gather information, he also had to be *proactive* (a word that he hated no less than the concept): he had to put himself forward. He hated the idea of putting himself forward or having to approach people—the thought made him anxious, it would bring nausea—talking to passers-by, making himself friendly, chatty and approachable, all the types of behaviour that were alien to him. But there was no other way. He could not employ anyone. Even if he could have confided in someone, he would not have trusted their skill and dedication. Fieldwork had to be done and he got on with it.

As part of his planning, and as part of his training for the fieldwork, Pavel had written out a list of necessary features, the features he considered essential for his task and he pinned one copy above his desk and another next to the front door: the first was to remind him of what was needed from his role while he was working on his more traditional research, on his reading and filing; and the second copy was a last-minute reminder, a reminder designed to strengthen his resolve and motivate him as he was setting out for his fieldwork, the fieldwork that was the key part of the business of parcels and that notion, the notion that without the fieldwork there would be no parcels (and without parcels he would not exist, not in any meaningful sense—he was convinced of that) was something that he had to repeat to himself again and again. I think this is an excellent example that refutes the allegation, the allegation that from my point of view would be unjustified and unfair, refutes the allegation that Pavel was arrogant for if ever there was a man who should have been confident of his ability, who should have been confident of his faith not to waver but to continue with the task, all the tasks of the fieldwork, that man was Pavel. He was not an arrogant man, he was not a man who overestimated his abilities and his strength and the list is a good indication of his lack of arrogance, as well as of his awareness of his own weaknesses, such as the reluctance to carry out fieldwork. But without it, as he knew very well, the whole operation of the parcels would collapse, if it could start at all. That was clear to him, there was no way he could argue with that, there was no way he could drop the fieldwork, there was no way he could replace the fieldwork with anything else, and yet he felt ambivalent about his role in the procedure, and he did mean his own role, for if only someone else, someone else could have done the fieldwork for him, he would have had no qualms. But that was out of the question. For who, who in the whole wide world could have possibly done it with such meticulous attention to detail, with such reliability, with such detachment? Clearly no one, and Pavel had not wasted his time even considering the question. Besides, there was no one that he could trust with the knowledge of the scheme, with the knowledge of the operation, let alone with the task of the parcels, there was no one he could possibly think of that he could trust with advice on his choice of the books, he would not even take a hint from anyone else but that was no surprise since there was no one he could trust with anything, anything at all, anything in his life or outside of his life. As anyone would have gathered by now, Pavel was not a sociable person, not sociable at all. Therefore, there was no one who could do the fieldwork and the research.

But the problem here was that he, he who was such a private person, he who disliked anyone asking any questions about him, he who could become suspicious if a colleague at school enquired what he had thought about some TV programme the evening before—not that he was the sort of person who would watch TV, or even the sort of person who would possess anything as vulgar as a TV (I think my hostility to TV must come from him)—here was he, Pavel the private person, the most private person you could ever come across, here was he, spying into the lives of four people, four people of Victor's daughter's family, here was he following the four people at least once a week and sometimes even more often, here was he speaking to anyone he could find who knew or had any information about the four people, here was he recording the words of the four people whenever he could be within reasonable proximity for his machine to catch their voices, here was he watching their front door, making notes of all the comings and goings, here was he archiving all his findings in ledgers labelled with the appropriate month and year and those four people had no idea about the amount of information that was stored on them.

How would he have felt had someone been doing it to him? How would he have felt had someone been prying into his life to such an extent so that they knew his grocery list, the details of his holidays, his social circle—had there been one—his ailments, his wishes, his fears, his aspirations? Had someone been doing it to him and he had discovered it, he would have probably been tempted to commit murder, but he was not a violent man and so it was more likely that he himself would not have been able to carry on and he would have died, died of shame, died of embarrassment, died of fear. No one understood better than him the seriousness of the business of collecting and storing information, such personal information and for so many years, almost fifteen, no one understood the seriousness of what was involved in the procedure of gathering information better than Pavel. No wonder he felt ambivalent about the fieldwork but ambivalent or not, it had to be done. Full stop. *Point final*. No discussion. End of story. *Basta*. Those were the words that he had to repeat to himself at the moments, and they were rare moments, the moments when he worried that one of the four recipients might discover what he, Pavel, was up to and when he worried what such a discovery might do to the four recipients of his parcels. But education was important, self-improvement was more important than anything else in a person's life, he kept telling himself, and he was doing his fieldwork to help those four on the road to self-improvement. The importance of that had to be weighed against the potential hazard of being discovered and besides, he kept telling himself, there were always tasks and duties in life, too many tasks and duties in life that he felt uncomfortable about but they were the ones that had to be done and so he did them, without complaint and without moaning and that was not only because he had no one to complain to, no one to moan in front of, but that was because he was not a moaning person; he was not a complaining person, for what good would that have done to him had he been a moaning or a complaining person? Perhaps Victor could do that, perhaps Victor was like that, that man he had known once but now Victor was dead, Victor was buried in an unmarked grave and what good was his moaning or complaining now? But perhaps this is giving the wrong impression about Pavel for not only had Pavel not needed to push himself, to remind himself of what he believed in, he was also pressing on regardless of any need for moaning, regardless of any need for complaining, regardless of any feelings of ambivalence, regardless of any fears, regardless of any close shaves, close shaves that resulted from his activities, from his necessary activities, such as that close shave in the cemetery after he had followed the family on their tour of the graves as he had done on so many previous occasions. Again, there was no point dwelling on those close shaves—each time it happened, he drew conclusions, he drew lessons from it and that was good, that was good and such an attitude helped him avoid similar situations in future—but he could not forget that episode, that particular episode had almost made him reconsider the manner of his activities or, rather, reconsider carrying out the fieldwork in the way he had been doing; but it most certainly did not make him reconsider his activities, even that close shave did not make him, for nothing would make him give up sending the parcels. For had it come to that, had it come to stopping the parcels, that would have been the end of his meaning, the end of his purpose, the end of him.

As he did that night after visiting the paper mill, he sits down and holds each album in turn, running the back of his hand across the cover. The excitement he felt then has not abated. He experiences the same anticipation of pleasure as he turns the leaves and touches the recto and verso of each. The back of his palm hovers above the textured surface, and he thinks how the beauty and pattern were created by death: pressed flowers and parts of broken butterflies and insects are worked into each side. It was this palimpsest of life and death that had attracted him in the first place, this *memento mori*, so appropriate on the pages of a photo album. It occurs to him that the albums serve to mock their user, the user who assumes that photographs are about living, the user who forgets that with each snap the subject is closer to death. That is why he keeps no photographs; he has enough of the past encroaching his memory, enough to mock him without those images that try to turn the ephemeral into the eternal. And then there is the sentimentality, the mawkishness of people melting into an irrational gooeyness as they look at family photos. But sentimentality always irritates him. Mary wasn't sentimental. Except, except perhaps when she remembered John Carleton, the young law student still genuinely in love with her like no one else had been, coming to see her in Newgate even after she had disgraced his family. A moment of weakness on her part. Comparable to his in the cemetery. He reaches a decision. He closes the album in his hand, wraps it in tissue paper and then in a wrapping sheet and does the same with the second album. He puts one in the box for the daughter of his *figlia che piange* and the other for the son. He closes the boxes and carries them to the hall, where he deposits them by the front door. First thing tomorrow, he will take them to the post office. His work for this calendar year will be done. He feels content, alone in his quiet, sparse, orderly home. He thinks how life consists of these little touches of solitude, gratifying touches of solitude, and he asks for no more.

Pavel did not know it at the time but the parcels we received at the end of December 1970 were the last. Fifteen years of parcels and then nothing. I missed them. It was exciting to have a distant, unobtrusive benefactor introducing me to new books. Pavel started me reading. What more could I have wished for from an ancestor? His gifts of Cervantes, Dostoyevsky and Kafka made me fall in love with the novel and they still form the core of my library. Oh yes, in the last parcel, one of the books was Beckett's *Krapp's Last Tape*. Even then, in my teens, I felt an affinity with the character. And as time passes and I grow older, I turn more into Krapp. Is that what Pavel would have wanted? The thought amuses me but there is no answer to that question and, in any case, I have no interest in it. The album, however, I lost somewhere on my travels. I don't know if my brother still has his copy. I have been meaning to ask him but on the rare occasions when we speak on the phone, I never do.

A COPY OF PAVEL'S DEGREE CERTIFICATE

SOCIALISTICA FOEDERATIVA RES PUBLICA IUGOSLAVIA
SOCIALISTICA RES PUBLICA CROATIA

UNIVERSITAS STUDIORUM ZAGRABIENSIS
FACULTAS PHILOSOPHICA ZAGRABIENSIS

DIPLOMA
DOCTRINAE ALTI GRADUS ADEPTAE

PAVEL HORVAT

nata die XXVI Iunii anni MCMXV Zagrabiae, in Socialistica Re Publica
Croatia, studia
HISTORIA ut disciplinae prioris (A) et

SOCIOLOGIA ut alterus disciplinae prioris (A)

per octo semestria se extendentia in hac Facultate die XIV Februarii anni MCXLIX
ad prosperum exitum perduxit.

Facultas philosophica Zagrabiensis PAVEL HORVAT omnibus
doctrinae alti gradus adipiscendae praescriptis satisfecisse et tali doctrina excultam
esse et disciplinae titulum

HISTORIAE ET SOCIOLOGIAE PROFESSOR

nec non omnia iura praescriptis inde provenientia consecutam esse confirmat.

Zagrabiae, die XV Octobris anni MCMLXXXI.

Num. IXID/MCMLXXIX

CHAPTER FOUR

The Poet

Photograph One: The Magi

An elderly man sits on a public bench with a young girl. The two are looking straight into the camera. She is smiling, probably encouraged by her father, an amateur photographer. In the manner typical of a young child, she has a finger inside her mouth. Her other hand is placed on the man's knee. She feels comfortable leaning against him. Her life is still to be lived and she is too young to imagine the difficulties that might lie ahead. Like any other two-year-old, she lives in the moment. It's a summer day (July—according to the date handwritten on the back) and she is wearing shorts, white socks, a light blouse and white ribbons in her blonde hair. She looks happy, as young children do when they have the certainty of being loved. Most likely, the picture would not have been taken had it not been for her. As the family's first child, she is the photographer's main interest . The man is thin and his woollen cardigan and tweed trousers suggest that, as is the case with older people everywhere, his aged body takes longer to feel the warmth of the

sun after the winter cold. His clothes are loose fitting; they belong to someone with more flesh on his bones. One of his hands is holding the girl's arm, the other one is visible behind her head.

The man is my grandfather, Francis Joseph. From the date on the back of the photograph I can tell that he is sixty years old and that he has recently retired from his job with a big newspaper and book publisher. He spent his entire working life with them, first as an apprentice and then as a typesetter. During that time, his employers changed the name of the company several times, surviving the social turmoil that characterized the history of that part of Europe, for centuries a buffer zone between the Christian West and the Muslim East and later, a non-aligned, socialist country squeezed between the Soviet bloc and the capitalist West. The company, and my grandfather, lived through five different states and political systems. He was born a subject of Emperor Francis Joseph I (with whom he shared both first names) and served him, as well as his successor Charles I, as a conscript in the Austro-Hungarian Army, fighting on what turned out to be the losing side. During the First World War, my grandfather was stationed in Postojna, famous for its caves, in the Carniola region that, at the time, formed part of the Province of Trieste. Later, Postojna was given to Italy but was then, as it is now, in Slovenia. Many years after the photograph was taken, I learnt that the young soldier had forged a liaison with a woman whose parents ran a guest house in Postojna and that she had become pregnant. Via an indirect contact, my grandfather discovered that the woman had given birth to a son and that after the War, she had moved to Italy. Throughout my teens, the story in the family was that the son had become a doctor, a psychiatrist. We didn't know his name, so he was always referred to as Francesco, the Italianate version of my grandfather's name. My father, who also became a doctor, was an only child and always longed to have a sibling. Sometimes he would refer to his half-brother, half joking, saying how one day he would meet his half-brother. I could not be sure how much of what was said was true and how much of it was rumour, or even wishful thinking. But I knew that my father meant it when he said how he would have loved to have met the Italian. Needless to say, to my teenage ears, the story of a long-lost uncle living in another country sounded romantic and appealing.

When I look at family photographs, especially photographs of people who are not smiling and therefore appear preoccupied, I wonder what was on their mind at the moment when the shutter opened. People who smile are posing; the smile doesn't say that they are happy but that they are aware of the photograph being taken. Other thoughts are pushed aside for a few seconds. And even if those other thoughts interfere, at the crucial moment the subject plays the required role—nothing but an image of happiness is to be preserved—and thereby actively participates in creating the photograph. I imagine that the act of smiling, even if for a split second, brings the concerns and worries that occupy the subject into an even-sharper focus: they are playing the role of happiness and content but they are torn inside, ridden with anxiety. But does it really matter since the oblivion of time will erase everything but what the photograph records. In this picture, however, my grandfather is not smiling. Why is that? I know that he loved me obsessively, more than he loved my brother who was born two years after this photograph was taken. I was his first grandchild and his only granddaughter and throughout the part of our lives that overlapped—I was almost fifteen when he died—we were close. He was the only adult who treated me as his equal and not as a child. Talking to him, I felt that my half-baked and ill-informed opinions, fuelled by youthful passion, mattered. He was the only person I knew that believed in socialism but who was critical of the so-called socialist system we lived in and openly spoke of the ruling party's betrayal of the ideals of social justice. His enthusiasm appealed to my young, idealistic self who dreamt of changing the world. Perhaps our love for each other was based on our shared interest in politics and lust for reading; or perhaps it was the other way around and I only became interested in politics because I valued our long discussions, often based on the moral dilemmas faced by contemporary politicians.

When I was five, my mother returned to full-time work and my younger brother and I attended nurseries and after-school clubs but whenever we were ill our grandparents looked after us. From the age of eight to ten, I suffered from various illnesses, such as jaundice, and spent long periods, for weeks on end, living with my grandparents. During that time, I developed the habit of listening to the extended, three o'clock radio news bulletin. My grandfather and I sat side by side next to his black Bakelite set. It was a serious occasion that required our full concentration. We sat still; there was no question of either of us doing anything else, certainly not eating or drinking. My brother was not allowed in the room. We didn't speak until the broadcast was over and Grandfather switched off the radio. It is likely that I became an avid reader because I wanted to be like my grandfather: later in life, when I started drinking Lapsang souchong tea, which I disliked at first but drank because I read somewhere that it was Samuel Beckett's favourite tea, I realized that sometimes love leads us to change our interests and tastes because loving someone may encourage us to fashion ourselves in their image and in the process we acquire particular habits and develop interests similar to the subject of our admiration. It was with Grandfather Francis, and not with my parents, who were far too busy making a living, and far too cynical to think of changing the world, that I learnt to appreciate the life of the mind.

On the occasion the picture was taken, I am sure that my grandfather was glad to be with me, as he was, I imagine, on all other occasions. During the first few years of my life, we lived in a small provincial town, where my father had reluctantly accepted his first post (for reasons that I do not wish to go into at this stage as they do not concern this story), in an area almost 900 kilometres from the capital where he grew up and where my grandparents lived. With poor roads and slow trains, it was an exhausting, two-day journey each way, whether travelling by car, as we did, or by public transport, as my grandparents did. The picture was taken during the week my father's parents came to stay with us for the first time, and I, their long-awaited grandchild, would have been the main purpose of the visit and the main recipient of the gifts they would have brought: the tinned frankfurters that I liked as a child and that were not available in the area, the educational toys and books that Grandfather wanted me to have and the clothes that Grandmother would have made for me. The last time they had seen me would have been a year earlier when I was six months old and when my mother and I left the capital to join my father in the provinces. My grandparents' visit would have been a joyful occasion for all of us and for my grandparents in particular; they were retired and our well-being was the main reason for their happiness.

Perhaps my grandfather is not smiling because he belonged to an era when taking pictures was an event that had to be planned, a time-consuming ritual that required dressing in your Sunday best and making a trip to a photographer's studio, where you assumed a dignified pose and a solemn expression, often next to a prop and in front of a curtain. It was a performance not to be taken lightly. Its purpose was to preserve an image of the subject for posterity or to record an important event. Once the camera was taken out of the photographer's studio and held by a non-professional, the act became commonplace and lost its gravity but the subject still retained the formality of its posture. These days, with the onset of digital cameras and mobile phones, the everydayness and indeed everymomentness of the images, the sheer quantity we can produce at no cost or consideration for running out of film, have made taking pictures as trivial and inconsequential as the instant they capture. Since you do not need to make an effort to take a picture and can erase it with a click, the act is too mundane, too banal to merit a serious expression. We pose all the time and we smile to pose.

From the year the photograph was taken, I also know that a few months earlier, my grandfather had undergone an operation for a gastric ulcer. Part of his stomach had been removed and he had lost a great deal of weight; people said that he had started to look older than his years. For the rest of his life he will maintain his fragile appearance. The sudden change in his physique, together with the necessity to retire and decrease his political involvement—he was an active trade unionist throughout his career—would have brought home to him his approaching mortality and might have contributed to the solemn expression.

I am now older than my grandfather is in the picture and perhaps that is why when I look at it, I feel a greater affinity with him than with the girl. The two-year old that I was then, and of whom I have no direct memory, is so far removed from how I see myself today that I think of her not only as another person but also a stranger I have never met. I know the story that she will live but I do not know who she is at the time of the picture. When I look at the two people sitting next to each other, with fifty-eight years between them, what strikes me most is the juxtaposition of the carefree outlook and the pensive countenance; the contrast between the girl's light, summer clothes and the man's heavy winter attire; and, most importantly, the juxtaposition of youth and old age. To me, a secular member of the Judaeo-Christian culture, the last of these is the central theme of all the representations of the Magi, of the myriad paintings, sculptures and tapestries that visualize one of the legendary moments of the New Testament. This ubiquitous image of the three kings, the three wise men—often represented as old—bearing gifts for the baby, the image of the celebration of the birth of the son of God, for an atheist like me, is entirely about secular concerns, namely, death and the passage of time. The moment is not about the baby but about the kings. This interpretation gains strength when you consider the conventional representation of the baby: unreal, like a plump plastic doll, often with adult features compressed to small size, as if the artist has no interest in him. In fact, the baby/the plastic doll, is no more than a prop that allows the kings to recognize that their lives are coming to an end. They are thinking: I was like that once and look what has become of me. And what have I got to show for my life? I can give presents, I have material wealth; but I am old, I will die soon. I hear them asking: Will there be anything else left after me? In other words, prompted by the presence of the baby, the wise men are taking stock and that brings a fear of what is to come. The same apprehension is passed on to us, the viewers. With them, we ask, like the King in Eliot's 'Journey of the Magi' whether our life, our efforts, our worries and concerns, whether they were all worth it? And perhaps, some of us come to the point in our lives when, again like Eliot's King, we can no longer be sure what it was all about, whether we were 'led all that way for/Birth or Death?'

Nowhere is the pathos of the kings' realization expressed more directly and more poignantly than in Leonardo da Vinci's *Adoration of the Magi*, which hangs in the Uffizi in Florence. Although, in this 1481 painting, the Madonna and the baby are in the centre of the composition, as convention demanded, the tone of the picture is set by the other figures. The baby's cherub face and full body contrast with the emaciated countenances of the three aged kings, kneeling in the foreground. Their skull-like heads are an unmistakable *memento mori*. This is a picture about death, a reminder of the transience of life, a visual representation of the inevitable ravages of time, rather than the celebration of a birth. The effect is enhanced by the surrounding figures, all of whom, with one exception, are writhing in an hallucinatory background next to an architectural ruin. Thought to be a self-portrait, the exception is looking away from the scene, as if Leonardo is distracting himself from the mayhem. The contorted bodies, holes instead of eyes, knotted fingers and hands raised in sharp gesture, like lunatics dancing in an asylum, all contribute to the nightmarish quality of the image. The final touch is provided by the lack of colour: the scene is bathed in red/deep orange, a late sunset light that makes us feel that the action takes place in a phantasmagorical haze. This is the picture that says: Look at us, the old kings, our lives are spent; you may be young now but like the buildings behind us, you will not endure; one day you will end up as old as we are. And then, like us, you will be down on your knees and you too will despair. Only art is immortal.

Since it is in the nature of interpretation that it comes from the reader—or the viewer in this case—I cannot attribute such sacrilegious thoughts to the painter. However, for me, Leonardo's canvas has a secular meaning that directly undermines the Christian doctrine of the purpose of Creation and the existence of an afterlife.

In the bench photograph, my grandfather's face is thin but not emaciated (that will happen thirteen years later, when he dies in hospital from the tuberculosis that had lain dormant in his body since his youth) but even in this picture, the occasion of his journey to adore the baby, the contrast between our faces and our body language is telling. I have nothing to think about beyond the present. Having my picture taken is a playful moment. I have put my feet up, a finger in my half-open mouth. My pose is erratic, casual. As much as the baby Jesus in countless representations of the Magi, my two-year-old self is a prop, a reminder for him, if reminding he needs, and for me now, the viewer, older than him at the time, of the scourge of time and our approaching deaths.

My grandfather is holding my hand and his upper arm is gripping my cardigan which I would have had taken off earlier. His body is tense, wiry. He knows the picture is being taken—he is looking into the camera—but his thoughts travel beyond the moment. He knows the score and his body is beginning to make it harder for him to push it to the back of his mind. Prompted by my youth, he too, like the three wise men in the Leonardo, may be looking over his life and taking stock. He had lived through two world wars: in the first as a conscript, in the second, a deserter from the army of a state supporting the Nazis and, as an anti-fascist activist, captured and sentenced to death by hanging. I remember him telling me how he escaped from prison towards the end of the war in the confusion created by the terrified guards joining the fleeing Germans, and how he stayed in hiding until the liberation a few weeks later. And I remember the stories about his trade-union activism (campaigning for better health-and-safety regulations for the members working with lead), his conviction about the need for free education ('That is what makes us enlightened people,' he said), and his belief in a fair distribution of wealth ('There is no civilized society without it.'). I remember his stories because that is how I came to share his ideas. Sitting next to me on the bench, solemn and pensive he may be, like Leonardo's kings, thinking about the future and the inevitable, imminent end.

Grandfather Francis believed in the power of the Enlightenment and in human progress both in public life and on a personal level. He thought it was cause for optimism that his life was better than his father's and that his son's was an improvement on his own. One day I heard him say to my father: 'My grandfather worked for the railways, I was only a printer and typographer and you became a doctor, a consultant. Who knows what my granddaughter will do. The sky's the limit for her.' He was wrong there but the point is that his words were optimistic, life-affirming. Leonardo's kings, however, appear dispirited to the point of cruel misanthropy. They have come to celebrate birth but all they see is death and destruction.

While my grandfather's colleagues in the trade-union movement had chauffeur-driven cars, as their rightful dues for the years of service, he insisted on using public transport. On his own initiative, he gave up the large flat which came with the position, for a smaller one: 'It's only two of us—why would we need a big place when there are people who live in cramped accommodation,' he reasoned. When he retired, he did not declare the years he had spent on anti-fascist activity, or his trade-union functions—both of which would have earned him extra points and a much bigger pension. Despite my father's objections: 'You're being foolish, everyone else looks after their retirement.'—Grandfather stuck to his guns: 'I was politically active because I believed in it. It was the right thing to do. I did not do it for personal gain. There are many people who are worse off than me.' The pension he was allocated was enough for a modest existence and he believed that in a developing country with a great deal of poverty it would have been immoral to receive more. 'Socialism means a good life for everyone,' I heard him say, 'not just for the few'. He was a *bon vivant*, used to the comforts of a bourgeois existence but he didn't mind giving them up when he believed it was for the common good. Following his ulcer operation, he was advised to drink a glass of red wine with his meals but half a bottle every day for him and his wife proved to be beyond their daily budget. His daughter-in-law, my mother, made a monthly contribution to cover the wine bill and I remember walking with him to a wine cellar down the road where they would fill his half-litre carafe from a barrel. (He never commented on who paid for the wine. In his shoes, I would have found it humiliating; he, however, felt it was better to remain loyal to his principles than worry about his dignity.)

When I was a young child, he took me on long walks around the city and every now and then we would run into an acquaintance, someone my grandfather had worked with in his youth as a young socialist or someone he knew from the anti-fascist underground, or the widow of someone hailed as a national hero, and who had a street or a school named after them, and whose name I would hear later in history lessons. They made a big fuss of seeing him and asked him to visit. Grandfather promised he would but he rarely did. On one occasion, we met an old lady outside her house and she insisted on going back in and bringing out boxes of chocolates for me ('They keep sending them to me,' she said) made by a factory that carried the name of her dead husband. Grandfather thanked her but on our next walk when I asked that we take the route past the old lady's house, he refused.

At the time the photograph on the bench was taken, prompted by the proximity of a new life, he might have looked back on his own but, unlike Leonardo's three kings, I doubt that he would have asked himself whether his journey had been worth it. He might have had regrets but his political commitment could not have been one of them. As much as the Magi representations place the baby Jesus in the centre, the photograph on the bench would have been taken because of the young child but to me today the image matters because of the old man, my Grandfather Francis, my wise man.

Photograph Two: *The Quick and the Dead*

A group of over thirty people, among them five women and four children, are posing for the camera. Some are seated, a few are crouching at the front but the majority are standing. They have gathered in an outdoor space. The top edge of a wooden fence, visible behind them, would suggest they are in a garden or a courtyard. Most of the adults appear to be in their early thirties but there is at least one much older face. Everyone is dressed in formal clothes; the men are wearing white shirts, suits and ties (several sporting bow ties) and the women are in elegant dresses, offset with pearls and clutch bags. In the same way, the children are well turned out: two of the girls are in smart white dresses and the third has an outfit with a white collar. The boy, crouching in the front row, is clad in a white sailor suit, a stylish, formal costume for young boys, especially in the 1920s and 30s, a fashion that was started by Queen Victoria's son Edward and soon spread across the continent, to Germany in particular, where it persisted well into the 50s. All the faces, except for those of one man and one girl, are serious, even solemn. Most of them are looking out, clearly posing. The frontality of the composition does not encourage communication between the people and the overall impression is one of a group of lonely, isolated subjects.

The image made me recall Edouard Manet's *La Musique aux Tuileries*, a painting that was influenced by the burgeoning new art of photography. Here the painter cut off parts of the figures

standing on the edge of the group to create the impression that they were left out accidentally from the frame of the camera. However, the painting represents a very different group of people from the ones in my photograph: the fashionable Parisian crowd, *la crème de la crème* of the French bourgeoisie, dotted with a number of identifiable faces of famous artists, writers and musicians. While the presentation, with its rapid brush strokes and unfinished patches, showing the texture of the canvas, is modernist in that it brings attention to the artist's technique, when it comes to the people represented, *plus ça change*: they are members of the class that has traditionally been the subject of oil portraits.

The *Tuileries* composition is a pastiche, a self-conscious imitation of a photograph and thereby it connects the old, bourgeois art of oil painting with the new, more democratic, more accessible art

made possible by the invention and spreading popularity of the camera. In that way, the painting expands the Manet project of becoming the painter of modern life. While the art of photography privileges its subject over the photographer, with painting, our interest is mainly focused on the artist. However, among the subjects of the *Tuileries* are celebrated artists and, therefore, the viewer is as interested in them as if they were the subjects of a photograph. Besides, the canvas is forward-looking in its wish to announce in a new era. Or at least, that is what we are meant to believe.

The pretensions of the photograph are very different. As much as the painting fakes its modernity, the picture of my grandfather and his friends and colleagues forges an image of relaxed, leisurely affluence. It aims to say: We are ordinary, working men and women but we aspire to better ourselves. Their smart clothes, starched and well ironed, belie the fact that most of them would have had no maids to do their laundry (essential help in well-to-do households at the time).

The boy in the sailor suit is my father and, since he appears to be four or five years old, the photograph must date back to 1929 or 1930. The woman sitting behind my father is his mother, my Grandmother Maria, and the man crouching to my father's right is his father, my Grandfather Francis. At the time, Francis would have been the leader of the local printers' union which regularly organized Sunday excursions for members and their families. The photograph was taken on one such occasion, which would have meant a trip to the countryside or a nearby small town by a tram or train, lunch at a local inn, followed by a constitutional. The people in the photograph represent a class that was socially mobile and their smart clothes, as well as Sunday lunch out, testify to that mobility. My grandfather, unlike my grandmother, came from a poor, working-class background, but he, like the other people in the photograph, can afford a comfortable lifestyle. He and his wife employ a home help (they do not use the word *maid*), their son is about to attend a prestigious, private school (although not themselves religious, they register as Lutherans in order to make him eligible for education in a German establishment) and from the age of seven he will start his violin lessons.

Francis is a socialist: he works hard, campaigns for workers' rights and believes that everyone has the right to a job and fair pay. He reads Marx in German and is intrigued by the philosopher's concept of alienation: 'That was a revelation, the equivalent of a secular epiphany,' he told me many years later. 'I could see it everywhere around me,' he said, 'but I didn't know what it was, disillusionment, laziness even. I had no name for it at the time.' He tries to address the problem. And as a result of his campaigns, he and his printer colleagues have the right to free newspapers and books. 'A worker should have access to his products—owning what he makes should never be beyond his means. We must not allow workers to be alienated from what they make,' he argues. (I am a reminded of his words from time to time when a checkout assistant in a supermarket picks up a packet of artichokes or an exotic fruit from the pile I have emptied from my trolley and asks me what it is, making me aware that perhaps it is not something they can afford.) Francis loves the company of like-minded people and, over good food and wine, he and his colleagues discuss their understanding of socialism. His view is that everyone should have a decent standard of living and that regardless of the society's wealth, the income ratio between the highest and the lowest paid should not be more than five, at the most, ten. The Sunday trips are occasions to exchange ideas and to raise the group's political awareness. (My father, the boy in a sailor suit, grows up in the middle of all that, absorbs the politics at an early age and, while throughout his life he is never politically active, at seventeen he is sufficiently aware to desert the fascist army of the 1941 Croatian puppet state within weeks of conscription.) 'Sunday is for leisure,' Francis says, but that leisure should have an educational aspect. The social activities he organizes provide him with yet more opportunities to mitigate the feeling of alienation that a worker must experience in a capitalist system.

The occasion on which the picture was taken would no doubt have been enjoyable and the company would have been cheerful. The people in the picture had the same social backgrounds and would have had similar ethnic and cultural origins. Moreover, they would have been united by their trade and their political orientation. They belonged to each other in more ways than one. Their demeanour, their clothes and facial expressions confirm that commonality and yet it seems to me that all of them, except the man who is smiling and leaning on the shoulder of my grandfather, the only man without a tie, the odd one out, are isolated, living in their own world, not communicating with one another. It is not only my grandmother, whose face suggests a deep reverie (but that is another story), or my father, who concentrates on the small toy he is holding, who seem to be alone in their own world. Everyone else, and particularly those who are looking straight out, challenging our gaze, appear thoughtful, as if they have something heavy on their minds. Perhaps, the discussion had been heated, perhaps they had been trying to understand one of Marx's more subtle ideas or perhaps they have been exchanging views about the world economic crisis, the Depression, from which these citizens of a new, rather poor, mostly agricultural country, in a pre-globalized world, appear to be strangely protected. Despite their physical proximity, united by the occasion and their shared values and aspirations, their serious demeanour, formal clothes and serene countenance isolate them from one another. That is certainly not the effect produced by the Manet painting where the figures are in a whirl of dizzy social intercourse. They are looking out, the composition is frontal, and yet, these people are together, communicating with one another.

Perhaps the contrast between the two images is enhanced by the nature of the media: photographs, unlike paintings, freeze a moment in the flow of time; in the process, they separate their subjects and emphasize their solitude. That was particularly true of the photographs at the time when the slowness of the film required that the subjects remained still for several seconds: the man with the broad smile would have had to hold it for an unnaturally long time. Even the position of his body would have been possible only for someone with strong leg muscles. Paradoxically, although the *Tuileries* canvas shows people interacting with each other, Manet painted each figure from a model in a separate sitting, most likely in his studio (although there is some speculation that he chose a relatively small canvas, uncommon for the genre, so that he could work *en plein air*) but his painting technique allowed him to create an image of movement and interaction. Looking at the *Tuileries*, we can almost hear the music, certainly the bustle of the crowd, the swishing of their expensive silks, and the murmur of their speech. But in the photograph, everyone is silent, alone with their thoughts.

In each of the images, the people are presented to the viewer as if they were on stage. With Manet, the Parisian bourgeoisie is attending an open-air concert, a fashionable and popular event where members of this class wanted to see and be seen by the other members of the same class and, while not all of them are facing the viewer, those who challenge the viewer's gaze do so in a manner that is typical of the painter's best-known canvases, such as *Le déjeuner sur l'herbe* and *Olympia*. These figures stand facing out frontally or sideways, as if they were posing for a photograph. In that way, the canvas is reminiscent of the early conventions of photographic portraiture. We, the viewers, are placed in the orchestra pit, and are therefore the object of the gaze of those presented, quite as much as they are the object of our gaze. As in the photograph, we are looking at them and they are looking at us, raising the question as to who is the subject and who is the object?

The people in *La Musique aux Tuileries* lived under the Second Empire. Despite all the difficulties of the reign of Napoleon III, and the rise of Prussia that was soon to threaten France and bring about the Commune with its associated hardship and social devastation, in 1860s, and for most of the nineteenth century, Paris was the cultural capital of Europe and, consequently, of the world. We are looking at the most privileged section of that society, economically prosperous, culturally confident. Although Manet's brushstrokes and composition make him the first modern painter, the *Tuileries* canvas shows us an old, decadent world, with a class whose whole *raison d'être* is to be on display. Note the cream-coloured trousers of many of the male figures; in those days, the colour was worn only by those who did not wash their clothes themselves. The women, too, wear sophisticated dresses which required careful maintenance and therefore signified wealth and social status. Here the class members turn themselves into objects of admiration and envy; even their casualness is carefully posed. The world is in motion but those that Manet portrays would prefer it to remain static. And while Manet, with his impeccable aristocratic pedigree (his mother was a godchild of the King of Sweden and his father, a judge, came from a wealthy family of judges, a family with an extensive estate), belongs at the top of that class, the *Tuileries* and several of his other paintings arguably reveal a more progressive politics of vision. He doesn't shy away from acknowledging his own class identity: he includes a self-portrait in the crowd and places his brother in the centre of the composition. At the same time, Manet creates an image that allows us to judge the world he represents as a world of leisure that has lost its *joie de vivre*, and has replaced it with *ennui*. The wealthy and the privileged, dressed in their finest, are listening to a concert but there is no indication of pleasure on their faces. Rather, they are on display and bored; note the two female figures in the foreground. They are not the subjects of their own lives; instead, they are turned into objects to be stared at.

The people in the photograph, however, are working men and women, citizens of a new age, their minds preoccupied by the world around them; they aim to be the subjects, active participants in the shaping of their present and their future. Their confidence and their place in society do not come from their family backgrounds but from their individual achievements, specifically from their trade and from the political awareness that they are developing during their Sunday outings.

No one can fail to be aware of the passage of time and the inevitability of death when looking at a photograph, particularly an old one. You see into the past, and with an image taken over eighty years ago, the mortality of those represented screams only too loudly. They were out on a day trip, they have just eaten their lunch and they are posing in their Sunday best. They have worries and hopes, desires and regrets, and yet all of those now seems insignificant as they are all dead, certainly all the adults. It is just possible that one, or perhaps both, of the girls are still alive, in their late eighties or early nineties. The boy in the sailor suit died seven years ago, aged eighty-six.

But why is it that when I see a vintage photograph, my first thought is that everyone in it must be dead? And why don't I have such thoughts when I look at the faces in an old painting? In the case of the images above, it may partly be to do with the fact that I knew and loved three of the people in the photograph, whereas, despite admiring Manet and Baudelaire whose portrait appears in the *Tuileries*, I know them only through their work and that, as long as it means something to me, cannot die. But I also think that my morbid thoughts are intimately connected with the genre and its attempt to stop time, to preserve the life of the living, a goal in which photography inevitably fails. The paradox is that a painter can make a painting of those who are dead and present them as living, while a photographer usually snaps those who are living but the product reminds us of death, or at least the passage of time.

Why was the picture taken? Why is any picture taken? A record of the group's activities perhaps but more importantly as proof of the occasion, tangible evidence to support the memory of the event. They had a day out, good or not, but they were going to remember it as good and the photograph will help them do so. My Grandfather Francis is in the centre of the picture and the fact that he is crouching might suggest that he, who would have organized the trip, might have also played a part in the way the individuals arranged themselves for the photograph. He might have been standing next to the photographer and gesturing to the people, all of whom he knew very well, to move to one side or the other, before he rushed back and knelt in front of them.

Why am I looking at the photograph? Because I want to see those who formed me in more ways than genetically. But also, looking at a photograph taken more than eighty years ago trains me to, if not quite accept, to try to come to terms with the passage of time and my own mortality. Manet's painting offers no help there: yes, it is fixed in time but the genre allows me to ignore the fact that the time of the Tuileries concert is more than a century and a half ago.

A final thought: as much as Manet tries to imitate the art of photography in his painting, mainly in its composition, the photograph of my grandfather's colleagues and their families after their Sunday lunch, has stylistic elements of an Impressionist painting, albeit by default: the girl in the middle and a man to the left did not keep still enough for the long exposure and their features are blurred beyond recognition. Similarly, some of the men's faces on the far right are out of focus, as if a painter had quickly sketched them, in the manner of Manet and his contemporaries. While this would have clearly been regarded a technical failure on the part of the photographer, I find it charming, precisely because it amuses me to think of it as a photograph imitating a painting. But this is a reading made possible only by the vantage point of the modern digital age, where computer software allows us to do so by distorting the crystalline precision of the photographic image and turning it into the imitation of a painting, thereby blurring the differences between the genres.

Photograph Three: Happy Birthday

A group of men and women are celebrating. At the point the picture is taken, the festivities have been going on for some time and everyone seems to have had a few drinks; four of the men look as if they have literally drunk themselves under the table. A white cloth covers the long table which holds bottles and carafes of wine, vases with flowers and a cake stand. The men are wearing white shirts, some with ties, others without—they might have taken them off— and their top buttons are undone. The woman right in the middle of the table has an elegant dark dress with a white collar and pearls. Some of the faces are smiling, a few are looking out with no defined expression, others seem to be unaware of the photograph being taken. The group are posing and the photographer, whose intention must be to capture the moment, has arranged them so that everyone is facing the camera. The atmosphere is cheerful. There

are decorations on the wall—hanging ivy?—and a poster in the middle, partially hidden by a man standing in front of it, wishing 'happy birthday'. From another picture, taken a year later in the same place which shows more of the space they are occupying, I can tell that they have gathered in a private room at an inn. A handwritten note on the back of this picture records the date as 1937.

The composition is frontal, as if the men and women were on stage, under a proscenium arch, facing the audience. While the four men on the floor may be drunk, and are therefore finding it easier to keep their balance on the floor, it is possible that they have just moved there in order to face the photographer and to avoid blocking the camera's view of the people sitting on the other side of the table. Or, it is possible that a more posed and ordered picture has already been taken and that the men stayed on the floor as their state of inebriation made it difficult for them to stand up. Perhaps, the photographer is catching the group in an unguarded moment, when some of them think the picture has already been taken.

This is not a large gathering but several stories seem to be unfolding.

Let us look at the four men on the floor. My Grandfather Francis is holding a carafe in one hand and a glass in another, as if to make sure he has a steady supply of wine. His expression is blurred; he does not seem capable of focusing on anything beyond his own world. But I know that this is not a one-off bout of drunkenness where he has forgotten himself and had too much at a jolly celebration. He is forty years old and by this stage of his life he has a drink problem, and not a simple drink problem: on paydays, he invites all his work colleagues who are willing to join him at the inn and he treats them. Not just to one or two glasses but as many as they can manage and alcohol flows until his money runs dry. When he goes home, his pockets are empty. His wife is used to a comfortable lifestyle but she does not complain. Instead, she accepts help from her family who run a successful upholstery business.

As Francis' habit continues, Maria becomes more and more self-reliant. Although, he goes out to work, she is the breadwinner. She attended a textile and design school out of interest; a woman of her background was not expected to work for a living. Maria makes her own and her son's clothes because it gives her pleasure and she is exceptionally good at it. She is always well turned out and aware of people's sartorial style. (In my early teens, I remember her commenting on a neighbour, saying she looked sloppy and had no dress sense.) Tall, with an enviable figure, she stays slim throughout her life and people often comment on her elegance. Her trademark style is a white collar, lace or embroidered, on a dark, fitted dress. Skirts have folds and reach under the knee. But with Francis drinking away his salary, not only does her hobby become a necessity but Maria also has to take orders for soft furnishings, mainly curtains and armchair covers, from her father and brothers. She becomes their freelance but regular employee. No doubt this arrangement has implications for their marriage, on how Maria and Francis relate to each other. I imagine that Francis could find his wife's silence, her acceptance of his behaviour, her choice to address the problem of family finances on her own, frustrating. (But lest anyone accuse me of taking his side, let me say that this is Francis' story and that is why I am primarily thinking of his feelings. Besides, no outsider, let alone one like me, so far removed by time, can tell what goes on in a marriage.) He must wonder why she doesn't talk to him. Why doesn't she raise the issue of his drinking, his unacceptable, irresponsible behaviour? I know that their son is closer to his mother and once Maria isolates herself in her own world, earning a living and carrying on as if there were no problem, the vicious circle is established: Francis feels increasingly lonely at home and seeks the company of his friends even more often than before. Perhaps that makes him turn to drink more regularly. He starts living for paydays when he can enjoy the company of those to whom he matters.

In this picture, I can recognize several of the faces from Photograph Two: Francis' trade union colleagues, the people he valued and yet, he seems to be isolated from them, too far into his world of drink to be able to partake in the general conviviality. But perhaps we should not draw too many conclusions from Francis' appearance; the photographer might have captured a moment of my grandfather's pensiveness or a moment when, for some indeterminate reason, Francis' eyes have a look of absence, a moment when Francis was thinking about something that is going on in the wider world. And plenty is going on. The fact that the two men on Francis' right project a different image, happily sharing a drink and enjoying each other's company, should not fool us. Some people find it easier than others to enjoy the moment and forget their troubles. Similarly, the man on his left is interacting with the group at the table. None of the men appears as alone as Francis.

Like him, the two women at the party seem isolated, secluded in their own worlds. Maria, his wife and my grandmother, is sitting directly behind him, right at the centre of the table. If this were an image of *The Last Supper*, she would occupy the seat of Christ but I am not going to pursue a narrative of betrayal and identify Francis with Judas. That would be too simplistic. But it is Francis' drinking and the financial consequences of his behaviour that invite the comparison. The added factor is that he was known to be popular with women—a euphemism my parents used. At some point, most likely several years before this picture was taken, Maria had an abortion. He was saddened when he found out but he didn't make a scene. From what I have heard, it is unlikely he would have had anyone to confide in. His feelings remained private. But Maria must have had good reasons not to want more children. Her termination spoke about her feelings towards Francis and their marriage; he must have understood that.

Here she is smiling, her attention caught by something to the photographer's left, her eyes looking awkwardly to the side. The only other woman in the group is next to her (there seems to be another woman present to the far left, or the right of the picture but her face is not visible; only an elbow and part of her skirt can be seen) but the two of them appear locked in their own worlds, cut off from the rest of the party. Maybe Maria feels uneasy with the trade unionists, the men drinking with her husband, the men spending the time he could spend with his family, and the men who know his philandering secrets. (In my teens, I came across a caricature of Francis that one of his mates had drawn, a cartoon my parents said would have been circulated among the group. It shows my grandfather with a padlock on his underpants, looking at a diminutive woman, dressed in high heels and a bathing costume who is standing in his palm. The caption is written in rhyme, and it says that Francis is suffering because he is having problems reaching his 'stuff' and therefore 'unable to score'. In his other hand, he is holding a string with a ball of a type used with skittles which are scattered on the floor. Perhaps the suggestion was that with the ball he will be able to break the lock and achieve his aim.)

I am not aware of Maria's politics at the time but I know that her family did not approve of Francis' socialism; indeed, they were opposed to her marrying a man they thought of both as too poor and too leftwing; later, they could have added his drinking. When I was a child, on one of our visits to a cemetery, my parents pointed out a large tomb made out of black marble, much grander than the surrounding graves, as if in death, too, the owner wished to flaunt

his status as a wealthy person, and told me that it belonged to the man that Grandmother Maria had been supposed to marry. From his dates, I could see that he was a generation older than Maria. He was a friend of her father's, my parents said, and very rich. I can see that a strong, independently minded woman like her would have gone against her parents' wishes but having done so and chosen Francis, Maria would have been too proud to complain to them about him.

While Maria sports an awkward smile, the woman, sitting next to her is glum, as if bored by the proceedings. Clearly, this is a men's gathering, a loud, drinking party and no wonder the women feel excluded. But why is Maria present at this celebration? To keep an eye on her husband? From what I remember and from what I heard about her, this would have been unlikely. Or perhaps, she is making an effort to become part of his social circle. How come she ends up sitting right in the middle of the party? Or, it is possible that in this predominantly male group, the two women might have been the focus of attention and could have been offered the best seats, as demanded by the chivalric mores of the time. Maria is an attractive woman, cultured and educated, fluent in German, well read and sociable. However, she had little contact with men coming from poorer backgrounds.

Maria would not have lacked male attention but there are no family stories about possible affairs. Knowing what she was like, I cannot think she would have taken a lover. Not that she was a prude, not even by the standards of my generation, or that she was constrained by prohibition to remain faithful. Rather, she was a woman who directed her energies and passions towards her dress-making and her son, and later in life, his family. If anything, she was resilient and self-reliant and, whatever difficulties she would have faced, she coped on her own, carrying the pain she felt deep inside her.

But while the two women and Francis appear lonely, other members of the group give the impression of enjoying themselves. The man to Francis' left is sporting an impromptu party hat made of newspaper. The four men standing behind the table, leaning against the wall, look well oiled and two of them have arms around each other. At the table, to Maria's left, five men are laughing, one is holding up a glass, another chewing on his pipe; they, more than the rest, are happy and relaxed, enjoying the camaraderie, without appearing too far gone. But who could tell what is going on in the lives of these people beyond their work and political activity?

Perhaps they are drinking out of desperation at the events of 1937 and of the preceding years.

We must remember that Francis and his colleagues are typesetters, working for a large publishing company and that, thanks to his campaigns, they have free daily newspapers and the occasional perk of a newly published book. They are well informed and politicized. These days it may seem unusual for people to meet socially to discuss current affairs, let alone to exchange views on Marx on a Sunday outing or at a birthday party. With my generation and especially with those coming after me, exposing our private lives, turning them into public display on Facebook, seems to have replaced discussions of political issues. Similarly, in the media, there has been a shift of emphasis from public and political issues to the superficial; some people become famous only because of the vagaries of their private lives. My grandfather's generation had a greater distinction between private and public life; I cannot imagine Francis talking to his friends and colleagues about his family or about his personal problems. Two other common topics of social conversation these days, sport and TV, are not available to Francis. Like everyone else in my family, Francis had no interest in sport and I don't remember him ever making any reference to it. (That may be one of the reasons why I grew up to regard spectator sport, as well as sports journalism, as firmly belonging to the second part of the *panem et circenses* phrase, or even less kindly, to associate such pursuits with the lack of intellectual acumen.) And since there was no TV to provide a common topic for conversation, Francis and his friends exchange views on what is going on in the world immediately around them and in the world at large. With their political environment as precarious as ever, there is a great deal to discuss. They are only in their late thirties or early forties but they are the citizens of a country that has changed its name, borders and political system three times in living memory. And in

1937, on the brink of the Second World War, Europe is already in flames. The Spanish Civil War has been waging for a year and with the direct involvement of Germany and Italy on the side of Franco, my grandfather and his fellow socialists are considering how to support the Republicans. They collect money and some of them join the international brigades. (I remember as a young child going for walks with Grandfather Francis and sometimes, after we had greeted one of his old friends, he would tell me that the man was a Spanish veteran. It didn't mean anything to me at the time but I heard the admiration in his voice.) In Paris, workers come out on general strike and Francis and his trade unionists, who themselves have resorted to downing their tools when necessary, would have marvelled at such action that paralysed a major European city. In Germany, Chancellor Hitler is consolidating his grip on power as he announces the need for more 'living space' for the German people. Within months he will declare the Anschluss of Austria which means that Nazi Germany becomes the next-door neighbour to the country where my grandparents live. In America, the Depression is still affecting the lives of millions and in July, Roosevelt signs the New Deal. And as Francis and his friends gather to celebrate a birthday in the middle of such political turmoil, and world peace teeters precariously, they wonder how many of them would be in jobs at the time of the next celebration and, indeed, how many of them would still be alive. Why not be merry and drink yourself to oblivion?

But perhaps Francis was thinking of something more personal, such as his inability to sing, a skill that would have been much admired at a social gathering such as this one. His wife Maria had a beautiful voice and was very musical. She sang around their home; she sang with friends but he could not hold a tune and it made him sad. 'There is a whole world of pleasure,' he told me many years later, 'that is unavailable to people like you and me.' At the time, we would have been remembering the four years, from when I was eight: every Wednesday afternoon he would take me to solfeggio classes in a private school that claimed their method had already helped many tone-deaf children. I knew within weeks that it would not work for me but did not dare give up and was relieved when my parents agreed that there was no point carrying on. Francis, too, was relieved. He said he had felt sorry for me but didn't wish to prejudge the outcome and it was worth a try. 'I hoped that you might not suffer in the same way I did.'

Whether, when the picture was taken, he was pensive or drunk, thinking about his inability to sing, worrying about the way the world was going, or all of that—such possibilities are part of the image of my Grandfather Francis that contributes to my memory of who he was. When he was widowed and lived alone, I was thirteen and went to see him once a week. I would watch him make us coffee in the kitchen—an elaborate ritual as he meticulously measured spoonfuls of coffee into a pot (Prufrock-like measuring his life?)—and then carry it on a tray with a plate of biscuits to the lounge, where we would sit at the table and talk about the political events of the week. He never said it but I could tell that he was pleased to see me so well informed. Often he would illustrate his interpretation of what was happening by reference to events in his youth and that is how I learnt about his life and political activity. Surprisingly, once he even mentioned the woman who had been pregnant by him and said that she had been in touch and wanted him to come and stay with her. I thought it was lovely and romantic but my cynical parents dismissed it as a fantasy of a lonely old man, trying to come to terms with the sins of his youth.

We continued our coffee afternoons for two years until he became ill and spent the last month of his life in hospital. Unlike his son, my father, let alone my brother, I felt I was a confidante, most likely the only confidante Grandpa Francis had in the final stage of his life. On my last visit to his flat, I was about to leave and was standing in the hall, my coat buttoned up, when he asked me to wait and disappeared into his bedroom. He came back carrying a faded envelope. 'This is for you,' he said. I pulled out three small volumes of poetry, printed on beautiful paper. The pale yellow cover carried the words: Poems of Lost Souls. There was no name of the poet. I asked him whose they were and he said they had been written by a colleague of his; someone who was no longer around. They had set and printed them together, working after the end of their shifts. There was only one copy of each collection, he added, and he wanted me to have them. 'No one has ever seen them and I think you would be the right reader for them,' he said. 'I am sure my friend would like you to be his reader, his only reader.' And then somewhat casually, half-laughing, he added: 'Let's say he wrote them for you.'

I asked him whether he ever wanted to write. He said no. I asked him why. 'I had nothing to say', he replied.

I took them home and something told me, I cannot remember whether it was to do with the style of the poetry or whether it was just a hunch, that the secret poet was my Grandfather Francis. As I read them, I thought that oblique reference to emotional pain, loneliness and desperation of the unnamed speaker belied the image I had of my grandfather: popular, sociable and confident. The memory of the conversation we had when he gave me the volumes was vivid but, as time passed, I could not tell whether it had really taken place or whether I had dreamt it. I kept the volumes hidden, or so I thought—I didn't think my parents were the kind of people who would appreciate them and worried that they might make fun of Grandfather Francis as they had made fun of his story that the woman from his youth had waited for him until he was single again. Besides, my parents thought that only young people in love wrote poetry. In their minds, being a poet was a phase of adolescence. For years I imagined that the slim collections were lying on a shelf under the jumpers in my wardrobe. When I was about to leave the country, for a year initially, I didn't think of taking them with me. But I never returned and, when my parents moved, some of my books were given away or taken by my brother and his then wife. When I asked about the three slim volumes, my parents were certain that there had been nothing under the jumpers in my wardrobe. But I know that they existed. I remember holding them. The paper felt beautiful to the touch. I remember reading the lines, savouring the words, marvelling at the rhymes. Besides, my Grandfather Francis was a dreamer, a fantasist, a lover of words, a seeker of beauty. For me, that's enough of a proof to believe that he was a poet, even if his poems are lost.

Photograph Four: Love and Other Affairs

A group of men and women have gathered around an L-shaped table covered with a white cloth. There are plates of food and bottles of alcohol. A row of coats hangs on the wall behind them. The year is 1938 and the people are in their late thirties or early forties. An older couple, that is, a corpulent, bald man in a dark jumper and an equally ample woman, wearing an apron and a dress with rolled-up sleeves, are sitting in front of the table, to the side of the composition. The man looks stern, with narrowed eyes but the woman is smiling in a friendly, relaxed manner. The group has gathered in an inn and the older couple are probably the innkeepers who would have been invited to join the group for the picture. Most likely the partygoers are regulars and friendly with the owners.

My Grandfather Francis stands at the back in the far-left corner of the picture. Like most photographs of Francis' social life, this

picture shows him in the company of trade-union activists and colleagues. He is wearing a white, open-neck shirt. He holds a cigarette in one hand while the other is resting on the shoulder of the woman in front of him and is touching her bare skin. He is in his early forties and she seems considerably younger. It does not look as if he has placed his hand there casually, just for the photograph. I cannot tell whether the woman is leaning against him but I can see that she has raised her arm and has placed her hand over his, clearly responding to his gesture. Maria, Francis' wife, is not in the picture. Both Francis and the woman are looking straight out; her lips are slightly parted as in an incipient smile and he is beaming. Tall and upright, he exudes confidence and has the air of a happy man. It is possible that something is going on, or is about to start, between him and the woman.

I imagine that it would have been difficult for Maria not to have some inkling of Francis' secret life and I can only speculate how hurtful she might have found the knowledge, even if his behaviour was a way of dealing with his wife distancing herself from him. It is likely that the woman in the picture is one of several that he would have been seeing. From what I have gathered about what my parents euphemistically called Francis' popularity with women, I know that there were no long-term, steady lovers. That might have been out of choice: he wouldn't have been the first person treading carefully not to become too attached to a lover to avoid jeopardizing his marriage. In any case, neither this young woman, nor any other, seems to have been sufficiently important for their names to have featured in family tales. But, apart from the cartoon where he holds a small figure of a woman in the palm of his hand, this picture is one of the few visual indications of Francis' infidelity that I have, which makes me wonder who she is and whether they are already lovers or are about to become so. At the same time, it makes me realize how insignificant such questions are in the context of the rest of my grandparents' life.

Nevertheless, the photograph is here: a record of his possible extramarital relationship, such as it was, with the woman. Would he have become careless after a few glasses of wine, unable to judge the trouble and pain such a picture could cause if it reached Maria or would he have been at a stage in his marriage when he didn't care any more and perhaps even subconsciously wished to be found out so that his wife would get the message? Those may have been big questions at the time but, almost a century later, they seem irrelevant.

Throughout the time I knew them, the time that remains in my memory—twenty-odd years after the picture was taken—they were supportive of each other in every way: if any of us criticized one of them, the other would always have something to say in defence. No one could doubt the strong bond between them. They ran their small household as a well-drilled team, sharing tasks and enjoying annual, out-of-season, seaside holidays. Maria never found fault with what my parents saw as Francis' stubbornness—or was it pride?—in refusing to sort out his pension rights and improve their financial situation. She would say they were fine and didn't need anything more although she still had to take in occasional jobs and carried on sewing curtains and armchair covers well into her late sixties. Even when she died, a couple of unfinished orders were stacked by her machine. I was too young to understand that she had to manage on a tight budget. I remember her keeping the pension money in an old wooden box with a lock but with the key always in it. Clearly, the lock was not there because she had to keep the contents safe from anyone but, I imagine, because it made the opening of the box a weighty, serious affair: it might have been there to make Maria stop and think before taking out a note. I remember seeing her bent over the box, which lived on an antique side table, and pausing before unlocking it and then, after another brief pause, she would lift the lid. When she was paid for her sewing, the cash went in immediately and the lock was turned, the key always left in. After the deaths of my father's parents, the box, together with the antique side table, reappeared in my father's study. While in his possession, it did not hold money; in fact, I don't think he kept anything in it. After his own death, I have inherited the box and it contains my favourite photographs of my grandparents and of my daughters as well as the cash I keep at home. It no longer has the key; it was lost somewhere on the way.

My grandparents' loyalty to each other and the sense of togetherness they exuded were, I realized later, a continuation of what happened to their relationship a few years after the picture with the innkeepers was taken. In 1941, Francis, aged forty-four, was drafted into the army which supported Nazi Germany. He deserted and joined the anti-fascist underground. As a prominent socialist activist, he was known to the authorities and a price was put on his head. Eventually, he was arrested and sentenced to death by hanging. In prison, tortured and malnourished, he became ill with a stomach ulcer and Maria, who by now had joined the underground movement herself, visited him every day with home-cooked meals. I remember the stories she used to tell me of carrying stacks of propaganda leaflets hidden underneath vegetables and coming across German patrols checking identity cards on trams. Good looking, smartly dressed and with her impeccable German, she would chat amiably to the soldiers and invariably escaped being searched. Had they caught her, she herself would have ended up in prison. I imagine her charm but, above all, her cool-headedness; her calm, polished manner would have stood her in good stead in sticky situations. (Francis, on the other hand, like me, I suppose, was a more excitable character, with a blunt manner and in a similar situation would have found it hard not to give himself away.) Busy with propaganda activities and looking after her ill husband in prison, she had no time for paid work and once their savings were exhausted, she had to sell her jewellery, at first on the black market and then to her brother whose upholstery business was doing very well. (But hang on, how come? That could be an intriguing story: Who had the money for soft furnishings at that time? People who profited from the Jews having been forced to flee and sell their property for next to nothing? Or did Maria's brother receive commissions from Germans and their collaborators? Who was investing in gold anyway?) When everything else was gone, she had to part with their wristwatches and wedding rings. Throughout the years I knew them, my grandparents wore no jewellery and the only watches they had were the chain, pocket ones—the watches they had inherited from their parents and which Maria might have kept for sentimental value. (After her death, my grandmother's watch, which in fact was my great-grandmother's, passed on to me.) I learnt about the jewellery sale from my father, who was appalled by what he considered shameful behaviour on the part of his uncle and for many years after the war he refused to speak to him. But all that is in the future. I suppose most families have such stories.

I cannot fail to be impressed by Maria's loyalty, even in an age when divorce was rare and, as a rule, women stuck by their philandering partners. But more than that, I wonder what ignited her political involvement and whether finding her own politics led her to see Francis in a new light. I remember once, in my pre-teens, telling her that I found a young neighbour of hers attractive, and she asked how I could possibly think so when I didn't know anything about his views, his politics. I was bewildered then that politics should matter as much as I am bewildered now that it wouldn't be a crucial part of someone's appeal to me.

It is possible that the behaviour of her brother, her favourite of her three siblings, was a crucial factor in her becoming politicized. She might have felt rejected or abandoned by her family (her father was still alive but he would have been unlikely to have any sympathy for his socialist son-in-law in prison) and I wonder whether suddenly Maria saw the difference between the values of her family and those of her husband and it became clear to her which ones she preferred. She might have thought that most decent people would help anyone, let alone their own sister, in such difficult circumstances. She would have seen that despite the authorities' collaboration with the Nazis, which included running concentration camps, the most notorious of which was Jasenovac, where 100,000 people were murdered, her family carried on with their upholstery business and behaved as if the political situation was of no concern. Francis, on the other hand, was guided purely by his idealism, with no thought for personal gain. Every day when she cooked his meal, taking special care to obtain fresh ingredients that would not further aggravate her husband's illness, and when she waited in prison to be allowed to pass on the food to him, often having to bribe the guards, she would have been driven by the knowledge that her husband was a better man than her brothers and her father. The scene I envisage is Maria preparing Francis' favourite dish of stew with potato gnocchi and, as she rolled out the dough and looked at the fine white flour covering her palms, her eyes catching sight of her unadorned hands, she would have thought that losing the wedding ring for the nourishment she could provide for her husband was a small price to pay. Perhaps that is when she began to see him in a new light and perhaps that is when she realized that she loved him. As I would realize in my own time, sometimes it takes a long time to appreciate those close to us. And even if it was not love, she would have felt respect and admiration. When she had married him, she might had done so more to oppose her parents and reject their choice rather than out of a passion for Francis; but as life threw its worst at them, she learnt to love and appreciate him. She might even have looked back over the years, difficult years, when she did not think she needed him, and she might have regretted not loving him enough. Caring for him now was the way towards a new beginning. And for Francis, there was a twist of irony: while he was searching for a woman who would not only give him love but also approve of his politics and ideals—he told me once that his best female friends, and by that he would have meant 'friends' as well, came from socialist meetings and trade-union groups— that woman had been next to him all the time. It took her many years to grow into the kind of woman he had been seeking.

When Maria died, suddenly and unexpectedly from a stroke, he was inconsolable. He stopped eating and had no interest in social contact. My parents would bring him with us on Sunday picnics in the countryside but he would sit in a camping chair, forever sad and aloof. Most days, he would come and have a meal with us, mainly to please my concerned parents. He wouldn't finish his food and my mother would wrap it up for him to take back. Once a week my father would throw out the pile of leftovers from Grandpa's fridge. If he had an afternoon nap in our home, he refused a blanket, even though any of us, had we lay down, would have needed it. My parents said he had behaved as if he wanted to catch a cold. When they thought he was asleep, they would ask me to cover him. I remember tiptoeing in and spreading the blanket over his bony frame, all curled up, and thinking how small he looked, as if his body had shrunk while he was asleep. Looking back on those last two years of his life, I can see that all he wanted was to die. Our coffee afternoons were probably the only times when I saw him animated. On one such occasion, he told me that as a child he had lived not far from Maria but later her family moved away to a bigger house and sometimes he would see her going to her girls' school. He said he had loved her ever since. 'She was the most beautiful woman I ever knew,' he said. 'And I wasn't the only one to think that,' he added.

How much of them remains in me? How much of what matters to me in my life have I inherited and how much of me is part of some self-electing affinities that travel across the space and time, such as my love for the Russian and German classics? It was from Grandfather Francis that I first heard of Gogol's 'Overcoat'—one of his favourite texts and which he often described as the perfect image of the absurdity of modern life—and it was Grandfather Francis who directed me to read *Crime and Punishment*. It was Grandfather Francis who read to me sections of Goethe's *Faust*. There can be no simple, straightforward answer; no way of providing a list and ticking this and that trait and tracing it back to any one of them. But who were they, my ancestors—those people with their secret lives? I don't know. All I have are my unreliable memories and the photographs, around which I invent stories, the photographs that capture a split second and turn a casual gesture, or a facial expression into forensic evidence, the photographs that fix an ephemeral moment into eternity. The photographs that have a meaning only after I tell a story about them.

There are also the few objects that survive from their lives: my grandmother's wooden box, the watch that used to belong to Maria's mother and a white porcelain tray on which I keep my pepper and salt mills. It is in the nature of objects to have autonomous lives: they, and the photographs, have outlasted my grandparents. They are likely to outlast me.

CHAPTER FIVE

The Suitor

Yes, things could have been different, there's no doubt about that. Not that I blame anyone. As my mother would have said, 'Gustl, it wasn't meant to be.' Her wise words, as always. They have guided me throughout my life and still provide comfort. But by the time of the events I am describing, my dear mother, my dear mother who understood the way of the world better than anyone, my dear, beloved mother who wished the best for me, was no longer around. Had she been living, it wouldn't have happened because I wouldn't have considered marriage. And why would I? After all, I shared her discomfort at seeing young women displaying themselves in cafes without chaperones, even young women from what one would think of as good families.

But were the Ondrušes really a good family? On the face of it yes: two sons and a daughter, all well brought up, a prosperous business, an ordered household, music and maids but who was this Adolph? Where had he come from? A man with no family except the one he created for himself. He was a friend and I couldn't complain about his friendship but did I really know who he was? A man of here and nowhere is nobody, as my mother used to point out. The story was that he had come to Agram from another part of the Empire—was it Bohemia?—as a young upholsterer to work on the building of the National Theatre. But how come that he never went back to visit his place of birth, how come that no one from his past ever turned up here? Was he some strange creature with no father or mother, no brothers or sisters, no one to call his own until he married Maria's mother? I did ask, yes, I did; after all, the stage we found ourselves in demanded that I knew who my future father-in-law was. No doubt that where you come from, your family, not to mention your country, is what makes you who you are. At the time I asked, we were talking figures, certainly offers were made on my part, and generous offers if I may say so; I felt I had the right to know, I needed an answer as the situation concerned me directly. Had I not made enquiries of such kind, I might have given the impression that I wasn't serious in my intentions; that I didn't care about the provenance of my in-laws. I asked, at first indirectly, perhaps too discreetly, but when nothing was said, I had to become more explicit. The answer was always the same. Adolph claimed to have been an only child and that both parents were dead by the time he came to Agram. But why come all the way, leaving the place where he grew up, unless there was some secret he was hiding or something he was running away from. And despite German being the language of the Empire, in Agram he had to learn Croatian, which he did, quite well, I agree. You could detect a German accent but that was fine. No one minded. If anything, it brought him more customers. But why the effort? What was it that had made it worth his while to come here and go through all that trouble? Was there a skeleton in his cupboard? But what kind of skeleton? Old bones do not make a good family.

Looking back, I know I should have been more circumspect, less excited by the prospect of marrying such a beauty. But that wasn't the only problem. I blame myself for rushing things. I know that now but, at the time, I grew impatient as I understood the urgency of marriage at my age. I feared I might lose her. And then there was also the necessity of saving her, saving her from herself. I was sure of that. Perhaps I invited the family to my country house too often, perhaps I was too insistent or perhaps I spent too long showing Maria around my wine cellar. I remember her nodding politely whenever I pointed out a particularly valuable vintage but did she really have any interest in my passion? Or perhaps I over-reacted when they didn't accept an invitation one Sunday.

Mother once said that, in every relationship, there was always an emotional imbalance as either the man desired the woman more than she desired him, giving her power over him, or the other way around. The best way to minimize the imbalance is to marry some-one equal in wealth and beauty. She didn't reckon on another ele-ment: the age difference. But then, I thought that my wealth more than made up for my twenty-five years' seniority.

Whatever it was, my impatience or the girl's unsuitability for a respectable marriage, nothing could have prepared me for what was to happen. Sometimes the girl responded to my greetings with an almost dismissive formality. She was polite, oh, yes, but I had a feeling, perhaps even less than a feeling, more a hunch, an inkling that I may not have wanted to accept at the time—and I have only become aware of this unwillingness with hindsight—that is, the possibility she was indifferent to seeing me, let alone talking to me. But at least she always responded. Even before I could raise my hat, she would smile, bend her head in respect and say, softly but clearly: '*Küstihand*, Herr Wagner.' (She used to call me *Onkel* Wagner when she was a child and I was pleased that she gave that up. The idea of a young woman like her referring to me as uncle would have made me uncomfortable. I say that without the slightest exaggeration.) But on the day when our paths crossed at the stairs by the funicular, she whizzed past me with not so much as a cursory glance. On that day, she was a creature insubstantial, a ghost, an eerie spectre that floated past and drifted through people or whatever was in her way. Nothing would or could have stopped her. Her eyes looked possessed; her body tightly wrapped inside her shell.

The 28th of May it was—a month to the day before the Sarajevo assassination. The day linked my fate to that of Franz Ferdinand. But who was my Gavrilo Princip? Maria, Adolph or even that poor printer from Laščina, not the most salubrious area in Agram, to say the least. I forget his name.

To say that I was shocked would be understating it. My left hand in which I held my hat, froze in mid-air, my cane dropped to the ground and rattled down the wooden stairs. I felt paralysed and stood there like a sculpture. Had I really seen what I had seen? A little boy, one of those dirty, skinny brats that litter the streets of Agram, picked up my cane and was trying to hand it to me. I half heard his shrill voice: 'Are you all right, sir?' Someone else stopped and asked if I needed help. Too right, I did. Steadying myself on the banister, I gasped for breath, unable to speak. Once I managed to collect myself, I took the cane from the boy and was about to give him a coin but the street urchin had already run away.

As for fate, another memory comes to mind: my gold pocket watch stopped at the very instant the girl flew past me. Seventeen minutes past three. I checked the time as soon as I recovered. The passer-by who had asked if I needed help, looked at my watch too and said that it was ten minutes slow. The ten minutes that I would have taken to recover. My first thought was that I had forgotten to wind up the watch and I was annoyed with myself for such an omission. Ever since my father had given it to me for my sixteenth birthday, telling me to wind it up every morning at exactly the same time—first thing on waking up—I had followed his instructions. Not once had I failed to remember, even when I was in bed with a chill. I wound up the watch and placed it back in my pocket. It was not before I reached Frankopanska Street that I checked it again and found it still showing seventeen minutes past three o'clock.

As I picked my way down the hill, I resolved to see Adolph straightaway. What I had witnessed had to be reported. Something had to be done before it was too late. I was doing them a favour.

Adolph wasn't in the workshop. I left a written message stressing the urgency of my need to speak to him on a matter of mutual concern.

Before nightfall, I received a note that Adolph would meet me in the Corso the following afternoon. A pleasant surprise. I had prepared what I wanted to say. I planned to ask formally for the girl's hand. Immediately. With no preliminaries. There was no time to lose. I was no longer young and she needed saving. Saving from her madness. The marriage would be to our mutual benefit. I could still have an heir and Maria would not lack for anything. She deserved my munificence. I saw us honeymooning in Paris, residing at the Ritz. We would walk through the Tuileries and attend the opera in the evening, like my mother and I did on our last visit.

Needless to say, I was apprehensive. Would Maria be a suitable wife? My good name could not bear the errant behaviour she was displaying. Perhaps we could stop in Vienna and visit a doctor. There must be a cure for her illness, I thought. I was sure it was an illness, a typically female complaint. But then, perhaps the marriage would be enough. A calm, orderly, respectable life to dispel her wild leanings. All these thoughts went through my head as I held the note delivered from Adolph that evening. I was encouraged by the speed of his response and his suggestion to meet the next day. Good portents. At the time, Adolph seemed to have neglected his social life and was rarely seen in cafes. People said he worked all hours, counting his forints. The wagging tongues of Agram. I didn't believe it. He clearly didn't need to be excessively careful with money. The boys were gradually to take over the business and the girl was bound to make a good match. There was no shortage of suitors. And now Adolph and I were meeting in a cafe to make arrangements. He must have understood what was on the cards. Well, I had dropped enough hints over the years. Besides, as a father, he couldn't have missed what was happening to his daughter and would have understood the need for urgent action.

I arrived early, took my table by the window at the front. The cafe was unusually peaceful. Since the death of the poet, more than two months earlier, the debates had quietened considerably. Oh, how all that used to bore me, the shouting between the Masaryks and the Viennese students; those disputes between the Old and the Young. I was aware that Matoš was fuelling it, by his very presence. Everyone wanted to impress him. Not that he was easily impressed. Why did they adore him so much? The Young began trembling as soon as he arrived. Once I asked one of them to explain to me the appeal of that gaunt figure. And you know what he said? 'Matoš is a poet, a great poet—the greatest Croatia has ever produced. A nation cannot be civilized without a great poet.' A poet. What kind of job is that? He certainly was not my kind of person. Why did he command so much respect? Only an arrogant person would allow so much adulation. As soon as he opened his mouth, the Young ones became silent. Thin as a rake. Poor as a church mouse. And yet all this veneration, even after his death. The Corso owner keeps his table empty as if the poet was about to return. I asked him why. 'We are proud to have had such a patron,' he told me. 'He wrote some of his great poems here.' Great poems? That's an exaggeration. The owner could see I wasn't convinced. 'They think that the first idea for the "Consolation of the Hair" came to him right here, at this very table,' he said. 'Consolation of the Hair'? What kind of title is that? But I didn't say anything. I had other things on my mind.

I told the waiter I wanted my usual but without the apple strudel. He nodded but I could see that he was dying to know why I didn't want the pastry. He turned to go, then changed his mind. 'The chef has just taken a batch out of the oven. Still warm.' He smiled. For a moment, I hesitated but then I reminded myself that I was there on an important task—business. Inevitably, the Corso cake doesn't match Mother's unparalleled creation. Her paper-thin, crispy, golden pastry and chunks of apples that melt in the mouth, a delicate hint of butter and a fine mist of vanilla *Staubzucker*. But that afternoon, waiting for my prospective father-in-law, I couldn't allow myself to think of Mother. I knew that if thoughts of her entered my mind, I would wonder whether what I was doing was a folly of a lonely, old man and I might lose confidence. I had to say what I needed to say without Mother by my side. I was on my own now. I, a single man, a bachelor. I had to speak for myself.

As I finished my coffee, I realized that Adolph must have been delayed. It was five past five. At that point, the owner approached the table and said that a boy from the Ondruš workshop had delivered a note for me. I opened it with trepidation. Adolph had been prevented from honouring our meeting by a family emergency. The girl. Something had happened to the girl. I left the cafe straightaway.

Over the next few days, I made enquiries and, yes, it was the girl. She had taken to her bed. She wasn't speaking and appeared to be in a semi-conscious state, mumbling something that no one understood. A doctor arrived from Vienna. He couldn't tell what was wrong. His advice was rest and more rest. No one and nothing was to upset her. She needed complete peace. I could have said that. The woman's thing. That was all. A wild, young woman. Had I been the only one who saw it coming?

There was nothing to do. I sent flowers to Mr and Mrs Ondruš and wished their daughter a speedy recovery. And then I waited. As is the way in Agram, rumours were afoot as soon as she took to bed. I took no notice of them.

Adolph contacted me. We met in his office. I repeated my wish that Maria would soon recover. He seemed in despair. Someone from the workshop came to ask for his advice about an order from, a customer who was a relative of the Esterhazys but Adolph dismissed the man. 'She has been in bed for close to two months,' he said, 'and there is no change. Her mother is losing faith.' I tried to reassure him, and said: 'Young people have the strength to weather any ailment.' I asked if there was anything I could do. 'Not for now,' he said and the words gave me hope. I hung on that 'for now'. Adolph promised to keep me informed. Several weeks passed but there was no word from him.

And then one day, with no warning, the girl got up and behaved as if nothing had been amiss, or at least, that's the story that was circulated. The family were told not to make any reference to her self-imposed confinement. 'Allow her to forget whatever trauma she has experienced,' the doctor from Vienna advised, 'and in time she will be able to resume her life.'

I was pleased when an invitation arrived for Sunday lunch *en famille*, a clear sign that Adoph had finally understood that I could make a new life for his daughter. My time had come and I was ready to play my part.

At the table, I was aware of the formality with which members of this family addressed each other. Whether they behaved so properly for my benefit or whether they were trying hard to forget what had happened—the atmosphere in the household pleased me. In the past, I used to think that the Ondrušes lacked a little of the quality of my family. But with money comes manners. In the afternoon, Adolph asked Maria to show me the garden. She disappeared for a few minutes to fetch her straw hat. We took the path through the middle and walked towards the orchard. Maria was excessively polite but at certain moments, her voice betrayed a touch of strain. Her demeanour was overtly cheerful as if she were playing a role.

I noticed, for the first time, that she was at least as tall as me. Had I shrunk or had she grown? If she were to wear heels, as fashionable women do these days, we would look an odd couple. That's the problem with tall women. Discomfited, I dared not offer my hand. I tried to tell myself that a rich man like me, a man respected in our town, a man past his fortieth birthday, should not be shy in the company of a young woman, even one as beautiful as Maria. But I couldn't help it. I became tongue-tied and we walked in silence. Yes, I have known her since birth but she was different. More fragile, like a porcelain doll. Not to be touched, only to be admired from a distance. Late summer flowers were in full bloom and we paused on the path by the pond to admire them. She looked up and smiled. 'Mama chooses the flowers,' she said. 'Don't you help her?' I asked. 'I prefer to read,' she said. That was part of the trouble with her, I thought. Too much reading. Not good for a woman. A frog jumped out of the grass and disappeared into the water. We watched as the concentric ripples spread out in perfect circles and perished. I wanted to say something as we turned back but nothing came to mind.

Later, Adolph and I had coffee and liquor in the lounge. I lit a cigar from a wooden box he proffered while he puffed on his pipe, as relaxed as a man with no care in the world. I could tell he knew what I was about to say but he waited for me to raise the subject. I put my cards on the table. He had a good idea of my wealth and I repeated that I loved his daughter. Did I? Yes, as a man who wishes for an heir loves a beautiful woman who can satisfy that need. I didn't say that.

'I would like Maria to be happy,' Adolph said.

'That is my desire, too. My aim in life is to make her happy. I will do everything in my power to make her happy,' I said, and I meant it.

For days before the lunch, I had resolved to dispel from my mind any possible difficulties I could envisage in a union with a woman of such an unconventional disposition. I thought I had pushed to the back of my memory, if not out of my mind altogether, the episode on the stairs next to the funicular, as well as numerous other incidents, less dramatic but nevertheless disturbing. I was determined to make a go of this marriage. I knew I should not but something made me ask about the cause of Maria's illness. The question just tripped off my tongue. I used the word illness. That was a mistake. Adolph tensed and he readjusted his trousers with an absent-minded gesture. But what other word could I have used?

'Maria was NOT ill,' Adolph said too adamantly. I was taken aback by the tone of his voice and must have recoiled in my chair. Adolph noticed my discomfort and forced a smile as if to make light of the exchange and of whatever was going on with Maria. 'She suffered from a trauma after visiting that circus. A minor trauma. All forgotten now. Done and dusted.' He continued to beam.

I could tell that it would be inappropriate to ask further questions. *Point final*, as my French governess used to say.

Adolph poured me another glass and, still smiling, repeated, 'All forgotten now.' And that was that. We smoked in silence. Our deal was done. Or so we thought.

A week later, I invited the family to my country house in Samobor. The day was pleasant but unremarkable. I had half an hour with Maria alone in my study, showing her my collection of stamps. Again, she was polite but it was obvious she was playing the role they had chosen for her. From the questions she asked, I could tell that she had very little interest in me or my passion.

I wished to have our engagement announced but Adolph said we needed to wait. The girl was still fragile, he said. 'Any change, anything new or sudden, might hinder her recovery.' But when I invited the family for lunch on the last Sunday in October, they apologized, claiming a previous engagement. I changed the date. Again, they were not available. Eventually they agreed but I wondered whether something was amiss.

Adolph came to see me. The girl didn't want to be married. She said she needed more time. He could have asserted his will but he was not that kind of father. That was a weakness on his part, I thought, but didn't say it.

Again, the waiting. Nothing to do but wait.

Three years passed, three years of occasional Sunday lunches; three years of visits to my country house; three years of polite role-playing on Maria's part and then it all gradually petered out. We hardly saw each other. But I was still hopeful.

One day I was strolling down Ilica, two years after the war had finished, when I passed by a typography shop and there was a banner, a handmade banner wishing a happy marriage to Francis P. Genus and Maria Ondruš. Was this a joke? I barged in and asked the meaning of that banner. A filthy little apprentice told me that one of their own, now a trained print-setter, had been married the day before to a beautiful young woman and that they were all so happy for them.

A banner in a shop window. How vulgar! To think that the Ondrušes could stoop so low. My announcement would have been in the *Agramer Tagblatt*, a respectable paper. Not on display for the street urchins to laugh at.

I walked out. I haven't seen Adolph since. He doesn't come to the Corso any more. If he did, I would want to know what kind of circus was he talking about when he said that the girl had suffered a trauma. No circus had visited Agram for at least five years. I checked that with the authorities. Why was he bluffing me?

I go to the Corso every afternoon. It's not the same as it used to be. Lots of riff-raff shouting. Young men who have returned from the front. I observe that world and tuck into my apple strudel— needless to say, not as good as my dear mother's—but times have changed and I with them. Soon I may be joining her in our black marble tomb. That printer from Laščina may have got the girl but I have my comforts that will for ever be out of his reach. Even in death I will be above him.

Today as I am leaving the cafe, I pause by the board at the entrance carrying tributes to Matoš—they are still harping on about him more than six years after his death—and I notice a panel with words scribbled by hand, in French: *Le monde est fait pour aboutir à un beau livre.* Humbug! My life is not going to end in a book, good or not.

I have no regrets. Yes, things could have been different but as Mother might have put it in her wisdom, 'Gustl' or 'Ottel', as she sometimes called me affectionately, the marriage to the Ondruš girl 'was not meant to be.'

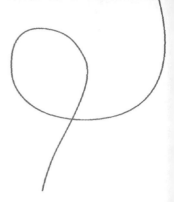

Acknowledgements

I would like to thank everyone at Seagull Books, especially Naveen Kishore. I am indebted to Sayoni Ghosh, the kindest of editors, for her professionalism and expertise and, above all, for her warmth that crossed continents to reach me in London all the way from Calcutta.

Anna Burns was most generous with her comments and I was lucky to have the privilege to share work in progress during the writing of this novel.

Thanks to Hannah Partos and Rebecca Partos for their love and support. Anthony Rudolf, great poet and writer, should be honoured for his selfless support of writers and I am most grateful to him as one of many recipients of his critique, kindness and friendship.

Finally, I wish to thank Peter Main, my first reader and, by his own admission, a lodger, too.

*

A Note on the Illustrations

The following images are now in the public domain, and are available at Wikimedia Commons:

Page 255 Leonardo da Vinci, *Adoration of the Magi* (oil and tempera on panel, c. 1480, Uffizi Gallery, Florence).

Page 261 Édouard Manet, *Music in the Tuileries* (oil on canvas, 1862, National Gallery, London).